The Finder
Brandon Fox

Dreamspinner Press

Published by
Dreamspinner Press
4760 Preston Road
Suite 244-149
Frisco, TX 75034
http://www.dreamspinnerpress.com/

The Finder
Copyright © 2011 by Brandon Fox

Cover Art by Catt Ford

ISBN: 978-1-61581-846-4

Printed in the United States of America
First Edition
June 2011

eBook edition available
eBook ISBN: 978-1-61581-904-1

For my partner, the find of a lifetime.

Chapter One

RHAN emerged from the forest and shielded his eyes against noon's glare. White stones jumbled on the ancient battlefield like ice floating in a green sea. In the distant foothills, red and black pennants fluttered above clouds of dust. He was relieved to see they were on time for their meeting with the imperial convoy. The empire of Tyume would have exacted a price if they had been tardy answering the summons.

A slice of shade behind a tumbled wall offered relief from the heat. Rhan sat, wrapped his arms around his knees, and sniffed the dry air. He was eager to smell this new place before it filled with his kinsmen's familiar scents.

The approaching Tyumens were upwind, and rivers of scent revealed what dust obscured. Many horses, as he had expected. Oxen, probably pulling supply wagons, as well as dogs and llamas. Sweaty men and women who smelled of the cheese and smoked meat favored by soldiers of Tyume. Beneath it all were undercurrents of grass and the arid smell of sun-baked stone.

"Rhan! This is no time for napping."

He jumped to his feet. The village tetrarch had emerged from the forest downwind and caught him unawares. Her weathered face glowered as if she'd caught him stealing apples from the storehouse.

"Help Catrin collect wood for the fires. They'll expect us to feed them and they won't want to wait." She didn't conceal her displeasure at the prospect.

"Yes, Marenka," he said, head bowed. He looked behind the elder and saw others leaving the forest. "There's Catrin. I'll go see where she wants to set the fires." Marenka waved him off and turned her scowl to the approaching Tyumen delegation.

He loped away, glad to escape before attracting more ire. Marenka was always stern, but fear had turned her mood foul. Three generations had passed since a Voice of Tyume last traveled this far west. Everyone knew the Voice's summons, with orders to bring the village's elders and finders, meant bad news. The empire's burden was sure to grow heavier.

The rest of Balmorel's representatives entered the meadow and began slipping packs from their shoulders. Though their burdens were lighter than a fortnight ago when they had left home, the relentless pace had been exhausting. Rhan ran over to a young woman with lustrous red hair and lifted her canvas pack while she pulled her arms from its padded straps.

"I see why you like to scout the trail," Catrin said as she rubbed where straps had pressed against her flesh. "You get to rabbit ahead and look at the scenery while the rest of us work like mules." Her smile signaled that she didn't hold a grudge.

Rhan lowered the pack to the ground and then offered his water skin. She accepted it and took a long drink. Even covered with sweat and dirt, she maintained a dignity that he never seemed to manage.

"Marenka told me to gather firewood and help you get ready." He took the water skin back and slung it over his shoulder. "Just as well. I don't think I want to get between her and the Tyumens."

"You're smarter than you look," Catrin said, eyeing his dusty leathers and unruly blond curls. "Besides, there's reason for her worry. There might be an Examiner with them. Best not to be noticed."

Rhan frowned. "It doesn't matter if I'm examined. I don't have marks or anything else wrong with me."

"Of course not." She held him with a steady gaze, commanding his attention like an elder even though they were the same age. "Just be careful. You know how they are. They'll cull you for anything, even if it's harmless. Remember Kev."

A clenched jaw was his only response. Kev had been his closest friend. They'd been seventeen when an Examiner passed through Balmorel and summoned them to be inspected. The official said Kev's gold-flecked eyes were likely a daemon mark and took him to Hoya for final judgment. Three years had now passed in ominous silence, and Rhan no longer held hope for his friend's return. His angry words about the Tyumens had alarmed Balmorel's elders and earned him increasingly severe warnings.

"I'll start on the fires," Rhan said, his expression tightly controlled. He pointed to the ruins where shattered walls spoke of ancient cataclysms. "Over there, all right?" He started for the forest before Catrin could answer. His argument wasn't with her, he could smell her sympathy, but he didn't want to hear another admonition. It didn't matter what the rest of the village said. He would never accept what had happened to Kev.

He plunged through underbrush, collecting dead branches, avoiding Catrin while his temper cooled. Knowing that she was only trying to help didn't soothe his pain. Kev had been abandoned by the village when his mark was noticed. Rhan still felt the ache of it like a dagger through his heart. Some marks showed on the outside and others didn't. But it made no difference. He would get no help if his uncanny sense of smell was discovered. It was a far deeper mark than gold-flecked eyes.

HORNS sounded in rich harmony as the legate and his escort neared. Rhan was awed despite his best effort to despise them. They were garbed in black leathers and wore silver chains with medallions proclaiming their rank. They seemed like giants as they gazed down at villagers waiting on bent knees. There were at least fifty, and they were only a fraction of the convoy that still flowed from the foothills and across the plain. The legate himself, a Voice of Tyume, rode at the procession's head. A shiver tingled Rhan's spine, and he averted his eyes. Being in the presence of such power was like teetering on the edge of a precipice. This man spoke for the empire and would be obeyed without question.

Marenka, still standing, thumped her staff on a rock before giving final instructions. "Remember not to speak unless spoken to. Don't show an interest in their finery or horses. Such things are not for us. We live by their leave." She turned to Catrin, who was kneeling near Rhan, and lowered her voice. "Keep a close watch, especially on the legate Jerolin. His face might reveal what his words hide."

Horns sounded again, a bright noise of imperial majesty unlike anything Rhan had ever heard. Even Marenka sank to one knee despite her stiff joints. She clenched her staff with a white-knuckled grip and bowed her head as the delegation reached them.

Rhan stared at the ground, curiosity fighting with dread as the riders came to a halt. New scents permeated the dust stirred by milling horses. Peppermint soap, oiled leather, strong perfumes mixed with the sweat of men and women, dried meat and biscuits stored in saddlebags, tobacco and other fragrant smoking herbs. The smells were fascinating. He breathed deeply, wishing he could share this pleasure with someone. But as far as he knew, only dogs and other lowly creatures shared his keen perceptions. If there were others, they wouldn't be foolish enough to reveal themselves. Hidden marks were feared even more than fleshly deformities.

Sounds of riders dismounting pulled his attention away from the tapestry of scents. Fear among the kneeling villagers grew to a stench.

"Arise, tetrarch." The man's voice was commanding. "I am Jerolin, who summoned you. Attend to my words. Tyume has a task for you and your people."

Rhan looked up. The legate standing before Marenka held a silver scepter that gleamed in the sun. The medallion on his breast sparkled with emeralds and rubies. His cloak was made of richer fabric than anything Rhan had seen at home in Balmorel.

Marenka slowly got to her feet, using her staff for support. The villagers followed her lead. Most kept their eyes downcast, but Rhan couldn't resist examining the legate and his entourage.

The Tyumen militia made no distinctions between genders, and the women looked as hardened as the men. Rank was another matter. Everyone was deployed in rigid formation and most wore insignia marking their function. Archers with crossbows flanked the party, soldiers with swords and spears occupied the center, and musicians with horns and drums stood at the back. Eight soldiers, grouped in pairs, stood immediately behind the legate and his orderly. Their clothing bore no military insignia. Curiously, each pair had an extra horse, saddled and laden with packs, in addition to their own mounts.

Jerolin handed his scepter to the orderly. His splendor beside Marenka's brown trekking clothes was like a flowering rose next to a withered weed. Resentment knotted Rhan's gut. The empire already had so much. Why did it have to demand more?

"From time out of mind, Tyume has brought you peace." Jerolin's voice rang with authority and conviction. "We have kept the daemons bound and the bloodline pure. Were it not for us, the daemon wars would have consumed the world."

"We thank you." Marenka's tight voice belied her words, but the legate didn't seem to notice. "We are honored to serve. Our elders and finders are here, answering your summons. What do you command?" Fidgeting among the villagers stopped as they waited to hear their fate.

Jerolin drew himself up. "First, the empire's needs have grown. Beginning with this harvest, you will pay tribute in proportion to the benefits we provide. Bring your elders forward so they may hear and remember."

Marenka turned. Tight-lipped, she gestured for the other nine elders to join her. They stood before Jerolin like a miserable herd of sheep while he began reciting the bushels of grain and other goods they would be required to send to Chakragil.

Rhan stopped listening, knowing the elders would remember every word. The assembled militia still beguiled his nose, and he was curious about the Tyumens. Despite their mastery of the world, he had only seen a few in his lifetime.

The archers looked tired but vigilant as they watched Rhan's kinsmen and the nearby forest. The musicians were hard to see at the back of the assembly, a disappointment as Rhan had never seen metal music-makers.

When he turned his attention to the eight soldiers behind Jerolin, he was startled to see one of them watching him as closely as he had been examining the warriors. Their eyes met, and the young man flashed a grin.

Rhan was too surprised at first to react. He stared at the young man like a deer transfixed by a hunter's poised spear. The Tyumens, at least this one, suddenly seemed less strange. It might even be possible to talk with them, a notion he had never considered.

The soldier who held Rhan's gaze stood last in the line of eight and was a head shorter than his companion. He looked to be close to Rhan's age and had short black hair. Dark blue eyes, alert and penetrating, enlivened a face of striking masculine beauty. His relaxed acknowledgment of Rhan's gaze made him seem very self-possessed.

Realizing he was being studied in return, Rhan blushed and continued his survey of the delegation. The man beside the friendly Tyumen was little older but unlike him in every other way. He was a bit taller than most, hulking rather than lithe, bored instead of curious, disfigured by a crooked nose and cruel mouth rather than pleasing to the eye. His expression was set in a sullen frown and lank brown hair hung in clumps over his forehead.

The next pair consisted of two middle-aged women, dark-haired and sturdy. One of them looked the way Marenka might have appeared thirty years ago. Rhan judged the second pair in line to be man and wife, since they wore matching wedding bracelets. At the front of the line stood a young woman and an older man who turned away from each other as if wishing the other was absent. It seemed the remote and powerful Tyumens weren't that different from his own kin in some ways.

Rhan glanced back at the short soldier. He was craning his neck to see as much as possible, as animated as the others were lethargic. Like a dog sniffing a new meadow, Rhan thought, idly wondering if this stranger might have abilities like his own. It made a pleasant daydream, though it seemed impossible any Tyumen could survive with a mark, even an unseen one.

A pause in the droning recital of new tributes drew his attention back to Jerolin. The legate dismissed the elders and turned to Marenka.

"Our other need concerns finders. How many did you bring?"

"Six," Marenka said. "That's all we have now. Two were killed in a cave flood last spring. Not many, but they have great skill." She held her head higher, justifiably proud of the relics Balmorel collected. Trading and working relics bought most of the village's luxuries. Just last summer they had even enjoyed searing spices from the east, after Rhan found a cache of metal relics their blacksmith could turn into plows.

"Show me the best four."

Marenka beckoned to Rhan and three others, leaving the two youngest finders with their parents. They came forward and stood in a row behind her.

From the corner of his eye, Rhan saw the short soldier looking at him intently. His features were remarkably expressive. When he saw that Rhan had noticed him, he smiled and gave a small nod. Rhan was embarrassed but entranced. The friendly gesture reminded him of Kev.

Jerolin frowned as he examined the finders arrayed before him. His contempt for their upcountry coarseness was plain, though Rhan knew that wouldn't spare them whatever task the empire demanded.

"Keeping the land safe is a struggle," Jerolin said. "Tyume is vigilant and heresy is never suffered to take root. Our task is never done. Rumors have reached Chakragil, telling of a pestilence growing in the west. We have come to rip it out." He fixed each finder in turn with a stare. "They say a heretic is using a relic to spread lies, perhaps even trying to release a daemon on the world. The heretic and relic must be delivered to an Examiner. Finders from the sea to Mount Tochal are set upon this task. Whoever succeeds will win the favor of Tyume. The victor's town will be forgiven its tribute for a full year."

He pointed at the eight soldiers behind him. "Each finder will be escorted. You will ride, to speed your search, and will depart without delay." He touched the jewel-encrusted symbol of Tyume on his medallion. "Half the world is poisoned and the bloodline is polluted. You dig in the ruins, you know why the daemon horde must remain bound. Do not forget the urgency of this quest."

He signaled the first pair of soldiers, the young woman and older man, to move forward with their three horses. Then he pointed at the first finder in the row behind Marenka. Lajos, a middle-aged man with a newborn child, looked at Marenka mournfully. She nodded with a stony face. He left the line and went to stand beside the first Tyumen detail, looking miserable.

Jerolin brought forward his second team, the man and wife. Second in line among the finders was Jana, wife of Balmorel's healer. She turned and waved to her husband, who ran forward to give her a farewell embrace.

Rhan was next in line and had no doubt Jerolin would follow his established order. The militia was known for its regimentation. Impulsively, he turned to the last finder in line. Keara was a small woman who had been a finder for only a year. She had always been timid. He leaned close, not allowing himself to wonder if Marenka would notice. "Maybe we should trade places," he whispered. He tilted his head toward the sullen man who comprised half the final team. "I don't like the looks of that one. You might be better off with the two women."

Keara nodded fervently. "He scares me. Thanks, Rhan." They exchanged places while the healer and his wife made their farewells. Jerolin scowled but didn't hurry the couple. If he cared about Rhan and Keara trading places, or even noticed, he gave no sign of it.

Still dazed by his rash decision, Rhan looked to see if any Tyumens had taken note of the switch. Half the soldiers were watching the forest and most of the rest seemed bored by the proceedings, which they had undoubtedly witnessed many times. But the short member of the fourth squad was watching him with wide eyes. He burst into a dazzling smile that Rhan couldn't help returning. A surge of optimism made him think the task ahead might not be so bad.

As expected, Keara was summoned next. She had nobody special to part with and promptly joined the two women on the third team. When Rhan was summoned to join the final pair, he waved to Catrin and then crossed to the Tyumen side. It felt like crossing an invisible divide, stepping from one world into another, but a welcoming nod from the black-haired soldier made it seem more exciting than daunting.

As soon as the last team was assembled, Jerolin retrieved his scepter from the orderly and held it aloft like a torch. Polished silver reflected the brilliant sun. "Tyume smiles on the faithful. Depart now and fulfill your duties."

Suddenly the orderly at Jerolin's side jerked and teetered, an arrow protruding from his chest, then fell against the legate. Another arrow flashed where Jerolin had stood a moment before and hit a horse among the newly assembled squads. The horse brayed its outrage and bolted.

Soldiers scattered to take shelter behind stones and crumbling walls. Two more arrows hit the ground near Jerolin before the Tyumen archers began sending bolts into the forest. Rhan and his companions moved behind their horses and tried to calm the panicked animals.

Whoever had attacked Jerolin seemed wary of a direct fight. No more arrows flew from the forest. The militia quickly regrouped, half protecting the legate and the remainder charging into the forest to give pursuit.

Rhan kept close to the horses as order returned. He had never seen combat and was shaken by the abruptness of it. "What do we do now?" he asked.

The surly half of the squad looked at him like he was a simpleton, but the other extended his hand. "I'm Aerik Rodan. I'm glad you'll be our finder." His voice was surprisingly deep for someone of his short stature. They clasped forearms in the Tyumen manner. The young soldier's smile held a hint of mischief. "I thank the gods of Tyume for our good fortune in meeting. They work in mysterious ways, yes?"

The other man made a sour face. "Try not to be an ass, Rodan.

Keep him from wandering off while I get our orders." He stalked away without giving them a second look.

"You can call him Maiko, though he'll probably ignore you anyway. And call me Aerik. Um, what should we call you?"

"Oh. Rhan Menkaure. I mean, you can call me Rhan." He realized he was still clasping the soldier's forearm and released it. Aerik's nonchalance about the turmoil around them was oddly reassuring. "Does this happen often? Who would do such a thing?" He was shocked that anyone would dare attack a high Tyumen official.

Aerik thumped him on the shoulder. "Later, my friend. We've just met. It's too soon for politics."

Rhan heard no evasiveness in the answer, though he didn't need to rely on intuition. Deceit had an astringent tang that sprang directly from the skin. A deep breath revealed only the healthy scent of an energetic male. Aerik's main distinction was that he smelled cleaner and fresher than most. "How soon do you think we'll leave?" he asked.

Aerik raised both hands to chest height, making a graceful gesture as if releasing a dove to take flight. "Who knows? It depends on Jerolin's quarry. He's in a hurry but can't ignore his enemies. They might try again if they escape, especially if they're from Chakragil. But if they slip away during the night, it will probably end the chase."

Rhan pondered the words, struck by the unexpected dangers and the sophistication of his new acquaintance. He was starting to suspect that Balmorel was even more of a sheltered backwater than he had imagined.

"Don't worry," Aerik said. "You're a finder with valuable skills. Jerolin won't be sending you to catch assassins. And I'm an Eye of Tyume, so he'll try to keep my hide in one piece." He grinned, a playful gleam in his eyes. "Now, Maiko, he's just a Hand. Catching arrows might be a good use for him, yes?"

Rhan stared. "You're an Eye? Aren't you a bit... I mean, I thought an Eye of Tyume would be a lot older." His growing sense of ease had vanished. An Eye of Tyume was higher than an Examiner. He had never seen one until now.

"I'm sorry," Aerik said, shrugging. "That probably sounds more imposing out here than it does in Chakragil. But you're right, an Eye is usually older. My case is... complicated." He sighed. "Well, you might as well hear it from me. Maiko will start mocking me as soon as he gets back anyway. My father gave me the title."

"Your father...." Rhan gaped, wondering just how foolish he had been to maneuver himself onto this team. He cleared his throat nervously. "Is there anything else I should know?"

Aerik shook his head, smiling faintly. "No, that's about it." He paused. "Oh, there's the bathing ritual. My attendant has to wash me every night, to maintain my symbolic purity. Maiko hates doing it, so that'll be your job now."

Rhan turned red and decided it would be unwise to say anything at all.

A radiant grin swept away Aerik's matter-of-fact expression. "I'm kidding, Rhan! I couldn't help it, you looked so worried." He suppressed his merriment, though it obviously required an effort. "I'm sorry. It's true my father is a Voice of Tyume and he made me an Eye, but it doesn't mean anything. Rank isn't always an achievement, you know. A Voice can do pretty much as he desires."

Rhan was still wary. "Doesn't it make you a high official of the empire?"

Aerik nodded. "In theory. But if I was really important, I wouldn't be in the provinces hunting heretics. My father just thought the title would help keep me safe while I'm doing my service in the militia."

Rhan was surprised by Aerik's honesty. And his smile was beguiling. Happiness magnified his beauty like a gemstone being held to the sun. It could be blinding.

Aerik looked past Rhan and sighed. "Here comes Maiko. I should warn you, he has no sense of humor. It's best not to provoke him. He'll complain to our subaltern if we give him any cause."

By the time Rhan turned, Maiko had reached them. If anything, his expression had become even more belligerent. "We stay here tonight," he said as he dug into a saddlebag. "The peasants stay too, so Jerolin can question them." He looked up and glared at Rhan. "They'll hang if they had anything to do with the attack. You'll camp with your own people tonight. And don't try to run away, either now or after we leave the convoy. Your village will pay if you do."

"Until tomorrow, then," Rhan said. Maiko had already turned away, ignoring him, but Aerik rolled his eyes and made a crazy-man gesture behind Maiko's back.

Rhan almost laughed with relief, comforted that he would have a friend in the days ahead. He nodded to Aerik before departing for the Balmorel encampment taking shape in the ruins.

TENTS and campfires were set among tumbled stones. The conscripted finders were spending a few minutes of their brief reprieve sitting around a fire, their shadows weaving across nearby rocks like dancing ghosts, trading impressions of the Tyumens. Keara liked her assigned team and had thanked Rhan effusively for trading places. All were sympathetic when he described Maiko's hostility, though it seemed many Tyumens had equal scorn for upcountry farmers. Rhan decided not to say anything about Aerik, reluctant to make a possible friend a topic of gossip. Besides, revealing that he was going to travel with an Eye of Tyume would draw attention, and that usually meant getting in trouble.

The fire had died to embers and Rhan was starting to feel sleepy when he smelled Catrin approaching from behind. He turned around and waved. She had been attending the elders all evening and looked grim.

"Marenka wants to see you," she said. "All of you. Be careful, she's not in a good mood." She looked directly at Rhan when she said it.

Rhan groaned. "What did I do now?" Resentment blossomed at the prospect of another lecture. The elders had probably noticed when he traded places with Keara and wanted to berate him. He was convinced it was their favorite pastime.

"You'll have to hear it from her," Catrin said. "Let's not keep her waiting."

A pavilion for the elders had been pitched inside a courtyard. Golden light seeping through its hemp walls made it glow like a lantern. The finders filed inside with Catrin following.

Marenka was alone in the pavilion, resting in a folding chair beside a lantern. Remains of the elders' evening meal still lay before empty chairs, wooden bowls containing scraps of stewed vegetables and bits of roast venison. The scents were thick enough for Rhan to taste.

As Marenka stood, the dim light made her seem wizened. She met the gaze of each finder without saying a word. Rhan started sweating. At last Marenka sank back to her chair.

"The Tyumens haven't caught the archers," she said. "Jerolin's not pleased and has a mind to hold us responsible for the loss of his aide. He says we should have made sure this place was safe before he arrived."

Rhan tensed, wondering if he was going to be blamed since he had scouted the trail. But Marenka was gazing at the lantern and no longer watching the finders.

"He demands compensation. Ten extra casks of hard cider in the fall. And four more conscripts to help with his quest." Her head hung as if she lacked the strength to lift it. "We answered the summons with thirty kinsmen. We'll leave with twenty-two, and the harvest starts in six weeks. Tyume demands too much."

"We'll be back soon," Keara said. "Maybe in time to help with the harvest. How long can it take to find a heretic?"

Marenka's frown deepened. "That's why I wanted to talk with you. The legate also mentioned a need for labor in Chakragil's brickyards and vineyards. I think that's the real reason he doubled the number of conscripts." She looked up from the lantern. "Be careful, all of you. One offense and I wager you'll still be serving the empire long after I'm dead and gone."

Her glare turned on Rhan. "You, especially. It's one thing to sass the elders. We're used to your ways and know you're just too damned full of questions. But the empire will do more than box your ears if you speak out of place." Her frown softened. "You're not suited for a life tending kilns. You're our best finder, and we can't afford to lose you. So promise me you'll behave yourself."

"I will." Rhan was embarrassed at the rare praise. "Have you decided who to send with us?"

Marenka nodded. "It wasn't an easy task." She smiled, which seemed to require a great effort. "You weren't a problem on that score, at least. Catrin offered to go with you. I tried to talk her out of it, but she insisted. For the others, the elders chose. Tomas will go with Keara, Elisa with Lajos, and Emil with Jana. They've already been told. They'll meet you in the morning."

Rhan felt numb. Jerolin's demands were bad enough, and Catrin joining the quest changed everything. She was a friend but was also Marenka's trusted aide. The prospect of someone from home watching over him chafed.

"That's all," Marenka said. "Rest well. You'll leave at dawn, and your first day riding will be hard." She sighed deeply. "For once they'll be sorry they levy such a high tax on horses. Learning to ride will slow you down. Take care, kinsmen. Come back to us when you can."

They left the pavilion in silence, feeling the night's chill. Rhan walked with Catrin to the meadow where they had pitched their tents. Once they were away from the others, he pulled her to a stop.

"Why did you do it?" He wanted to shake her, tell her she was stupid for leaving the village's safety, but knew it would serve no purpose. She was stubborn once she made a decision.

"Someone had to," she said. "Why not me?" She seemed small, as if trying to disappear into the darkness. "I know how you feel about Balmorel. I guess I'm a bit like you. I'd like to see what lies beyond our fields and orchards."

He knew she wasn't telling him everything, but her scent made him stop. He didn't want to hear the rest. What she wanted, he wasn't prepared to offer.

"Well... I guess I should thank you." He released her arm and stepped back, eyes downcast. "I'll see you in the morning."

He slipped away before she could say more and spent a long time walking before going to his tent. When sleep finally came, it was not Catrin who filled his dreams.

Chapter Two

AERIK woke at sunrise, a long-standing habit. Dawn exercise was still his favorite part of the day despite Maiko's ridicule and the rigors of being on campaign. This morning he had found a secluded spot at the forest's edge for the ritual, next to a creek deep enough for bathing.

A few minutes of stretching prepared him for the fluid movements of a dance retelling the victory of mankind over the daemon Shinigami eight hundred years ago. Music filled his mind as his body flowed with life and strength. Martial arts had demanded more attention than traditional dances the past several months, but love of movement had settled in his bones and sinew at an early age.

Sweat slicked his bare torso when the reenacted struggle was done. His chest rose and fell with deep breaths, though he felt vibrant and ready to keep going.

Then he remembered the upcountry finder he had met, Rhan. All buckskin and tousled curls, reticent yet bold enough to choose for himself his companions for the quest, and favored with looks that rivaled the fairest men in Chakragil. But unaware of his allure, Aerik felt sure. Life in the country would have spared him the excessive attention that spoiled so many.

He stripped off his pants and waded into the creek. It was cold but not as bad as the icy reservoirs that supplied water to Chakragil. He washed quickly and dressed so he could get to the mess tent and have breakfast before Maiko woke. The arrogant Hand's company was the surest way to spoil a morning.

AERIK was among the first to arrive at the corral and had his choice of horses. He was surprised to hear there would be more conscripts than originally planned and took care to select gentle mounts for them. The priests of Tyume believed peasants should stay close to their fields, so the empire made it hard for any but the wealthy to own horses. The recruits would likely be new to the saddle. Thoughts of leaving the convoy and embarking on his own explorations kept him happily occupied as he set about collecting tack for the horses.

Maiko was still absent, which Aerik counted as a blessing, even as villagers began drifting over to the corral. By the time horses were saddled, he saw Rhan approaching with a redheaded woman. Both carried canvas packs.

"I just heard the news," he said as they arrived. He bowed slightly in the woman's direction. "You're the addition to our little group?"

"This is Catrin," Rhan said. "I've already told her it's all right to call you Aerik." He paused, looking uncertain. "Should I have done that? I don't know what the rules are."

Aerik smiled warmly. "It's fine. I'm pleased to meet you, Catrin." He extended his hand for a clasp, which she accepted. "Please give me a chance, whatever you've heard about me. Rhan and I didn't really have time to get acquainted yesterday. I probably made a bad impression."

"No, you didn't," Rhan protested. He blushed, and then pushed on. "I haven't told her anything. There hasn't been time, really."

Aerik nodded. "A problem soon to be cured." He showed them the horses he had chosen for them. "I hope these will do. They're both calm, and friendly enough. Have either of you ridden before?"

"No," Rhan said. "Balmorel can't afford horses. We use oxen for pulling our plows and wagons." He let the larger horse sniff his hand and then produced an apple from his pack. The horse whinnied and started eating the fruit. Rhan looked entranced.

"You've made another friend," Aerik said. "A wise move. A horse can make your life miserable if it has a mind to."

Rhan laughed as the horse licked his palm. The sound was full of wonder and made Aerik grin. The prospect of spending time with someone so good-natured was enormously appealing.

"So, now we have two."

Aerik turned to see Maiko sauntering over, leading his horse. He eyed Catrin like she was a whore. "My luck is improving."

Aerik grimaced. "Catrin, this is Maiko. One of the militia's finest Hands, without a doubt. A charmer too."

"Shut up," Maiko said, his eyes never leaving Catrin. "You talk too much."

"You're probably right. But now I won't have to hold up both sides of the conversation." He gave Rhan a sidelong glance while securing their packs with the other gear. The finder's sour expression as he watched Maiko spoke well of his judgment but raised a question about his relationship to Catrin.

Talk around the corral subsided, and a barked order brought the Tyumens to attention. Rhan and Catrin followed along, though they couldn't hide their apprehension.

Jerolin and two aides were standing at the corral's woven rope gate. The legate was wearing his full regalia, creating an impression of nobility that seemed out of place among the ruins. "You have your orders," he said, looking sternly at the assembled soldiers and conscripts. "Be diligent, for heresy never sleeps. Remember your duty and the rewards of success. Find the poison that pollutes the body of Tyume. Do not fail." He turned and walked toward the mess tent without waiting to see his soldiers off.

Maiko mounted first. "Hurry up. You heard what he said. We have a job to do."

Aerik turned to Rhan and Catrin. "Ready to go? Let me know if you need any help."

"I'm ready," Rhan said. He put a foot in the stirrup and swung smoothly into his saddle. Excitement filled his face. "I've always wanted to do this. Ride, I mean."

Aerik grinned at him. "We'll see how you feel about it by day's end. But at least you're off to a good start. Catrin?"

"I'm ready too." She climbed into her saddle, more awkwardly than Rhan but showing no fear of the horse. Aerik checked their saddle belts one last time, and then they were off.

THE sun warmed their backs as they set out for a remote fishing town called Eben. Branching off from the route the convoy was following as it conscripted finders from other villages, they left the plain and entered forested foothills. Aerik set a leisurely pace to accommodate the novice riders.

Maiko soon tired of their company and rode ahead to scout the trail. Aerik was glad to see him depart. Catrin and Rhan had kept their silence while the Hand ridiculed their riding but their irritation was plain.

Aerik slowed their pace as soon as Maiko disappeared around a bend in the trail. Riding abreast was easy despite trees that were erasing the ancient roadway they followed. "How are you doing?" he asked.

Rhan beamed at him. "This is so much faster than walking, and easy on the feet. They ought to let finders use horses without paying the tax. We'd bring in a lot more relics."

"I think you're right. Finding more relics would benefit everyone. Besides, I can't imagine what it would be like, never going far from where you were born."

Catrin looked at him nervously. "You're questioning the priests? Isn't that... well, sort of like heresy?"

Aerik shrugged. "Maybe if the priests hear about it. But who's going to tell them? I'm sure Maiko tells his Examiner everything, but I don't." He made a sweeping gesture to encompass the sun-speckled forest. "In some ways, you're lucky to live out here. You don't have

Tyume looking over your shoulder all the time. How often do you even have to see an Examiner?"

"Often enough," Rhan said. All enthusiasm had vanished from his voice. "But in Balmorel they don't shrive anyone except the elders. The rest of us aren't important enough. They only check us for marks. Someone is culled most every year."

"That's a lot, especially for a small village. In Chakragil we sometimes go three years without a culling. Of course, that's why the city was built where it was. The mountains were less touched by daemons in the wars."

"Not everybody gets to live in a refuge. What happens to children of the powerful when they're culled?"

"Rhan, don't pester him." Catrin's voice held a clear warning. "We're here to serve."

"Questions don't bother me," Aerik said. "You're right to be careful, though. Some people like nothing better than to take offense." He turned back to Rhan. "They're taken into the temple and never return. I've heard they're given two potions to drink. The first puts them to sleep in a few minutes. The second is a poison that kills while they slumber. The family grieves, of course, but the bloodline has to be protected."

"Nobody goes to the brickyards? Gets sent to the river to dig clay? Or is that saved for upcountry folk?"

"Rhan!" Catrin's fierce glare discouraged any argument.

"Sorry." He was flushed, his back stiff.

Aerik thought Rhan looked more defiant than sorry, and resentful of being silenced. He sympathized. His father had cautioned him countless times to keep his own counsel, especially around strangers. Perhaps life in the country wasn't as different as he had imagined.

They rode in silence while birdsong and a gentle wind smelling of decaying pine needles softened hasty words. He pondered what Rhan had said and the spirit it had taken to speak so bluntly. It was refreshing. His new companion had far more candor than was common in Chakragil.

"There's truth to what you say," Aerik said after a few minutes. "The rules aren't the same for everyone. I think that should change."

Rhan looked surprised. "How? I don't think asking nicely will do much good."

"Well... I agree it won't be easy, but that doesn't mean we shouldn't try. Maybe we should talk about it. Can we start over?"

Rhan gave him a cautious smile. "I'm willing. I'd like to be friends, if we can."

The offer sounded sincere, and Aerik was charmed. His father said that an open heart was rarer than a fair face, and Rhan seemed to possess both.

The trail soon emerged on a bluff overlooking a river valley. Calm waters flowed by in a broad jade ribbon. Maiko was lying in the shade of an old oak with his eyes closed. He gave no sign of hearing their approach. Judging by the food littering the ground, he had been there quite a while.

Aerik suppressed a smile when his companions dismounted and walked their first steps. Catrin's wince was what he had expected. Rhan concealed it better, but it was obvious he was discovering muscles he hadn't known he had. Aerik helped them unsaddle their horses and then carried a saddlebag with provisions to a flat rock well removed from Maiko.

Rhan settled into a cross-legged position. With no hesitation he peeled off his tunic and tossed it aside. His hairless torso was almost as tawny as his hair. He closed his eyes and basked in the sun like a cat, completely at ease.

Aerik forced himself not to stare. Clothing was the single greatest sign of one's rank. For someone to shed it in public was remarkable. But Catrin took no notice, so perhaps this was just another unexpected facet of rural life.

He knelt on the rock and removed their lunch of pemmican, nuts, cheese, and apples. As he distributed the food, he was keenly aware of Rhan's lean form an arm's reach away. The finder's sensuality was effortless, as if the effect his sleekly muscled body might have on others had never occurred to him. Artists in Chakragil would have paid him generously to sit for paintings.

Aerik noticed Catrin watching him. He blushed and picked up a water skin, wondering if she had seen his interest in their companion. "Care for some water?" he asked. She accepted the skin and took a drink, her eyes never leaving his.

Rhan stirred and leaned forward, choosing a piece of pemmican. He chewed it slowly while watching the river below them. His eyes nearly matched the river's jade.

"Have you been here before?" Aerik asked, anxious to escape Catrin's scrutiny. "This is pretty far from your village, isn't it?"

Rhan nodded and swallowed his pemmican. "It is, and not the kind of place where finders usually work." He pointed at the forested slopes on each side of the river. "The ancients didn't often build where it's steep like this. Maybe because of landslides, I think." His brow furrowed while he twisted off a bite-sized piece of pemmican. "What about the mountains around Chakragil? Are there many ruins there?"

"Not a lot. Remoteness is what spared it from the daemon wars. That's the main reason there are almost no finders in Chakragil. There's nothing much to find."

Rhan washed down his food with a swig of water and then fixed Aerik with a challenging gaze. "There are other reasons too, aren't there? Why should Tyumens risk their lives when they can take what others find?"

Catrin nearly choked on the cheese she was eating. "Don't be a dolt, Rhan! They have to make sure the relics are safe." She looked like she was ready to gag him if he said another word.

Aerik glanced at Maiko, who still seemed to be dozing. He leaned forward and lowered his voice so only Rhan and Catrin could possibly hear him. "I can't deny it. I'll tell you what's happening in the capital if you swear not to repeat it. Talking about such things can be dangerous." He gave a nod toward Maiko. "He has no fondness for me."

Rhan didn't hesitate. "I swear," he whispered, holding out a hand

and curling his fingers into his palm in the oath sign. Catrin looked wary but soon made the same gesture.

Aerik sprang to his feet. "Let's give Maiko a bit more space." The others stood less gracefully, the morning's ride obviously being felt. They gathered their food and carried it down the slope until Aerik called a halt at a slab of sun-warmed granite where they could resume their meal.

Aerik sat so he could see if Maiko got up and then turned to his companions. "I'm relying on your oath," he said. "Even though nothing I say is disloyal to the empire and I'm sure nothing you say is meant that way."

"Why are you doing this?" Catrin demanded. "Isn't it enough you drag us away from home just before harvest? Is this some kind of test?"

"No test." Aerik held up a placating hand. "I'm doing this because Rhan asked a fair question and he deserves an answer. Some of us, my father's faction, think tributes have grown too high. That the empire's power is not used wisely." He looked at Rhan. "There's another reason we should talk. I welcome your questions. But it would be best to ask them when Maiko's not around."

Rhan's eyes narrowed. "Why are you worried about him? He's just a Hand and you're an Eye. You see for the empire and he just follows orders."

"You're an Eye?" Catrin's voice squeaked like a snake had just landed in her lap.

Aerik gave her an awkward smile. "Hard to believe, isn't it? It's true, but doesn't mean as much as you think. Rhan didn't tell you?"

"No." She glared at the finder.

"It comes through a family connection." He shrugged. "I haven't even undergone the ritual yet. That won't happen for nine years. That's when I turn thirty and can enter the Oireachtas. So for me the title is more like a family heirloom." He glanced up the slope. "As for Maiko, don't doubt the trouble he can cause. He's devout and will report anything he thinks is heresy."

Catrin looked skeptical. "So are you saying Rhan's right? That the empire takes too much and doesn't do enough in return?"

"In part. Despite its demands, the empire does provide a great service. Keeping peace for five hundred years is no small thing. But some in Chakragil think power has been held by too few, for too long. The archon is old and his successor hasn't been chosen. The factions are positioning for a fight."

A movement up the slope drew his attention. Maiko was standing and looking out over the river. "He's up. We'd better get back. We'll have another long ride this afternoon."

THEY pitched their tents on scattered patches of ground along a meandering stream, anywhere they could find enough space that was free of rocks, trees and bushes. Aerik assumed the chore of preparing a stew from dried venison and vegetables, insisting that Catrin and Rhan rest their sore muscles. Maiko watched his labors in disbelief before turning his gaze to Catrin. She ignored his stares but kept her distance.

They had ridden into twilight and it was dark by the time the stew was ready. Stars filled the clear sky like sparks thrown across the heavens. Aerik realized he was enjoying himself. Discipline in the convoy was rigid, and their subaltern dispensed punishment freely. While Aerik had obeyed the rules and avoided the lash, he had not truly relaxed since leaving Chakragil.

"We made good time today," he said. "It's lucky there's an old road keeping the trees down." He glanced at Rhan, who had been eyeing Maiko warily while finishing his meal. "How much do you know about Eben? Does it have trade with Balmorel?"

Rhan looked away from Maiko, his features easing as if he was abandoning an unpleasant thought. Blond locks fell over his forehead, and he peered through them like a watchful cat. When he smiled, Aerik blushed. He was amazed that someone so recently met could affect him so strongly.

"No, it's too distant. I heard someone talking about it a few months ago but didn't pay much attention. I was getting ready to go on a dig."

"Any mention of a relic? Do you think something might have turned up way out here?"

Maiko tossed his bowl aside. "Why do you think we're going there, runt? Yokels dig up relics all the time. If it weren't for us, the idiots would wake a daemon. Then we'd be back at war."

"Hmm. Jerolin told you this?"

Maiko leaned back against a rock, crossing his arms behind his head. "You know the missals. Or didn't you learn them? Maybe all that singing and dancing addled whatever brains you were born with."

Aerik gave Catrin a wry smile. "You see how exalted my rank is, yes? If Maiko the Hand can mock me, you have nothing to fear."

"She can fear me instead," Maiko said. "I have a mind to make her serve Tyume the way a woman should."

Rhan was on his feet in an instant. "Don't touch her." His voice was low with menace. "You have no right."

Maiko got to his feet and stood toe to toe with the finder. He was a bit taller than Rhan and outweighed him by half. "I'm a Hand of Tyume. You're nothing, and neither is she. I'll take whatever I want."

Aerik saw Rhan's fists clench and the flush of anger coloring his face. He'd seen the reaction before, back in the barracks. Maiko liked to incite a brawl with someone smaller for the blood sport. He jumped up and stepped between them, facing the Hand as his heart suddenly hammered. Maiko was far heavier and the top of Aerik's head only came to Maiko's chin, but there was no turning back.

Maiko started to shove him aside, but Aerik grabbed his arm and gave it a sharp twist, forcing Maiko to spin around. The man bellowed, but he held tight.

"Don't touch either of them. If you do you'll answer for it here and now. Against all of us."

"Let go! This isn't your affair!"

Aerik gave the arm another twist. "I say it is. Yield, Maiko. Swear on Tyume's name you'll leave them alone."

"Fuck you!"

A fierce twist made the man yowl.

"I swear, by Tyume, I swear!"

Aerik released Maiko's arm. He would have jumped away except Rhan still stood at his back. The finder hadn't retreated an inch and his fast breath was hot against Aerik's hair.

Maiko spun around and glared at Aerik with barely controlled rage.

"Tyume took your oath," Aerik said. "It's done. Now apologize to Catrin and forget about it."

"I won't drop this, Rodan. Just wait till the subaltern hears you attacked me. You've gone too far and your family's not here to get you off. You'll get the lash, I promise." He turned and stalked into the forest, leaving his threat hanging.

Aerik took a deep breath and let it out slowly, only then realizing he was shaking. A hand on his shoulder made him jump.

"Thanks," Rhan said, squeezing his shoulder. "That could have come out a lot worse."

Aerik nodded. "He could have easily broken free, you know. I guess he was afraid to injure me. Maybe that title is good for something, after all."

Rhan turned him and stepped back to look in his face. "I don't think that's it. He's big, but he knew you'd fight. And that he'd have to take on all of us."

"A cheerful thought." Aerik laughed, still shaky. He found himself unable to look away from Rhan's concerned gaze. "Um, you have my thanks too. I was more tired of his abuse than I care to admit. That felt good." A corner of his mouth quirked up. "Now that it's over, anyway."

"Are you sure it's over?" Catrin asked. She was still huddled by the fire. "He might come back, and there isn't a clearing big enough for us to move our tents in sight of each other."

Aerik thought a moment before answering. "He won't do anything to either of you, at least not directly. He's superstitious to the core and won't break an oath he made on Tyume's name. He'll have it in for me, though." The prospect of explaining this to his superiors was sobering.

"Superstitious?" Rhan regarded him curiously. "You're not afraid of breaking an oath?"

"I keep my word, but not from fear of the gods."

"You don't think they're watching us?"

Aerik glanced toward the forest. "I think we should be sure we're alone before talking about this."

Catrin stood, her cloak pulled tight around her shoulders. "I'll wash dishes, since you did the cooking."

"I'll take care of it," Aerik said. "Maiko has notions about a woman's place, but I don't. You should rest. I know how hard the ride must have been for you."

She grimaced. "I hope you're right about it getting easier. Thanks." She handed him her bowl. "My turn tomorrow."

Aerik accepted the bowl. "Get a good night's rest. We'll be starting early."

She nodded and left for her tent.

"I'll do it," Rhan said, taking the bowl from Aerik's hands. "You've worked enough today."

"We'll do it together. I'd welcome the company."

They carried utensils and the cooking pot to the nearby stream. Rhan peeled off his shirt again, then knelt by the water and gathered a handful of long grass for scouring. Though lean enough for ribs to show as he bent forward, his arms and broad shoulders were strongly muscled. Aerik pulled up his sleeves and went to work.

They did the chore in companionable silence, leaning close and occasionally touching as they worked. Aerik wondered if the fleeting contacts were intentional, but Rhan's inscrutable expression gave no clue. When they were finished, Rhan used his shirt to dry his arms, then pulled his knees up to his chest and wrapped his arms around them. Moonlight painted him silver. He looked at Aerik and for a time they were quiet, listening to the rippling brook and wind stirring the reeds.

"You're not what I expected," Rhan said at last. "You're different than most of them, aren't you?" It was more a statement than a question.

Aerik shrugged. "I'm not much of a soldier, I guess, but there are other Tyumens like me. How many of us have you met, anyway?"

"You're the first I've talked with. The Examiner doesn't count. He just made me strip so he could look for marks and then shoved me out of the elders' hall."

"Let's forget about the empire, all right? Just be friends. It will make this trip a lot more pleasant. And, um…."

"What?" Rhan laid his head on his knees and watched Aerik calmly. His chaotic curls glowed in the moonlight.

Aerik felt a blush warm his cheeks and was grateful for the darkness. Perhaps it was the light playing tricks, but something about Rhan's gaze made him feel the finder could look right through his skin and see his heart. It was disconcerting.

"Well… I noticed what you did when Jerolin was calling finders to join our teams. You changed places with the woman next to you. I'm glad you did, but I'm curious why you did it."

Rhan grinned. "It's good to be curious."

Though he burned with embarrassment, Aerik returned the smile. "This is strange. You've never been far from your village and I'm from a noble family in Chakragil, but you make me feel artless."

"We're age-mates, within a year. And you're far more experienced than me." He held Aerik's gaze. "I'm sure there are many things you could teach me."

"Maybe it's your questions that make you seem older. They say that asking questions is a sign of wisdom."

This time Rhan lifted his head and laughed. "That's not what Balmorel's elders say! They think questions are the sign of a pest."

Laughing in turn, Aerik felt a growing sense of ease. He felt sure Rhan's qualms about the empire concealed no personal hostility. "I'm sorry about Maiko," he said. "Hands are a rough lot. And he's more oafish than most."

"I noticed." Rhan's eyes held a mischievous sparkle. "I also noticed what he said about singing and dancing. What was he talking about?"

"I did the usual temple service when I started my schooling. Learning traditional songs and dances is part of it. I was better at it than most, though. My father let me study the arts at Chakragil's academy. He thought it might come in useful someday."

"Has it?"

"Not the way he thought. He hoped I'd meet people who'd become influential, and I don't know if that will ever happen. But learning to sing and dance was one of the best things I've ever done. I love it."

Rhan released his knees and leaned back, supporting himself on arms thrust behind his shoulders. He seemed oblivious to the cooling air and displayed his smooth torso as if posing for a sculptor. "I'd like to hear you sing. So would Catrin. I imagine your music is different from what we have at home."

"Probably. I'd like to hear your songs too. Um, I still don't know Catrin very well. You two seem close. Are you and she, um…."

Rhan cocked his head. "Are we what? Bed mates?"

Rhan's directness threw him off balance. He wondered what it was about the finder that made him so tongue-tied. Lack of words wasn't his usual problem. He nodded, afraid his voice would betray him.

"No. We're not." His attentive gaze implied there was more to be said.

"Sorry, I didn't mean to intrude. It's none of my business."

"It's all right. Catrin's a good friend, and that's the way I'd like to keep it." He stretched, arching his back and straightening his legs along the ground. "Time for sleep. My legs have never been this sore. Tomorrow is going to be tough."

"I have balm for sore muscles. Dances can be very demanding. Want to try it?"

Rhan stood, wincing at the movement. "How does it smell? Some balms really stink."

"Mine is odorless and works really well. My friend who made it is studying to become a healer."

Rhan picked up his shirt and then nodded. "Thanks. It's in your tent?"

"Yes. Let's leave the dishes here until morning." Aerik got up and led the way upstream to where he had pitched his tent. "I almost decided to sleep under the stars tonight," he said. "But last time I did that, it rained, and I don't want to start this journey with a wet bedroll." He opened the tent flap and crawled inside, emerging a few seconds later with an oilskin pouch the size of a man's fist.

"Just rub it on?" Rhan asked, accepting the pouch gingerly.

"Yes. Well, that's not really the best way." He was painfully aware of Rhan's wild beauty but was determined not to let awkwardness vanquish him again. "It works best if you relax and somebody else massages it in. The massage helps as much as the balm, probably."

"Oh." Rhan suddenly grinned while looking Aerik straight in the eyes. He made no move to leave.

Aerik was dazzled, although the friendly appraisal made him feel naked. "Um, I could show you, if you'd like."

"Only if you want to." Rhan still held his gaze. "You've already been very kind."

Aerik took back the pouch. "Perhaps I have a lot to make up for." He gestured at his tent. "Want to use my bedroll? It's on the smoothest spot I could find. There's enough room if we move the saddlebags out."

Rhan crawled into the tent and handed the gear to Aerik, who stacked it by the entrance before going inside. The tent was designed for a single soldier and his gear but removing the saddlebags created enough room for two. They sat next to each other on the bedroll, letting their eyes adjust to faint light flowing through the open flap like mist.

"Whenever you're ready," Aerik said after a few moments. Anticipation filled him.

Rhan pulled his boots off, then unbuckled his belt and loosed the fastening of his pants. Leaning back, he lifted his hips and slid the leathers to his knees in a single quick tug. He pulled them off and crouched while Aerik moved off the bedroll. As soon as the way was clear he folded his shirt into a makeshift pillow and lay face down. His body from the waist down was as tan as his torso.

Aerik pulled off his boots and knelt at Rhan's side. He poured a trickle of balm into one hand, then put the pouch aside and rubbed his palms together to warm the fluid. "Feeling it mostly in your thighs?"

"That's the worst spot. And a bit in my back too."

"I'll start with your back so you can get used to it before I hit the really sore spots. Try to stay loose, even if I push hard." He moved around to kneel above Rhan's head. "Keep your arms along your sides. That way your muscles can relax more."

Rhan complied, muscles shifting as he positioned his arms.

Aerik placed both palms on Rhan's upper back, fingers pointed toward the spine, then leaned forward and pushed his hands down in a smooth glide. His fingertips traced along Rhan's backbone, probing the furrows on each side. When he reached Rhan's buttocks, he slid his hands apart and pulled them along the sides of the torso. He kept a strong grip, pulling hard. As his hands reached Rhan's armpits he slid them to the upper back and pivoted them so his fingers could again trace the spine. Once the pattern was established he began repeating it, putting more weight behind his hands.

"You've done this before," Rhan said. "I really like it."

Aerik laughed softly, exhilarated as he caressed Rhan's muscular flesh. His cock had gotten hard within seconds and was creating sweet torment in its confinement. He hoped the tent's darkness would save him from embarrassment. "I had a good teacher. Another dancer at the academy, a year older than me. Stian's in the city guard now, but we're still good friends." He kept up his steady movements as he talked, probing for the deep layer of muscle in Rhan's tapering back. The strong body felt wonderfully alive beneath his hands. He stretched down and worked Rhan's lower back with his thumbs, alternating strokes close to the spine and just below the waistline. The finder's groans were rewarded with deeper and stronger strokes.

"Now for your legs," Aerik said after Rhan's lower back was thoroughly explored. "That's what you need most, after a day in the saddle."

He moved to the other end of the bedroll, sliding one hand down Rhan's body to maintain contact, and straddled the finder's calves. After pouring more balm and warming it between his palms, he placed a hand just above each knee. He worked his way upward while stroking the inside of each thigh with circling thumb movements. When he reached the buttocks he raked back down, pressing firmly with just his fingertips, before repeating the upward stroke.

Rhan started breathing faster and Aerik felt the powerful muscles quivering beneath his hands. He moved slowly and deliberately, repeating the pattern but introducing variations in pressure, exploring with touch what had been hidden from his eyes. He used all his skill, and Rhan's moans told him the effort was not wasted. He would have liked to continue all night, but the confinement of his erection was becoming painful.

"Time for the front," he said, moving to the side. He took a last look at the virile sweep of Rhan's back and strong legs, wondering how long he'd have to wait before this marvel of symmetry was again revealed to him.

Rhan stretched, his chest and feet lifting off the bedroll as his back arched. Then he rolled over and propped himself up with elbows beneath his shoulders. He looked at Aerik through half-closed eyes.

Heat suffused Aerik in a rush. Rhan was fully erect and made no attempt to conceal it. His cock speared up like a smooth horn, making a low arch from his groin to above his navel. The dusky head was slick and clear liquid smeared his flat belly.

"You're right," Rhan said, giving Aerik a friendly grin. "The balm's better if someone else rubs it in." His head tilted. "I hope I'm not giving offense. You know how it is when this happens. There's no way to stop it."

Aerik swallowed, shocked but entranced by Rhan's candor. It made Chakragil's formal manners seem absurd. He blushed furiously but couldn't look away.

"I didn't mean to make you nervous," Rhan said. He drew up his legs and rocked onto his knees, facing Aerik and putting a hand on each shoulder. "I know we're newly met. But we're alike, I think. What you want is the same as what I want."

"What... how do you know what I want?" Aerik felt strange, as if Rhan were the experienced one and he the provincial, but the finder's confidence made him think this moment had been inevitable. Rhan was an equal.

"Am I wrong?" Rhan asked. "If you doubt, listen to what your body tells you." He leaned forward and brought their lips together.

Any reluctance to admit his desire burned away. Heart pounding, he put his arms around Rhan and parted his lips in response to his new companion's urging. They kissed deeply. Rhan's gentle insistence never faltered, his hands moving down Aerik's back and holding him strongly. Aerik was light-headed and fiercely aroused. "Let me take your shirt off," Rhan whispered.

Aerik raised his arms while Rhan pulled the shirt up. He felt the heat of the finder's body against his skin, warm as the afternoon sun. Rhan gave him a dazzling grin and put an arm around his shoulders, drawing him down to the bedroll. He followed willingly.

They lay side by side and renewed their kisses while caressing each other with eager hands. Aerik had thought he was skilled at love, but Rhan's directness left him breathless. The finder's lips strayed over his face, neck, and chest as Aerik's fingers tangled in thick curls.

The leisurely pace of Rhan's exploration was intoxicating but agonizing. Aerik's cock ached and its confinement was becoming torture, but Rhan made no move to release it. He wondered if Rhan was waiting for him to act first and decided to find out.

He pulled away and looked Rhan in the eyes. The finder seemed dazed, glowing with friendly lust. Aerik slid a hand from where it rested on Rhan's ribs down to his waist. He was rewarded with an expectant smile.

Encouraged, he moved his hand between their bodies, lightly caressing his friend's flat belly. This time Rhan responded by leaning in for a kiss. Their lips met as Aerik's fingers found the thick shaft of Rhan's erection.

There was no doubt that the finder was eager for more. His tongue slipped between Aerik's lips and his smooth cock throbbed in the encircling fingers. Aerik squeezed gently and felt slickness on his forearm where Rhan's hard flesh strained against it. Rhan moaned and broke their kiss. "You too," he said urgently. "Can I?"

Aerik answered by releasing Rhan long enough to unfasten his pants and shimmy out of them. His cock slapped against his belly as it was freed.

Rhan rolled on top of him, supported on knees and elbows so their skin touched. "You feel wonderful," he whispered, his lips an inch from Aerik's ear. "Even better than I imagined." His slid his hands beneath Aerik's shoulders and nuzzled his neck while their slippery cocks rubbed and jousted.

As much as he was enjoying himself, Aerik was set on returning pleasure as well as receiving it. He slid his hands down Rhan's back and briefly squeezed his buttocks before pulling him tight and rolling him onto his back. Moving to the side, he picked up the pouch of balm and dangled it above Rhan. "It's good for more than sore muscles. Let me show you." He dribbled salve into his palm, then laid his hand flat against the underside of Rhan's cock and slowly moved it in small circles. The phallus felt stiff as oak yet silky smooth.

Rhan bucked. The muscles sheathing his abdomen etched clean lines as Aerik's slippery fingers caressed the sensitive underside of his glans and tugged at his foreskin.

Aerik leaned down and kissed Rhan deeply, wrapping his fingers around the rampant cock and squeezing it with a milking motion.

Rhan moaned and put a hand behind Aerik's head. His body jerked and hot liquid splattered Aerik's cheek. Aerik continued the kiss while gently stroking. Five more jets of semen splattered his face and shoulder while Rhan shuddered. The air was thick with his seed's musky scent.

When Rhan was spent, Aerik kissed him on the cheek. "I'm glad I found you," he whispered.

"Not as glad as I am," Rhan said, his chest rising and falling with fast breaths. His nostrils were flared, and his eyes had lost none of their intensity. "Lean back."

Aerik needed no persuasion. Sitting on his haunches, he thrust his arms behind his back and let his erection spear the air. Though an inch shorter than Rhan's, it had the same thick shaft and upward curve. The flaring glans was slick with his arousal.

Rhan rolled onto his stomach. Instead of reaching for the offered phallus as Aerik expected, he raised himself on his elbows and licked the erection from root to tip. Then he took the glans in his mouth and engulfed it in wet heat.

Rhan's lovemaking was as confident as his kisses. He was completely focused as his lips and tongue teased the sensitive flesh, slowing whenever Aerik reached the brink of release, prolonging pleasure until it soared to a sharp intensity.

At last no further delay was possible. Aerik shook as his ejaculation spewed over the caressing tongue. Rhan made no attempt to contain it, licking the cock's head and tugging on it with his lips until the orgasm finally subsided. Aerik tumbled to the bedroll, gasping. Rhan moved to his side and kissed him, his lips slick with come.

Something tugged at Aerik's mind as they lay in each other's arms. He remembered and rolled onto his side to face the finder. "Remember what you said? About it feeling better than you expected?"

Rhan smiled faintly and gave him an amiable squeeze without opening his eyes. "Far better."

"I was just wondering... was that your first time?"

Rhan opened his eyes and nodded. "Balmorel is small, and the elders think it needs to grow. They say love between men is a waste of seed."

"Oh." He lay back again and rested his head against Rhan's shoulder. "The priests say the same, but only the pious take them seriously. Everyone else does what they please."

Rhan remained silent for a time, then pressed his cheek against Aerik's hair. "It feels like my life is finally starting. I've waited a long time for this."

Aerik found Rhan's hand and clasped it. "You could have fooled me. Some people have natural talent for love. You're—"

Rhan sat up and peered out the tent's entrance. "Did you hear that?"

Aerik rolled to his knees and stuck his head outside to look around. The forest seemed bright after the tent's shadows. He caught a flash of movement among nearby trees. "Something fairly big, I think. Couldn't make it out, though."

Rhan slipped outside the tent and stood motionless. After a moment he padded over to the place where Aerik had seen movement and examined the ground.

Aerik followed, mystified. "You see anything?"

He crouched and pointed to a place where dirt and pine needles had been disturbed. "Maiko was here. I'm sure of it."

"How can you tell?" Rhan sounded confident, but it was hard to see how such small traces could prove anything.

"I... I can't really explain. Reading signs comes with practice, that's all. I've been doing it all my life. Believe me, Maiko was here."

He stood, looking troubled. "How much do you think he heard?"

Aerik felt a chill. "No way to tell. All I know is, he's a bastard and has it in for both of us." He took a deep breath. "All we can do is wait for tomorrow and see what happens. It probably won't be pleasant."

Chapter Three

LOW-HANGING clouds were threatening rain when Rhan woke. Impassioned dreams lingered in his mind, and his erection ached as he remembered the musky fragrance of Aerik's arousal during the massage. He closed his eyes and breathed deeply, still smelling Aerik's heady scent on his skin.

After bathing in the brook, he followed it upstream to the clearing where Aerik's tent was pitched. A gentle breeze flowed from the direction of his destination. It carried the scent of Aerik's sweat, healthy and fresh. Curiosity stirred. He slowed as he neared the clearing and peered between the trees.

The tent was already down, leaving a rectangular area where meadow grasses had been flattened. Aerik was in the open space, wearing only his pants. His perfectly proportioned body glistened with sweat, and he moved with athletic grace, limbs speaking an acrobatic language meant for eyes rather than ears. Concentration gave his face a more reserved aspect than the night before, but he was still beautiful. He danced with masculine conviction to music that only he could hear.

Entranced, Rhan kept still and watched the friend who had so unexpectedly changed his life. Being torn from his village should have been a hardship, but instead it filled him with hope. His first taste of freedom, and of love, was intoxicating.

Aerik was doing a slow back flip in seeming defiance of gravity when Maiko emerged from the forest, carrying with him a sour body odor. The Hand looked dangerously smug. He walked into Aerik's exercise space, not giving him enough room to continue.

"We don't have time for this," Maiko said. "We're supposed to ride hard. You heard our orders."

Aerik stepped back, beads of sweat running down his face and chest. "We're moving fast enough. Besides, Catrin and Rhan need an easier pace. You know what it's like for new riders."

"They don't matter and you know it. They're just peasants."

Aerik's eyebrows pulled down. "Don't bother them, Maiko. Remember your oath."

"I was thinking about that last night. You're going to release me from that oath. And I'm going to make sure those dirt-grubbers know their place."

Aerik wiped his brow with a forearm while watching the Hand warily. "Not a chance. You've taken a vow, it's done."

"Not if you value your skin, runt. I know all about you. Things you don't want your Examiner or your high and mighty father to hear about. Release the oath, or you'll be in so much trouble you'll wish you'd never left Chakragil."

"You're a clumsy liar, Maiko." Rhan could smell Aerik's alarm, though his face concealed it well.

Maiko towered over Aerik, his hands balled in fists, but Aerik stood firm. "Tell people whatever stories you want. It'll be your word against mine. I'm not releasing you from the vow, and you'll leave them alone. You swore on Tyume's name and there are three witnesses. Breaking the oath would be an affront to the gods. Want me to tell your Examiner about that?"

Maiko spun and stalked off, leaving an acrid stench of rage in his wake.

Rhan faded into the forest. He yearned to talk with Aerik, but it was too dangerous when Maiko was near. He retreated to the spot where they had cleaned dishes and collected their gear before heading to the fire pit.

Smoke told him that someone had already started a fire long

before he arrived. Catrin was warming her hands over the flames and seemed relieved to see him. "Give me that pot. I'm dying for some tea."

She filled the pot with water and hung it on a forked branch she had propped above the fire. "You look more tumbled than usual," she said. "Did you sleep well?"

Rhan crouched near the fire's warmth. "I guess so. Lots of dreams." He immediately realized it was an unwise topic. "What about you? Were you worried about Maiko?"

She removed several pieces of fragrant bark from the supplies she had packed and then tossed them in the pot. "Not really. Though I made sure my knife was within reach." She glanced up. "Do you trust him? Aerik, I mean? I wasn't sure whether to believe what he said about Maiko keeping his vow."

Rhan nodded. "I trust him." He was afraid to say more. Catrin was watching him intently.

"Well… maybe you're right. But be careful. He's a Tyumen and he can't help but think like one. Like Marenka said, their way of living isn't for us."

Rhan stood and ran fingers through his loose curls in a futile attempt to impose order on still-damp hair. "He can't help where he was born, Catrin. I think he's interesting. Aren't you curious what the capital's like? Did you know he was a temple dancer?"

"I think you'd do well never to set foot inside a temple of Tyume. You belong at home, Rhan. We need you."

Rhan crossed his arms. "Well, the elders don't act like it most of the time. If complaints were coins, I'd have enough—" His frown faded as Aerik entered the clearing, carrying his gear. "Come warm yourself," Rhan said. "You look cold."

"A cold bath is better than none." Aerik carried his gear to where the horses were tethered. His hair was still wet, but he seemed calm and refreshed. He joined them and peered into the pot. "Good. We also have dried apples and hard biscuits."

"Where's Maiko?" Catrin asked, looking around.

Aerik shrugged. "He usually eats alone, when he can. I've always considered it his best feature."

Catrin's smirk showed her agreement. "Tea's about ready."

Aerik dug food from his saddlebags while Catrin used the bowls to ladle tea from the pot. They settled around the fire and passed the simple fare around.

Rhan was sipping from his bowl when he noticed Aerik's sidelong glance in his direction. Their eyes met and he blushed. He was sure they were thinking about the same thing. In moments he was hard.

He shifted to conceal his erection from Catrin, though Aerik could now see it outlined against his leg. The happy gleam in Aerik's eyes dissolved his embarrassment instantly. He took a bite of dried apple, trying to concentrate on its sweetness and make his body forget its other demands. The scent of his new friend's arousal was making it difficult.

"How far from Eben do you think we are?" Catrin asked.

Aerik started to answer, but stopped when Maiko strode into the clearing with his gear. The Hand threw his load to the ground and started saddling his mount. "Time to get started," he said, keeping his back to them. "Quit loafing if you want to stay out of trouble." He glanced over his shoulder at Aerik. "I'll be giving a full report on what happens out here."

Rhan bristled at the menacing tone and the man's angry scent, but Aerik glanced at him and shook his head slightly. He was still troubled and had no doubt Maiko would take vengeance if given an opportunity.

They finished their breakfast while Maiko rode ahead. Sun was starting to break through the clouds by the time they left the clearing and followed the Hand's trail.

THEY caught up with Maiko late in the morning. The Hand stayed ahead, a small display of hostility, and Catrin lagged behind. She seemed pained by the riding, but she bore it stoically. Rhan had to admire her determination. He had always felt she'd make a fine wife for someone. Just not for him.

Maiko's threats had failed to dampen Aerik's enthusiasm. He remained an engaging travel companion, full of observations and questions. "Why did you become a finder?" he asked Rhan when the path cleared enough for the two of them to ride abreast. "Did you choose for yourself or do your elders decide such things?"

"It seemed to happen by itself," Rhan said. "I've always been good at finding things. Even when I was too small to walk far from home, I'd find buried relics in the fields." He shrugged. "Maybe I was just more interested in looking." He wished he could admit that his nose led him to most finds, but the dangers of ever revealing that secret were too great.

Aerik swerved to dodge a tree and then moved back to his side. "Most people are afraid of relics, but finders usually aren't. That's the main difference I think. Have you ever found one that scared you?"

"Well, I've found things that make me careful. But nothing that hurt me. I'm not sure relics are as dangerous as they say. Some of them are even beautiful." He stopped short, realizing he was straying into heresy. Priests of Tyume held their own beliefs about relics and had no tolerance for dissent. He turned to see if Aerik had caught the slip and was surprised to see a friendly grin. It was the most entrancing sight he'd seen all day.

"My father has heard rumors of secret vaults carved deep in Mount Karfax, beyond the archives," Aerik said. "Galleries filled with beautiful relics from all over the empire. The priests deny it, of course. They'd have to pay the finders if they admitted keeping relics. It's cheaper to say the relics are daemon work and claim they were destroyed."

"I knew it! Some of my finds have been confiscated too. Beautiful, fine ones. Just because you don't know what something's for doesn't mean it's dangerous. Balmorel could have made a lot if we'd kept them."

Aerik nodded. "If the stories are true, it's an injustice. But maybe there's more to it than greed. If you don't know what a relic does, how can you be sure it's not harmful?" He swept an arm in an all-encompassing gesture. "There's no denying the ruins. The daemon wars destroyed so much. And even now, the bloodline is still poisoned. Can you be sure it's wrong to hide relics we don't understand?"

"The priests should pay if they keep relics instead of destroying them," Rhan said, still hot. "That's the rule. You don't know what it's like, going hungry because a third of the harvest went in tribute."

"Easy, friend." Aerik pointed ahead, where Maiko kept an impatient lead. "He's thickheaded, but has good ears."

Realizing he had raised his voice, Rhan took a deep breath and settled back into his saddle. He was relieved to see no resentment in Aerik's expression. "Sorry. You don't know what it's like, though. To dig for days and find something good, then have an Examiner take it away." He paused. "These secret collections, do you think they really exist?"

"I'd bet on it. My father uses the library in the archives. There are doors his key won't open. He's a magistraat, not a cleric, and doesn't know how much the priests are hiding." He lowered his voice. "According to my father, many priests don't even believe what they teach. The lessons are meant to keep people in their place. To make men like Maiko behave." He nodded in Maiko's direction. "Can you imagine what he'd be like? How dangerous he'd be if he didn't think the gods of Tyume were watching? There are a lot of people like him."

"That doesn't make it right for Examiners to keep finds that aren't dangerous without paying."

"You're right. I'm just saying that part of what they're doing is trying to prevent chaos. Like the dark years after the daemon wars. Tell me, do you think things would be much better if your elders were running the empire?"

"Well... that's not the point. Bossy elders don't justify bossy priests."

"We've found something to agree on. It's a good start."

Rhan looked over his shoulder to see how closely Catrin was following. She was about fifty feet behind, riding with a stiff back and looking like she wished she were someplace else. "She could have used some of your balm," he said, turning back to Aerik. "But I'm glad you offered it to me instead. I dreamed about you last night."

Aerik's grin dispelled the forest gloom, and the sweet musk of arousal spiced the air. "Perhaps we met again last night, in the place where dreams are made. I dreamed, too, of things we didn't have time for last night. Things I'd like to show you." He squirmed in his saddle, reaching down to adjust the swelling at his crotch. "See, you're doing it again."

Rhan laughed softly. Upwelling affection filled him, marvel compounded with lust. He could imagine the elders' outrage if they knew he was bedding a Tyumen man. He pushed the thought from his mind. The elders weren't near, and he didn't want to think about them. "What about Maiko? I'm as eager as you, but I think he's watching us. Isn't it dangerous?"

"I suppose. We'll have to be careful." A sly smile lit his face. "He has to sleep."

Rhan's body responded to the randy enthusiasm. In moments he was aching and wishing his leathers were less confining. "We'll have to think about Catrin too. She's—"

"What? Is something wrong?"

The odor was so faint he doubted at first it was real. He turned to face upwind, sniffing the breeze while pretending to search with his eyes. This time he was sure. Concrete and rust, the smells of antiquity. The combination of scents drew his attention like a lodestone. A moment later he saw a subtle thinning in the forest.

"There," he said, pointing. "Ahead on the left. The road forked here. You can tell by the trees. There's a pretty good chance of some ruins around here."

Aerik peered in the direction Rhan had pointed, full of curiosity. "I don't see the signs. But you're the finder, not me. Want to explore?"

"Who knows if we'll have another chance? Besides, it's time for lunch soon, anyway."

Aerik put two fingers in his mouth and produced an ear-splitting whistle. Maiko turned, not trying to conceal his irritation.

"We're going to look over there," Aerik said, pointing. "Rhan thinks we might find something."

Maiko looked pained but didn't argue. Rhan was glad the Hand was avoiding them, and wondered if it was because of the prior night's confrontation or what he'd heard while lurking outside Aerik's tent. He hoped Aerik was right, that an oath would be enough to keep Maiko at bay.

Rhan took the lead as they left the path. Their new route took them lower, toward the river at the valley's floor. They reached a bench overlooking the broad expanse of water and found a score of hillocks dispersed among massive oaks. He sniffed the air, seeking the scent of people, but the site seemed long deserted. They rode into a clearing beside a mound and dismounted.

Rhan approached what looked like the top quarter of an encrusted boulder rising some thirty feet from the forest floor and started throwing aside fallen branches that leaned against it. His efforts quickly revealed the smooth lines of an ancient concrete structure.

Maiko made a warding sign and stepped back. "Leave it alone. There must be a reason this place is deserted. Maybe the daemon wars touched it."

"Or maybe they ran out of food," Rhan said. "Or fled to hide from enemies." He kept clearing debris and tearing ferns from the mottled surface. Catrin and Aerik joined in, and soon they uncovered an indentation the vegetation had hidden.

"Look," Rhan said, carefully scraping dirt off the recessed area. A shiny brown surface emerged at about eye level. "Have you ever seen one of these?"

Aerik examined it. "Glass of some kind?"

"It's a window. It's been covered a long time and earth has seeped into it." He wiped dirt away, defining the rectangular shape more clearly. "There used to be shutters; you can still see a bit of hinge. The shutters rotted or rusted a long time ago, but the window's not broken. We might be the first to find this. There could be some good relics here."

"We should go," Maiko repeated. "This isn't part of our mission."

Rhan smelled the stink of fear in Maiko's sweat. For all his swagger, the man was as fearful as a beaten mongrel when confronted with something beyond his experience. "It won't take long," he said. "We'll just dig enough to see if it'll be worth coming back here."

"It's time for lunch," Aerik said. "Go eat something, Maiko. We'll probably be finished before you are."

The Hand scowled his disapproval but retreated without further argument.

"What about you?" Rhan asked Catrin. "Want to dig, or have lunch?"

"With Maiko?" She wrinkled her nose. "What do you want me to do? And are you sure this is safe?"

"Safer than most digs. You don't usually find things on the surface like this. The deeper you go under the ground, the more dangerous it gets." He selected a dead branch and used his foot to break it into three pieces, then handed one to each of his companions. "Not as good as a hardened digging stick, but it'll have to serve. We'll dig until we find a door, then see about getting it open." He peeled off his shirt and tossed it aside. Aerik raised an eyebrow.

"Digging is hot and dirty work," Rhan said as he started prying a thick layer of decayed leaf debris from the mound. "This saves having to wash your shirt. If the rest of you weren't here, I'd take off everything but my boots."

Aerik tugged off his tunic, and Catrin hesitated only a moment before doing the same. They set to the task with enthusiasm.

Digging felt good after so many hours sitting in a saddle. Rhan put his back into it and fell into a rhythm, straining and prying, while Catrin worked to move dirt aside after it came loose from the concrete shell. Aerik kept up with him, his paler skin glistening with sweat. Rhan found it impossible to ignore his friend's virile scent. Keeping arousal at bay was harder than the digging.

They were streaked with dirt and sweat by the time they uncovered a portal. Rhan traced its outline with his finger to show them how the door followed the dome's smooth curve. "They covered the doors with concrete too," he said. "We think to protect their houses from fires. Nothing made of exposed wood could have lasted this long."

"How old do you think it is?" Catrin asked.

"Don't really know," Rhan said as he felt around the door for irregularities that might reveal a latch. "The window is ancient, but whoever built this might have just found the material and used it. We'll see when we get inside. Ah!"

His fingers felt a hand-sized indentation about four feet above the ground. He used a stick to gouge dirt out of the groove, then reached inside with two fingers and felt around. Sweat dripped down his dirty face, unnoticed. Soon his eyes narrowed to slits and he angled his hand to push upward. There was no sound, but he removed his fingers and wiped his brow.

"I found a latch and was able to move it a bit. If we're lucky we shouldn't have to smash our way through. Let's see if we can pry the door now."

They sharpened the points of their digging sticks and then wedged them into the vertical groove near the latch.

"Go easy," Rhan said. "If we break something, it'll be harder to open." On his cue, they began prying. At first the door was as unyielding as a real boulder. They pushed harder, Rhan's stick starting to bend as he put more muscle into it. Just as he thought it was going to break, concealed hinges squealed and the outline Rhan had traced opened to a crack an inch wide. Dry air puffed out. It smelled of dust and age.

"Gently now." Rhan dropped his stick and wedged his fingers into the crack. Aerik moved below him and matched his grip. Steady tugging opened the door in small jerks until something gave way and it suddenly swung fully open.

Maiko came over, scowling. He had hung an amulet bearing a religious symbol around his neck. "I'm going to report this. We have a job to do and shouldn't be wasting time here."

"I'll get candles from my pack," Rhan said, ignoring Maiko. "Anybody else going in?"

"I will," Aerik said. He was flushed with excitement, eyes shining.

"Me too," Catrin said. She was far less eager and her wary glance at Maiko suggested her real reason for going along. She picked up her shirt and put it on, keeping her back turned while fastening the carved buttons.

Rhan returned with six short candles, a bundle of sulfur matches wrapped in oilskin, and a small leather pouch. He gave candles to Catrin and Aerik, and tucked two in his pouch after fastening it to his belt with metal clips. All but one match went into the belt pouch before he struck a light on the exposed concrete. They each lit a candle in the blue flame.

"I'm not going to rescue you if there's trouble," Maiko said. "And don't waste time. I won't wait all day."

"Leave whenever you want," Aerik said. "We'll catch up." He turned to Rhan. "What do we do?"

"Just follow me. And if you see something, ask me before touching it. Things aren't always what they seem."

Holding his candle aloft, Rhan stepped through the door. The air already told him that no animals had found their way inside. It smelled of dust, dry wood, and crumbling concrete, but little else. He walked into the spacious room with Aerik and Catrin crowding behind.

"It doesn't look like much," Aerik said, a tinge of disappointment in his voice.

Rhan turned around slowly, inspecting the arched ceiling and bare concrete walls. Inset windows circled the dome at eye level and near the top, all of them long since covered by forest detritus. The flagstone floor was barren except for a darker area near the chamber's opposite side. "Over there," he said. "It's probably nothing, but let's look."

They crossed the room, footsteps echoing around the dome. As they neared the far wall their candles revealed an opening with stairs leading down into darkness. Flagstones surrounding the opening were carved with graceful runes, like letters formed by flowing water. Aerik knelt to inspect them, his torso gleaming like marble in the flickering candle light. After a few moments he looked up at Rhan. His usual assurance was gone.

"Um, this isn't a warning, is it? Does it look like daemon writing? I've never seen anything like it."

Rhan knelt at his side. He pretended to study the runes while testing the darkness at their feet for scents. He detected nothing aside from a faint smell like damp sand. "I can't read it," he said. "But I know what some of the warding symbols look like, and don't see any here." He stood. "Nothing here to stop a finder, that's for certain. I'm going to take a look. It's all right if you want to stay here. If there's a cave-in or some other problem, it's good to have someone waiting in a safe place who can help."

"No, I want to go too," Aerik said. He stood and looked at Rhan with disarming trust. "I'm curious what it's like, being a finder."

"Well, I admit I wouldn't mind waiting here," Catrin said. "I'll come if you call."

"Thanks." Rhan took one of the spare candles from his pouch and gave it to her. "We won't go far, I promise."

A slow smile spread on Aerik's face. "My father would be speechless if he could see me now. Even if we don't find anything, that's enough to make this worthwhile. I'm ready."

"Then let's go." Rhan held out his candle and started down the steps.

Chapter Four

AERIK stayed close as they descended, encouraged by his friend's self-assurance. He was glad for the chance to be alone with Rhan and wondered if their explorations might take a different turn than searching for relics, but the thought was short-lived. His friend was a finder. Trying to divert him now would only irritate him.

The shaft angled steeply before intersecting a tunnel. Aerik's throat was tight by the time they reached the bottom. The stairwell's closeness had been oppressive. "Which way?" he asked, lifting his candle to illuminate a faded fresco on the wall. Faint images of wolves peered back at him from behind trees and boulders, ghosts of another world.

"Doesn't matter," Rhan said. He took a lump of chalk out of his belt pouch and made a mark on the floor, an arrow pointing to the passage they had just left. He stood and peered down the corridor in both directions, breathing deeply, and then turned to his right. "Let's try this way."

They set off, going slowly and examining the frescos adorning the walls and ceiling. Throngs of beasts and birds surrounded them. The deserted tunnel felt strangely crowded.

"Is this common?" Aerik asked, pointing at the decorations.

"No, and these are in better condition than I've found before," Rhan said. "This place has stayed dry, which probably means we're the first to find it." He turned and grinned. "You're bringing me luck. I wish I'd found you sooner."

Aerik was tongue-tied, caught by the play of candlelight on Rhan's face. The finder's smooth torso gleamed like bronze and his jade eyes reflected the flickering light. Arousal blossomed despite his effort to suppress it. "You've found me now," he managed to say. "And I'm glad you did."

Rhan's sultry smile left no doubt he knew what Aerik was talking about. He reached over and cupped the mound swelling beneath Aerik's leathers. "We'll go somewhere tonight? After the others are asleep?"

"The moment their eyes close," Aerik said fervently. Abandoning caution, he put his free hand around Rhan's waist and pulled him close. They pressed together, skin hot against skin in the cool air.

"I'm eager too," Rhan said softly as he nuzzled Aerik's ear. They kissed, Rhan bending to meet Aerik's upturned face. The moment seemed timeless yet ended all too soon.

Aerik was light-headed as they moved apart. His experience in Chakragil seemed inadequate preparation for the finder's fearless tenderness. Rhan gave his heart as well as his body. "We'd better not do that again while we're down here," he said. "I want to lie with you under the stars, not under the ground. Kisses like that make it hard to wait."

Rhan grinned and stepped back. "Now you know what I feel like. I've been waiting for years." He gestured down the corridor with his candle. "There's only enough time for a little exploring. Let's see where this leads."

They kept to the main passage and paused briefly at each intersection. Side tunnels branched off in all directions, some containing narrow stairwells that led up or down through concrete shafts. At each intersection Rhan chalked an arrow on the floor to mark their route. It seemed like excessive caution since they made no turns, but Aerik was glad for it. The flickering light reminded him that it might become necessary to find their way out in a hurry.

Their candles had burned a third of their length by the time Rhan stopped at a complex intersection like the hub of a wheel with six radiating spokes. The walls in the circular room where the spokes intersected were richly painted. The fresco depicted a ravine surrounded by snow-capped mountains that seemed to recede to vast distances. The entrance to each tunnel was cunningly painted to look like the mouth of a cave.

The first thing Rhan did was mark the entrance of the tunnel from which they had emerged. "Time for a decision," he said. He walked around the room, which was smaller than it appeared, and looked into each tunnel. "Let's try this one," he said after completing the circuit, picking a passage and marking it with his chalk.

Aerik nodded agreeably. He was finding it hard to concentrate. Watching Rhan kept turning his mind to the possibilities that awaited them after nightfall.

The corridor Rhan had chosen angled up in a gradual incline. It soon became a staircase, wide enough for them to walk abreast. Niches in the wall showed where oil lamps had once cast their warm light. The forest murals were gone, replaced with life-sized paintings of men and women garbed in chainmail armor.

Soon the corridor leveled and they entered a domed space at least three times bigger than the one they had pried open. Rune-carved columns spaced along the walls seemed to support an inverted bowl of sky. The room's far side held a dais with an ornately carved throne like an unfolding flower.

A white figure, garbed in a chainmail tunic and leather clothing, faced them from deep within the throne's shadows.

Aerik's stomach clenched. "Is it a daemon?" he whispered. He felt as if a thousand eyes watched them.

Rhan put a hand on his shoulder. "Whatever it is, I think it's long dead."

"You're sure?" The figure had not moved, but it seemed intact, almost like a statue.

"We haven't seen any signs of life. This place has been sealed a long time. Did you notice how dry the air is?"

Aerik sniffed, detecting a trace of Rhan's sweat but nothing else. "Um, maybe you're right. But look at it. If it's dead, why didn't the corpse rot?"

Rhan released him and started across the room. "I've heard of this from other finders but never seen it myself. Come on, it's probably safe."

Aerik followed, thinking that finders were like soldiers in their casual acceptance of risk. But unlike soldiers, Rhan seemed uncommonly free of superstition. Or at least unusually knowledgeable about the ancients. The priests claimed to know everything, but it was finders who touched the past with their own eyes and hands.

The throne loomed over them as they approached. The figure had not stirred, and now Aerik could see that its eyes were closed. Skin white as bone covered desiccated features and gray hair in thick braids framed the face. The ancient ruler, if that's what it was, had been a woman.

They stopped when they reached the steps beneath the throne, three broad terraces made of blue slate. It seemed to Aerik that the long-dead matriarch still held sway in her underground realm.

"Well," Rhan said at last. "Let's see what we've found. We don't have much time."

"Doesn't it bother you? I mean, isn't it desecrating a tomb or something?"

"We prefer to call it finding. And the empire doesn't mind, as long as it gets its share in tribute. Come on." He strode up the steps. Aerik followed with more misgiving.

Rhan leaned over the seated figure and examined its ivory skin without touching it. "So it's not just a story. They could preserve a body even in death." He turned to Aerik, excited. "Do you know what this means?"

"Um, no. Should I?"

"It means these people lived close to the time of the daemon wars. The finder who told me about preserved bodies said they're at least seven hundred years old."

Aerik stepped back, eyes wide. "Was it done by daemon work? Be careful, Rhan. Daemon works can mark you, corrupt even a pure bloodline."

Rhan's sudden frown was like a splash of cold water. "Can't you forget about bloodlines for once? Being Tyumen doesn't—" He stopped himself with a visible effort. After taking a deep breath, he met Aerik's startled gaze. "Sorry. Look, life is different out here. We do what's needed and let the Examiners worry about purity. I'm just trying to survive, that's all."

"Maybe I should keep my mouth shut," Aerik said, still stinging. "You're right, I guess. It's just that I wouldn't want to see you get harmed or marked somehow. I... I'd hate it if something happened to you."

Rhan grimaced, not the reaction Aerik had expected.

"Forget it, all right? Let's not talk about it."

"As you wish." Aerik knew he had blundered but wasn't sure how. "So, what do we do now?"

Rhan knelt beside the seated corpse. "We see what there is to find." He glanced at Aerik, as if watching for signs of disapproval. "If there's something here, she's long past caring if we take it. The needs of the living are greater than the needs of the dead, they say."

"I'm not arguing." Aerik crouched at Rhan's side and pointed at a strap crossing the mummy's shoulder. It was connected by metal hooks to a leather sack that was almost hidden behind the body. "Did you see this?"

Rhan leaned over to get a better look and then nudged Aerik in the side. "You're still bringing me luck. Let's see what's in it." He unhooked the sack from its strap and tugged it out from where it had been lodged.

Aerik held his breath as Rhan opened a clasp that held the sack shut. The finder carefully shook it and its contents poured out in a rush.

Aerik was stunned. The unassuming sack held treasure. Gems

glistened in heavy gold settings and loose stones spilled across the floor. Coins large and small, in both silver and gold, bore the likeness of long-forgotten men and women. There was even an enameled brooch that might have been an insignia of office.

"I don't believe it," Rhan whispered. He was motionless, rapt.

"A fortune," Aerik agreed. "Even in Chakragil, I've seen no finer pieces. Your elders will be very pleased."

Rhan looked up, bemused. "The jewelry, you mean? Yes. But the real treasure has to be our secret. I'd never be allowed to keep it."

"You… you're going to keep…." He trailed off, not wanting to think Rhan would steal from his own village. "Um, aren't finders supposed to give everything to their elders?"

Rhan sighed. "Remember what you said about how priests aren't always fair to finders? Did you mean it?"

"Well, I guess so." His unease grew by the moment. "What is it? Are you saying you want to keep these jewels?" He felt sick saying it, even though it wasn't exactly an accusation.

Rhan's gaze didn't falter. "Jewels don't matter to me, except for what they'll buy for Balmorel. But look at this." He reached for the pouch and touched the end of a cylinder that had fallen halfway out. He tilted the pouch again and the half-inch thick rod rolled free. It was about six inches long. The last inch of each end was clear as glass and the rest was black as deepest night except for three red dots arranged in a row near one of the clear ends.

Aerik lurched back. "Don't touch it! It's daemon work!"

Rhan sighed and sat on the floor beside the pile of finds. He seemed half amused and half exasperated. "So, you know who made it? And what it's for?"

Though his heart was pounding, it didn't seem the relic had done anything. Aerik blushed at his panicked reaction. "Who else could have made it? It has the look of daemon work." His certainty began to falter. "I mean, doesn't it?"

Rhan grinned and picked up the cylinder, holding it by the

middle. "The past is a puzzle, Aerik. That's why it's so interesting." His grin got wider. "But I have an advantage. Finders consider these the best of all relics."

Aerik moved closer, hearing the confidence in Rhan's voice. "What is it then?"

Rhan touched his hand. "You understand this will have to be our secret? We'll lose our heads if an Examiner finds out about this."

The warning was dire, but exerted an irresistible attraction. "Our secret, yes," Aerik said softly. His stomach fluttered as the boundary was crossed. Mocking priests was one thing, but actually committing heresy felt very different.

Rhan was clearly delighted to be sharing his discovery. He patted the floor, and Aerik settled cross-legged at his side.

"I might get this wrong the first time," he said. "I've only heard about these, never seen one."

"But you're sure what it is?" It seemed like a bad time for Rhan to be confessing doubts.

"Well... I think so. It fits the description. Watch." He held the cylinder upright, perpendicular to the floor, and then rotated it upside down. After a few seconds he turned it upright again. He repeated the process several times with no visible effect.

Aerik felt a strange combination of disappointment and relief. He glanced at Rhan's face. Though the finder showed no sign of being upset, he prepared to offer consolation if his friend's hopes were dashed.

After a full minute of the odd ritual, Rhan put the rod on the floor in front of them. "I guess that should be enough." He chewed his lower lip, staring at the object intently. "I'm not exactly sure about this part. But I don't think it matters." He touched one of the red dots near the cylinder's end.

Nothing happened.

Rhan's brow furrowed. "I hope it isn't broken or something. Let me try another one." He touched a different red dot. At first nothing happened. Then Aerik saw the cylinder's clear tips start to glow with pearly light that seemingly came from nowhere. He jerked back.

"What's it doing? Its daemon work, Rhan. There's no denying it."

Rhan bent close to the floor and examined the rod with childlike awe. "It's just making light," he said. "That's what it's for. It's like a candle that never burns out. And you don't need fire to light it." He looked up, beaming. "Isn't it amazing?"

Aerik had to swallow before he could answer. This wasn't just heresy. They were in the presence of ancient forces, like men had faced during the daemon wars. He wondered if his desire to impress Rhan had led him into terrible folly.

"It's… is it magic, then? Did you work some kind of spell by moving it the way you did? And are you sure it's not harmful? Maybe you're too close to it."

Rhan grinned and picked it up. "It's meant to be held, see? It fits the hand. A human hand. This wasn't some daemon weapon." He nodded toward the seated corpse. "It was hers, wasn't it? Does she look like a daemon to you?"

Aerik looked skeptically at the unnaturally preserved body, but had to admit the finder was right. "Just how much do you know about these things? Have the finders been keeping secrets from the rest of us?"

Rhan's smile faded. "You have to understand. We spend our lives exploring. Mostly underground, because that's where the relics usually are. It's easy to get lost if you lose your light. Having one of these could save my life. Should I give it to an Examiner so the priests can destroy it or hide it in a secret collection?"

"I didn't say that." Remembering his promise, he touched Rhan's arm. "I won't tell. I stand by my word. But do you really know how safe this is? And what Maiko will do if he finds out you have it?"

Rhan looked exasperated. "Do I look so stupid?" His eyebrows pulled down. "It's this damn hair. It makes me look like the village idiot."

Aerik laughed despite the outburst. "I love it," he said, touching the loose curls. "I'm sorry I doubted you. Now, what do you know about these things?"

"Finders call them cold torches." He held the rod in his open palm. "These dots make it do different things, but I'm not sure which is which. Let's find out." Before Aerik could protest, he touched the dot that had made it start glowing. The light instantly vanished. Touching the dot again made the light reappear. They soon established that the second dot made the light get brighter or dimmer, depending on which end of the rod was pointed up. The third dot made the light cycle through a rainbow of colors, but only if the rod was held with the triangle of buttons pointed down. Turning the rod the other way around instantly changed the light back to white, as if a fragment of sun was trapped inside the black part of the cylinder.

Their candles had burned down to stubs by the time they learned all the device's variations. Aerik's fear had vanished, replaced by deepened respect for his friend's adventurous nature. Risk presented dangers but also offered rewards.

"We should start back," Rhan said, using his first candle to light two spares. "Catrin is probably getting worried."

Aerik helped him return the treasure to its leather sack, then pointed at the cold torch. "What about that? They'll see it if we put it in the bag with the other finds."

Rhan tried squeezing it into his belt pouch, but it was too long to fit without removing a divider and he wasn't carrying the knife needed for the job. He pondered the problem and reached a quick decision. "Make sure Catrin leaves the dome first," he said. "I'll put it near the door. I can fetch it when everyone's getting ready to leave, after putting my shirt on."

Aerik didn't have a better idea, so they began retracing their steps. He followed Rhan with mounting excitement. Their shared secret strengthened a bond he couldn't yet name but that made him want to sing. If songs could take human form, Rhan would be a lusty ballad.

His reverie lasted until they neared the stairwell to the dome where Catrin waited. Rhan turned, candlelight making his hair seem to dance like flames. "I can't wait either," he whispered, watching Aerik with wide-eyed innocence. He bent his head and kissed Aerik, catching him completely off guard.

Though startled, Aerik didn't waste the opportunity. He returned the kiss hard. When they finished he slid a hand along the finder's side. "Am I that obvious? Or do we just think alike?"

"Finders are observant." Rhan brushed his fingers across Aerik's cheek. "The truth is, you've barely left my mind since last night. I was hoping it might be the same with you."

"I've never been so eager for nightfall."

Rhan's grin flashed. He removed the torch from the sack of treasures and stuck it in his waistband behind his back, then handed the sack to Aerik. "You go first. Let Catrin look inside when we get up the stairs. It'll distract her."

They reached the upward passage and started climbing the narrow steps, Aerik leading. Faint light from Catrin's candle reflected off rock above them.

"Rhan? Is that you?"

"It's us," Aerik called back. "We found something for you." A few more steps and he saw Catrin peering down at them from the top of the stairs. As they left the stairwell, he opened the sack and held it out for Catrin's inspection. She looked inside and then drew back, astonished. "I see what took you so long. This is the richest find I've ever seen."

"We need more light to judge the jewelry's quality," Aerik said. "Let's get them outside so we can get a better look." He gestured for Catrin to go first.

They crossed the dome quickly, with Catrin leading the way. Aerik suspected she was more than ready to abandon darkness. Waiting alone had probably been harder than exploring with an amiable companion.

The skies had cleared and shafts of light shone through the tree canopy like golden spears. He had no chance to enjoy it. Maiko marched toward them, looking furious. "We ride now. No more delays."

"Look what we found," Aerik said, meeting Maiko halfway and then spilling treasure across the ground. He saw that Rhan was just leaving the dome, closing the door behind him but not far enough for the latch to catch. "I think you'll agree the time was well spent."

Maiko stopped in his tracks and stared at the bounty with narrowed eyes. He bent down and ran his fingers through scattered coins. For once he lacked an insult for the occasion.

"We still need to eat lunch," Rhan said. He retrieved his shirt from where he had left it while digging. "It won't take long."

Maiko ignored them while sorting through the find. Aerik was sure the Hand had never been close to so much wealth.

"I'll get some pemmican," Catrin said. She left to rummage through a saddlebag.

Rhan slipped his tunic over his head but didn't tuck it into his leathers. "That door didn't close all the way," he said. "I'll secure it. Maybe we'll get a chance to explore here again." He turned back to the earth-covered dome.

Aerik crouched near Maiko and picked up a gold bracelet. He angled it to catch the sun. "How old do you think it is?" he asked, waving the trinket. From the corner of his eye he saw Rhan open the door partway, as if inspecting the latch.

Maiko glanced at the bracelet before his gaze flickered back to the pile. "Who cares? All that's important is how much it's worth."

"It's not ours. Rhan found it. It belongs to his village."

Maiko's grimace was more eloquent than words. "Don't side with him, runt. I know he's your lover already. Didn't take you long, did it? Temple dancers are all the same." Anger twisted his face. "A share of this should be mine. You wouldn't have found it if I hadn't allowed this delay."

"Don't be stupid. There are rules for finds. Everybody knows—"

Maiko sprang to his feet. "You! Finder! What are you doing?"

Rhan turned, his expression bland. "I'm getting this door closed. Like I said."

"Don't try to lie, I saw you take something! Saving the best for yourself, thief?"

Rhan hesitated. "You're mistaken."

Maiko closed the gap between them in four strides and shoved Rhan back, pinning him against the ancient building. "You're a thieving liar! Show me!" He reached for the bottom edge of Rhan's shirt.

Rhan tried to twist away, but Maiko grabbed him around the chest. Rhan yelped and struggled to break the Hand's grip.

Aerik's shock lasted two heartbeats before he barreled into the fray. He rammed his shoulder into the middle of Maiko's back, hard enough to make him stagger. The blow allowed Rhan to break free as Maiko and Aerik tumbled to the ground.

Maiko tried to get up, but Aerik grabbed him around the waist and wrenched him back down. Maiko bellowed and jabbed with an elbow, catching Aerik on the side of his head.

Pain shot through him like a hot spike, but Aerik doggedly kept his grip. He was dimly aware of jarring blows and blood in his mouth. Nausea swelled. His vision faded, narrowing to a tunnel, as Rhan pounced on Maiko. Another flailing blow hit him on the back of his head and darkness engulfed him.

AERIK swam up from nightmares and immediately wished he hadn't. His stomach lurched and his head felt like it was being crushed in a vise. He moaned, choking back bile as he took in the stars overhead and the embers of a campfire close by.

A damp cloth touched his forehead, moistening it with cool water. Catrin leaned over him. Relief filled her face, and a sympathy he had never before seen there.

"You had us worried," she said softly. "It's past midnight." She dipped the cloth in a bowl of water and dabbed his temples. The pain seemed to ebb a bit.

"What happened? Is Rhan all right?"

She paused before answering. At last she gave him a small nod. "Maiko didn't hurt him, if that's what you mean. In fact, I was afraid we were going to have a dead Hand to deal with. I hate to think what the empire would have done about that."

"He bested Maiko, then?"

Catrin nodded. "I've never seen him so fierce. It frightened me. He's usually a gentle creature, but today… well, Maiko got more than he bargained for."

Aerik chuckled and then regretted it as his head throbbed. "I wish I'd seen that."

"I think Maiko is going to be more careful from now on." She picked up the bowl. "You should drink some, if you can."

Aerik was thirsty but could only manage a few sips before nausea threatened to overwhelm him. He lay back, groaning.

"Do you mind if I let Rhan sleep?" Catrin asked. "He told me to get him if you wake up, but he needs to rest. Maiko might try to make trouble again if he thinks he can get away with it."

"He was standing watch against Maiko all day?" The news was troubling, especially if it meant the ancient torch was no longer a secret.

"No. He was with you. All afternoon and almost to midnight."

"Oh."

"Is that all you have to say?" She watched him with a thoughtful expression.

Aerik sighed, wondering at the signs of friendship Catrin seemed to be offering. She had been wary of him since the trip began, but the sense of distance appeared to be fading.

"Catrin… are you mad at me? I can't help where I was born. And, uh, maybe you can tell, I like Rhan a lot. I couldn't help it, even if I wanted to."

She dropped the cloth in the bowl and leaned back, shadow hiding her eyes.

"I don't want to be your enemy," Aerik said. She didn't respond, so he plunged ahead. Better to get it over with now, while they were alone, than when the others might be listening. "You and Rhan are good friends, I know. I don't want to change that."

She stirred but kept her silence.

Aerik's throat felt dry. "Can I ask you for some advice?"

After a moment she nodded. "Go ahead."

"Is it going to hurt Rhan to be my friend? Because I'm Tyumen, or… or for other reasons?"

"I wish I knew." She turned her head, moonlight painting her features in silver. Her expression held no malice. "But I finally realized it doesn't matter. Rhan is stubborn. If you're what he's looking for, nobody can change it."

"You're not angry, then?" He lifted himself on an elbow despite the pain. Catrin was watching him calmly.

"No," she said at last. "It surprises me, but I guess I'm not. Rhan's a friend and I've known him all my life. But he's never pretended to be more than that. If he cares for you in a different way, that's his decision. I'd have to be blind not to see how he looks at you." She gave him an apologetic smile. "And I've decided he hasn't lost his senses. At first I thought you were just a rich Tyumen playing with him for amusement. That did make me mad. But then I saw how you fought for him. I misjudged you. Sorry."

Aerik thanked the darkness as heat rushed to his cheeks. Catrin's generous assessment was more than he deserved. It was true that his original interest in Rhan sprang from the finder's beauty and boldness. But their easy camaraderie, and the powerful way he had responded to Rhan's calm confidence, felt like signs of something deeper taking hold. "I see why Rhan values your friendship," he said. "You care for him. And you see clearly."

She shrugged. "I could tell he was lonely, the way he kept to himself most of the time. And he wouldn't have found a friend like you at home. The elders make sure of that."

"What do you think will happen when our mission is over? I haven't had a chance to ask Rhan about it, and I'm afraid to. Where is there a place for us?"

"As lovers?" Catrin stood, shaking out her hair with a toss of her head. "I don't know. But here's one more piece of advice. Always be honest with him. I think he can tell if a person is hiding something. Show him your heart and see what happens."

She put the bowl close to his side. "It's not going to rain tonight, so I'm sleeping outside too. My bedroll is on the other side of the fire. Are you well enough that I can get some sleep?"

Aerik nodded despite the pain that throbbed every time he moved. "I'll be fine. Rest is what I need. Thanks for keeping watch, Catrin. And for the advice."

"I hope it serves you well. Good night."

"Until morning."

He listened while she slipped into her bedroll and as the pace of her breathing slowed. He watched the stars, brilliant points sprayed across the sky in uncountable profusion. It seemed incomprehensible that the world could be so large yet lack a place where he and Rhan fit into it. Yearning swelled until it ached, but he could see no haven.

Chapter Five

RHAN woke with a start, and anxious memories rushed back in a torrent. The tight-woven hemp of his tent already glowed amber with dawn's light. He scrambled outside without pausing to put on his shirt or boots.

Maiko was nowhere in sight or scent, but Catrin was curled in her bedroll. Aerik lay motionless near the dead fire. Rhan went over and placed two fingers on his throat, feeling a strong pulse. Aerik yawned and opened his eyes.

Seeing Aerik waken felt like a storm clearing. He glanced at Catrin to make sure she was still asleep, then bent down and kissed Aerik's cheek. "How are you feeling?" he asked. The ache that had filled him for many hours was already starting to fade.

Aerik stretched, twisting his head and moving his shoulders without sitting up. "Sore and stiff. But not anything to worry about."

Rhan raised an eyebrow.

"Really, I'll be fine. Did Maiko see the cold torch?"

"I tossed it into a bush when you knocked him down. He's suspicious, but he couldn't have seen it when I put it under my shirt. My back was turned. Now it's in my belt pouch, I made enough room for it."

"He's suspicious, all right. You should have seen him fingering the finery. It's a good thing he's a true believer. He'd have killed us on the spot and stolen it if he didn't think he'd pay for it in the next life."

Looking behind Rhan, he propped himself up on an elbow and nodded.

"Morning, Catrin. You got some rest, I hope."

"Morning." She was disheveled but still lovely, with long hair stirring in the wind. She crouched beside Aerik. "Do you think you'll be able to ride today? Maiko complained about the delay all afternoon. At least when he wasn't counting coins and gems." She rolled her eyes. "It's people like him that give Tyumens a bad name."

"Don't judge us all by Maiko," Aerik said. "Though the truth is, he's not the worst. At least you know where you stand with him. And yes, I can ride."

She patted his shoulder. "No time for a fire this morning. I'll get some jerky and we can eat on the trail. It's better than listening to Maiko."

Aerik sat up and winced as a bruised muscle pulled his side. Rhan started to help him, but he shook his head and got to his feet unaided. He looked shaky but determined. Rhan could tell his friend was not likely to disappoint.

THE sun was a huge orange ball, low in the sky, when they finally emerged on a bluff above Eben. A vast lake spread to the horizon like a sheet of molten bronze. Dozens of boats skimmed its surface.

On the shore, circular buildings lined narrow streets paved with half-sawn logs. The structures had roofs like flattened cones and were painted in a riot of colors. They reminded Rhan of mushrooms sprouting around a pool except that no mushrooms had such profuse variation.

"They're called yurts," Aerik said, pointing. "These people make their living from fishing, mostly. Everything can be taken apart and moved if there's flooding or they need fresh land somewhere else along the shore." He was visibly relieved to be at their destination. Rhan had smelled his suffering during the long ride.

Though the others didn't comment on it, Rhan was overwhelmed by the smell of fish. Raw, grilled, smoked, sun-dried, baked, and other fishy concoctions saturated the breeze that engulfed them as they rode down from the bluff. His stomach rumbled, reminding him how meager their meals had been all day.

Vegetable gardens were laid out in neat plots at the village's outskirts. Laborers in straw hats were still at work gathering ripe produce. The scent of eggplant and sweet melons mingled with fish smells, an unusual but entirely agreeable mixture. They stopped at a trough to wash their faces and let the horses drink. Rhan was entranced by the new surroundings and scents. He wondered if this was why the Tyumens kept horses to themselves and those with wealth. If they didn't, people would spend all their time traveling.

"This is lovely," Catrin said as they left the fields and rode among the yurts. "It's like being inside a painting."

"Well, that's more or less where we are," Aerik said. He gestured toward a row of yurts. Some were painted to resemble a thickly wooded forest, others portrayed schools of fish darting through blue waters, and there were countless other designs. "It's their version of architecture, I suppose. And it's good commerce. They do a healthy trade selling these to merchants who travel with a large retinue."

They dismounted when the street grew crowded and started looking for a market they had seen from the bluff. The people thronging the road were as colorful as their lodgings. They wore robes woven of brightly dyed wool and hats sporting feathers or fish bones painted with rich enamels. Some men even had beards, a rarity, and had braided them with ribbons.

"Peacocks," Maiko said, frowning at a woman whose blouse glittered like fish scales. "Peasants who put on airs are fools."

Rhan had adopted Aerik's practice of ignoring Maiko whenever possible. "How do we find out if there's a heretic here?" he asked. "Eben is bigger than I expected."

"Listen for talk of things that might be relics," Aerik said. "Heretics often use them as props, to make people think they have old knowledge. That's why Jerolin conscripted finders." He looked around, his view obstructed by the natives who crowded around them. "I wish these streets were wider. Can you tell which way it is to the market, Rhan?"

"This way." They went through an intersection and down another log-paved road. One side of the street bordered a grove protected by a bamboo fence. Alders and flowering shrubs on the other side of the fence obscured several yurts, each painted with designs featuring a different animal. A larger one next to the road was decorated with geometric patterns and ornate writing.

"Lodging," Aerik said, pointing. "Let's make arrangements so we can leave the horses here. They make us conspicuous. Then we'll get dinner. A busy tavern is probably our best bet for catching some gossip."

They tied their horses to a bamboo rail outside a large tent serving as a barn. Maiko stayed with the horses while the others crossed the street to the yurt. The flap was tied open, and it looked invitingly cool inside. Before they entered, Catrin drew Rhan and Aerik aside. "You should let me talk to the proprietor," she said softly. "I've had a lot of practice dickering with merchants. I'm pretty good at it."

Aerik shrugged and unhooked the coin purse from his belt. "Maybe you're right," he said as he handed it over. "If nothing else, it'll irritate Maiko when we tell him you struck the bargain. Always a worthy cause."

Catrin accepted the purse and led them inside. Greenish light filtered through its canvas walls, making the round room seem like deep forest. It was comfortably furnished and even contained curved wooden shelving along one side. A portly man rose from a cot where he had been reading a leather-bound book. His gray robes swept the polished wooden floor. He bowed and gestured to a tray holding a glazed water pitcher and several matching cups.

"Welcome to Eben, travelers. My name is Hovan. Please, refresh yourselves." He smiled broadly. "You've come to the right place to feel at home. Clean bedding, a washhouse, and peace of mind are all at hand."

Catrin bowed. "Thank you for your hospitality, sir. May I ask the price for a night's stay? There are four in our party."

"How many yurts do you require, my lady? Each comes with one cot, and there's room for bedrolls on the floor as well."

"Two of your smallest, please." She smiled shyly and reached over to clasp Rhan's hand. "And if you have it, a third with a bigger bed. It's a special occasion, you see."

Rhan barely managed to conceal his surprise. His stomach felt hollow. Catrin had never forced herself on him before.

The man's grin widened, his eyes crinkling. "I have just the thing. It costs a little extra, but the furnishings are as lovely as yourself, if you'll pardon my saying so. It's a place for nights you don't want to forget."

"Thank you," she said, looking down demurely. "Will two gulden be enough?"

The ensuing negotiations were conducted with polite formality, finally settling on four gulden with care of their horses and breakfast at a nearby grill included in the price. Catrin seemed well satisfied.

Once payment was made, Hovan opened a wooden box nestled among the books on his shelf and withdrew three wooden disks. He held all three in his palm. "Tokens to mark your lodgings," he said. "And to reclaim your animals in the morning." He bowed ceremoniously and handed the first token to Catrin. A lion's head was painted on it. "Look for a pair of slumbering lions. A small cot, but adequate." He handed her the second disk. "Look for the yurt painted with monkeys swinging in trees. Another small cot." He held up the third token, admiring it. "And for a special night, look for the stallion and mare. It's in the back corner, very private." He handed it to her with a wink.

As soon as they were outside, Rhan stopped and looked at Catrin severely. "Catrin, what—"

She held up a hand to silence him. Sorting through the tokens, she picked out the disk painted with a leering monkey's face. "This is obviously meant for Maiko," she said. "And I'm partial to cats, so I'll keep this one." She slipped the token bearing a lion's likeness into her shirt pocket. The disk painted with a stallion's head lay in her palm. She handed it to Rhan with mock sympathy. "Sorry, I guess you and Aerik are stuck sharing a bed. I thought somebody should keep an eye on him in case he's not fully recovered."

Rhan was speechless and Aerik blushed crimson.

Catrin looked at them and laughed. "You can thank me later." She gave Rhan a wistful smile. "We need to talk, but not today. Let's find some food. I don't know about you two, but I intend to eat well and get a good night's rest."

A stable boy emerged from the barn across the street. They joined Maiko and showed the awed boy their tokens. He had never cared for so many horses at one time.

"Let's stow our gear and meet here in ten minutes," Catrin said. Leaving their horses in the hostler's care, they slung saddlebags over their shoulders and went to find their yurts.

Rhan and Aerik followed a path into the back of the grove. Village sounds faded as trees surrounded them. The trail ended at a yurt with two horses painted on its curved wall, noble beasts racing across a grassy plain beneath a starry sky. They opened the flap that served as its door and carried their bags inside.

Their yurt was twice the size of the small ones they had passed and was finely furnished. A low table and two floor pillows occupied one side, and the other side held a plush bed on a bamboo frame. The pine floor was polished to a golden glow. "Hovan wasn't lying," Rhan said. "No wonder Catrin had to double her price."

Aerik put his saddlebags on the floor beside the bed before sitting on the thick mattress. "Soft," he said, giving Rhan a winsome grin. He shook his head as if he couldn't believe his eyes. "Did you have any idea what she was planning?"

"None." Rhan put his gear down. "She's quick. I'm not surprised she figured out what's between us, but I didn't think she'd accept it so well." He sat on the mattress and put an arm around Aerik. "I'm glad, though. She's right about it being a special night."

Aerik leaned against him, a compact and solid presence. "I'm really getting to like that woman."

Rhan squirmed, anticipating nightfall. He cleared his throat. "We'd better get back. Ten minutes, she said."

Aerik nodded. "The sooner we're done with dinner, the earlier we can return here." His hand slid over to Rhan's crotch and cupped the mound of flesh beneath the soft leather.

Rhan's heart raced, but he forced himself to stand. "Until later, then." He intended to make sure there were no complications this time.

"THIS looks promising," Aerik said. They stood in front of a pavilion large enough to cover a house with room to spare. The canvas was painted with murals of fisherman hauling in their nets. "It's lively enough that we might hear some gossip. And the food must be good to draw this crowd." Several flaps in the tent's sides were tied open for ventilation, and they could see trestle tables being tended by harried servers. An open-air kitchen smelled of hickory smoke, grilled fish, and roasted corn. Even Maiko was agreeable to the suggestion.

They claimed an unoccupied table near a middle-aged woman who was playing a lute. A server brought them mugs of dark ale for their refreshment while waiting for their meals of grilled lake trout, roasted vegetables, and cornbread to be prepared.

Contentment filled Rhan as he sipped the creamy ale. The cheerful surroundings had smothered Maiko's complaints for the moment. Aerik and Catrin were both taken by the lutenist and listened raptly as the performer executed a difficult passage. It was wonderful to be here, Rhan decided.

When the piece ended Aerik turned to Rhan, even more animated than usual. "She's good. She could attract an audience in Chakragil, if she wanted."

"I'm impressed too, though I don't have much to judge by." He put his mug on the table and looked around. "Who should we try talking to? A server, maybe? They probably hear what's happening in the village."

Aerik tapped the table with a finger and then shook his head. "They're too busy. I have a better idea. Let's buy the musician a drink."

"I see where you're heading," Catrin said. She signaled a server and arranged to have a mug of ale delivered to the performer. When she received it, the woman smiled and waved before starting her next piece.

"Buying drinks for peasants is a waste of money," Maiko said. He had already finished his first mug and beckoned impatiently for another. "We should find whoever's in charge of this backwater and tell him what we need."

Aerik sighed. "Tyume is feared, Maiko. Not loved. That's why we're not wearing militia uniforms. Start making demands and people will talk. Any heretics around here will go into hiding."

The musician started playing again, a slow and lyrical melody. Aerik's frown vanished as he turned to listen. Rhan watched him from the corner of his eye, struck by his friend's intense concentration. His unguarded expression was like a window into his spirit and was as beautiful as the music that inspired it.

When the piece ended, the woman drank from the mug they had sent her before raising it in their direction. Aerik raised his right hand with fingers spread in a musician's salute. She bent her head in an abbreviated bow.

Aerik pushed back his chair and stood. "Be right back. I'm going to invite her to come over when she takes a break." He went to the woman's side and whispered in her ear. She smiled and nodded, obviously pleased by whatever words of praise had been offered. They spoke briefly and she stood, leaving her lute on her chair and picking up her ale before following Aerik to the table where the others waited.

Rhan and Catrin stood as their guest reached the table. "May I introduce Kara Miklos," Aerik said. The musician greeted them graciously, even managing to win a nod from Maiko.

"This is our first visit to Eben," Aerik said, waiting until she was seated before sitting. "They're lucky to have someone of your skill in a town this size."

Laughter lines creased her face when she smiled. "I travel some, but not too far the last few years. Teaching takes most of my time now. Do you play?"

"I always wanted to learn, but never managed it. Between dance, singing, and school, there wasn't enough time left over."

"A pity. Singers often play well. And it's profitable to be able to do both." She sipped from her mug before continuing. "Thanks for the drink. You'd be surprised how many people pay no attention. Is there anything you'd like to hear? I know most of the popular songs."

Rhan had been watching their exchange with keen interest. Aerik's respect for the musician was a revelation. While he used wit as a defense against those who judged him by his size or his family, in the world of music, people were judged only by their talent. Aerik seemed more relaxed and confident around the musician.

Sudden curiosity made Rhan bold. "Do you ever accompany singers?" he asked.

Kara nodded. "It's often requested for banquets and the like."

Rhan wondered if he was overstepping, but pressed on. "I was wondering if you and Aerik know any of the same songs."

Aerik looked surprised but showed no annoyance.

Kara nodded agreeably. "Split the coin half and half, if we get any? It's harder to ignore a singer than a lute, so we might do well."

Aerik paused briefly before answering. "That's generous; your skill is finer than mine. Tell you what. If you'll take dinner with us and tell us about Eben, we'll split the coin two for one in your favor. We're thinking about lingering here a while."

"Done." She clasped his forearm to seal the bargain. "Two songs to see if the crowd likes you, more if they're feeling generous?"

"That's fair." Aerik's nose wrinkled. "How good are manners around here? Will they throw food if I displease them?"

Kara laughed. "You've had training, so I expect you're better than nine out of ten songbirds they've heard. Now, what shall we give them?"

Maiko belched and pushed his chair away from the table. "I've already heard enough," he said as he stood. "There's a gaming house down the street, I'll eat there. This place is starting to make me sick."

Kara watched with narrowed eyes as he departed. "Tone deaf?"

"Don't mind him," Aerik said. "He always has a bellyache." He grinned. "And now your supper is already ordered. I'll have to thank him in the morning."

It took a few minutes for them to decide on several songs they both knew, heads bent together to softly hum tunes and fingers tapping the table to agree on tempos. Rhan and Catrin watched silently, exchanging glances as the performers pursued their business. They seemed far more professional about it than the musical folk back in Balmorel.

The huddle soon broke, and Kara drained the remaining ale in her mug. "Ready to start?" she asked.

"We'd better," Aerik said. "We want to be done by the time dinner arrives." He nodded to Catrin and Rhan. "If you'll excuse us." He lowered his voice and winked at Rhan. "I hope you don't regret this. Remember, it was your idea."

Few noticed when Aerik stood beside Kara while she checked her lute's tuning. A few moments later she played a short flourish that slid into the opening passage of a traditional lament about a soldier preparing for war. Heads turned as Aerik started singing. The piece was soft and simple, chosen to give his voice a chance to warm up.

Though the song presented no real challenges, Aerik's natural and unaffected voice was beguiling. He sang with his eyes closed, making it easy to imagine he was a young soldier leaving home to risk death in the daemon wars. The room was hushed by the time he was halfway through. Rhan was dazed. He felt as if he was truly seeing Aerik for the first time.

Nobody moved when the song ended, silence stretching for

several seconds before the audience collectively let out its breath. Kara didn't allow an interruption. She launched into a spirited introduction to a ballad on the virtues of love. Aerik opened his eyes and smiled, radiant. He sang more boldly this time, but still with relaxed grace. His hands moved in subtle gestures that were plainly echoes of dance, and his face reflected the joy of the song's lyrics. When he reached a stanza praising the friendship between lovers, he sang it straight to Rhan. If the crowd noticed, nobody bothered to turn and follow his gaze. The singer's magic had ensnared them.

This time there was no delay when the song ended. Applause erupted and requests for other songs were called out. Kara put her lute's case on the table at her side as if to suggest how to win her attention. The invitation for bribes was quickly accepted. Energy filled the tent as if a slumbering beast had stirred to excited life.

Kara and Aerik performed four more songs before food arrived at the table where Rhan and Catrin waited. Other diners begged for the show to continue, to no avail. The musicians glowed as they took their last bow.

Kara bought a round of drinks to accompany their meal after counting out the coins they had received and giving a third to Aerik. "Better than the last five days combined." She thumped Aerik on the back. "Anytime you want to sing, let me know. And next time it's half and half. You're too modest."

"Thanks for the offer," Aerik said. "I had fun too. But I'm not sure how long we'll be in Eben. We're on a holiday, looking for adventure. Is there any to be found here?"

During the meal Kara regaled them with stories of local scandals and disasters, monstrous storms roaring in from the lake, and an earthquake that had knocked down an ancient tower and split the earth a few miles up the shoreline.

The mention of ruins caught Rhan's attention. "A tower was still standing near Eben? Does anyone know how old it was?"

Kara shrugged while breaking off a chunk of grilled trout. "Every storyteller has a different theory, so probably nobody really knows. It was said to be haunted, of course, and venturing near was supposed to mark you somehow. Tales to frighten children, I expect. But they say nobody ever breached the walls. Nothing grows there, and it might be poisoned like the old cities."

"Have any finders explored the area since the earthquake?" Rhan asked. He kept his eyes downcast as he sliced a roasted pepper, but could see Kara ponder the question as she chewed. He barely breathed as the silence stretched.

"Depends on whether you believe old man Odette," she said at last. "Personally, I think he's just crazy. Always has been. But he lives out that way and claims to have explored." She leaned closer to Rhan and lowered her voice. "I never talk religion, no good comes of it. But Rolf Odette does. Now more than ever, and he's suddenly full of crackbrained ideas. It'll get him in trouble someday if he's not careful."

Catrin picked up the thread without a pause. "I have an aunt like that. She even says she has visions." She gave Kara a conspiratorial smile. "She didn't have any ruins to blame it on, though. She prefers to blame everything on Uncle Ruslan."

"Odette's a widower. Pestered his wife right into her grave about ten years ago, the poor woman. Didn't shut him up, though. He still yaps about religion and relics. Some folks say he's onto something, but I think they just like to get together and gossip." Her disapproval was plain. "Some people don't have enough to do."

The server returned to their table and started clearing away empty plates. Night had fallen, and people were waiting out on the street for their turn at dinner. Kara snared the last of her cornbread before the earthenware plate was snatched from the table and then gave Aerik a hopeful smile. "Looks like a new audience is showing up. Want to earn some more money?"

"I'd enjoy it, but Rhan and I already have plans for tonight. We'll be busy all evening."

Catrin sputtered into the ale she was finishing.

"Perhaps tomorrow, then? I'll be here at the same time."

"I'll come by if we're still here, I promise." He clasped hands with Kara before they parted company. She stayed inside to resume busking while Rhan and his companions stepped into the night.

Darkness changed the town's character more than Rhan had expected. Narrow streets were filled with the soft glow of lamplight shining through painted pavilions and yurts. Silvery fish seemed to swim through the air, and bright eyes seemed to peer from behind dark foliage all around them. Stars glittered brilliantly overhead.

Catrin nudged Rhan in the ribs as they ambled back to their lodgings. "So you two have been making plans? Want to tell me about it?"

"Do you think we should find Maiko and tell him we're leaving?" Rhan asked. Catrin poked him again but didn't pursue it.

"He'll find his own way back," Aerik said. "If he's not too drunk, that is. Besides, why ruin a beautiful evening?" He gave Rhan a sunny smile as if to promise the best was yet to come. It made Rhan feel light-headed and aroused at the same time. Perfume from night-blooming vines scented the breeze and mingled with the exciting scent of his friend's body.

The grove was dark when they arrived at Hovan's establishment. It looked like a forest encampment, blanketed with serenity. When Catrin started to bid them goodnight, Rhan touched her arm. She stopped, questioning.

"Thank you again," he said. "You're a true friend."

She gave him a resigned smile. "I'm just practical, and something tells me I don't have any choice in this. You are who you are." She looked to Aerik, who was standing at Rhan's side. "His heart is in your hands. You know the value of what you hold?"

"I know." Aerik was solemn. "If the future is something I can shape, he'll be safe."

"An honest answer." She leaned over and kissed him on the cheek before retreating down a dark path.

"You've impressed her," Rhan said. "I was worried what she'd think about us. Maybe I shouldn't have."

"You never know." Aerik seemed sad. "Everyone's different. My father understands, but my mother's a true believer. When she found out about my friend Stian, she wanted to send me to the priests for a cure." He brushed Rhan's arm with a light caress. "But never mind that. Catrin gave us a gift. We shouldn't waste it."

Rhan pulled Aerik against his side. "Let's find the washhouse. I need to cool off before, uh. Before."

Aerik laughed and returned the hug. "I saw it earlier. It's not far from our yurt. This way."

The washhouse was at the grove's back edge but was visible from the trail leading to their yurt. Bamboo walls created separate rooms for men and women. The side they entered held a wooden trough large enough to sit in, about two feet deep. Water trickling continuously from bamboo piping kept the trough constantly overflowing onto surrounding sand.

"Go ahead and climb in," Aerik said. "I'll fetch some soap from my saddlebags. Much better than scrubbing with sand." He slipped away without waiting for a reply.

Rhan stripped and stepped into the tub, enjoying the rich smell of wet oak. He bent forward and ducked his head beneath the surface. The cool water felt wonderful.

He soon heard the crunch of someone running on the pebbled path. Aerik appeared at the open door with a white lump the size of a plum in his hand. The scent of peppermint filled the air. He closed the door and held up the soap. "Want me to wash your back?"

"What if somebody comes in?"

Aerik walked over, admiring Rhan's body with open enthusiasm. "Then they'll see me washing your back. So what? Besides, it's pretty dark in here." He pulled off his shirt and knelt beside the trough. After working up lather on his hands, he gave the soap to Rhan. Grasping the finder's shoulders, he pressed firmly and started rubbing.

The feel of hands sliding over his flesh made Rhan hard in seconds. He bent forward as Aerik massaged his back and sides with slick fingers, using the soap on his hair before ducking his head underwater again. Aerik never broke his rhythm, exploring with his hands. He was plainly enjoying himself and he ventured further beneath the water with every stroke.

Rhan rinsed his hair and washed his face before coming up for air, then shook his head like a dog. Before he could open his eyes, he felt Aerik's arms slide around him from behind. His erection bounced against Aerik's knuckles. Jolts of pleasure made him shiver.

"Your turn," he said, eager to return to their yurt. Slipping free of the wet grasp, he climbed out of the trough and reached for his pants. The air felt good on his bare flesh, but the prospect of other lodgers entering the bathhouse was much too embarrassing at the moment. His cock swayed in front of his flat belly like an upthrust spear.

Aerik unfastened the catch and slid out of his leathers with a graceful shimmy. Despite being a year older than Rhan, his compact form and expressive features made him appear younger. He too was aroused and wasted no time taking refuge in the water.

Rhan found the lump of soap and slid it over Aerik's back until the skin was slick, then put the soap aside and rubbed with both hands. Muscle shifted beneath his fingers as he stroked the sturdy body.

Aerik sighed and flexed his shoulders. "This was a good idea," he said. "I can almost forget that long ride." He turned his head and smiled. "I'd make the ride every day, though, if I knew it would end like this."

"Wet your hair and I'll wash it for you." Rhan nuzzled behind Aerik's ear and sniffed. "You still smell like a horse."

Aerik laughed and splashed water over his shoulder. "You're hung like one, so don't complain." He cupped water in his hands and dumped it over his head. "Good enough?"

Rhan answered by making lather and working it through the short hair, massaging his scalp and neck in the process.

Aerik settled back in the trough. "That feels great. You know, you're really different than people I've known in Chakragil."

"Is that good?"

"Yes, I think so. I have close friends at home, but they mostly see things the same way as me. You see everything differently. And you're more... I don't know, humble, maybe. Nobody at home would think of offering to wash my hair."

"It has nothing to do with humility," Rhan said, his hands sliding down to Aerik's shoulders. "I just want to touch you. Everywhere I can." His hands slid lower, gliding over biceps before slipping under Aerik's arms to encircle his torso. Aerik's heart beat strongly beneath his hands.

"I'm clean enough," Aerik said, his voice eager. He rinsed his hair and then stood up, glistening with water. Droplets streamed down his broad back and between the solid mounds of his buttocks. Rhan handed him his leathers as he stepped onto the sand.

They collected their shirts and boots and left the washhouse, walking barefoot on smooth pebbles. The alders shimmered in moonlight, and crickets chorused in the distance. After entering their yurt, Rhan tied the cords that secured the flap while Aerik retrieved a candle from their gear.

Rhan watched as Aerik lit the candle and put it in a metal stand, adjusting the mica reflector until he achieved a glow like hot coals in a campfire. His leathers fit him like a second skin, and his ribs etched clean lines along his torso as he reached to place the candleholder at the table's center. The dim light made him seem intimate and quiet, a stark contrast to the outgoing performer who could confidently sing in a room full of strangers.

Rhan felt a surprising calmness now that they were together in a private place. When Aerik straightened and turned to him, it seemed as if time had stopped.

"What is it?" Aerik asked. He held out a hand in invitation. "Am I rushing you?"

Rhan answered by going to him and wrapping him in a fierce embrace. "I've waited so long for this. Now here you are, better than any of my dreams."

"Let me show you how much better." Aerik reached between

them and unfastened Rhan's pants before sliding his fingers beneath the waistband and moving his hands down. The leathers fell to the floor. Aerik continued the caress, hands sliding to buttocks and cupping them as he gently kissed Rhan's neck.

The peace that had filled him while watching Aerik light the candle was forgotten as Rhan's flesh responded to his friend's touch. He put a hand to Aerik's cheek and turned his head until their lips met. As they kissed, he unfastened Aerik's pants and nudged them down until they slid to the floor. They pressed close and kissed deeply.

At last they parted. Rhan was intoxicated by his friend's virile scent. Desire radiated from his skin like heat from a sun-baked stone. "You promised to show me what I've been missing," he said softly. "I'm ready."

Aerik held his hand and drew him toward the bed with an enticing smile. "Whatever you've been dreaming of, just ask and it's yours." He reclined on the mattress and pulled Rhan with him.

As they rolled together on the clean bedding, Rhan marveled at his compact friend's strength, testing it during playful wrestling and yielding to it when Aerik rolled on top of him and pinned his arms during a demanding kiss. They eventually came to rest on their sides, facing each other, hard cocks slick between their bodies.

Acrik gazed at him tenderly, his eyes black pools surrounded by thin blue rings in the near-darkness. "I'd like to return the gift you gave me on our first night," he said. A grin flashed. "I hope I'm skilled enough." He reached between them and held Rhan's erection, his hand covering half the shaft's length. "Did you know that you're, um, big?"

Rhan pushed his hips forward and rubbed his cock against Aerik's. "You're the one who makes it grow."

Aerik kissed him and then pulled back a few inches. "Let me try from above first. It's easier that way." He pushed Rhan onto his back and moved around so they were head to toe. Rhan's phallus stretched across his lean belly, hard and potent.

"You're sure?" Rhan asked, realizing his friend's size made his challenge more formidable. "I'm content with your hand if that suits you better."

"You deserve more than that. Don't worry, I'll be fine." He lowered his head and gently kissed the underside of Rhan's glans.

Rhan's cock jerked and fluid seeped from its tip to coat Aerik's lips. Aerik ran his tongue around the flared head, eliciting soft moans as he bathed the sensitive flesh with warm spit.

Rhan tensed, his body curling as pleasure soared. "Wait," he said. "This is new to me."

Aerik pressed his cheek against the slick shaft. "Don't worry, there's no rush. Try to relax. And say something if you need me to stop."

Rhan started to reply but broke off in a moan as Aerik returned to giving pleasure. His lips slid around the head of Rhan's cock and tugged gently. After a few seconds of teasing, his lips started a slow slide down the thick shaft.

Rhan watched through slit eyes as his flesh slowly slipped inside his partner's body. Aerik paused halfway down, moving a hand up to cup Rhan's balls, then continued his feat. The shaft's remaining half slid into his throat like a sword into a snug scabbard. Aerik squeezed with his lips as he let the ivory column slide back into view, glistening with his spit.

Rhan's erection strained in a rigid arc, its dusky head smearing Aerik's tongue with slippery fluid. For a moment he feared he was going to succumb to pleasure, but Aerik sensed his excitement and squeezed the base of his cock. The orgasm that had seemed inevitable gradually retreated, leaving him panting.

"You have a lot to teach me," Rhan said. He traced his fingers along Aerik's erection, making it twitch and drool. "Show me what you like, and I'll do the same. I want to learn."

"A fine idea." Aerik spread his legs further apart, making the head of his cock graze Rhan's lips. A sensuous lick along the underside of Rhan's erection began their play.

Rhan imitated the leisurely movement, letting his tongue mold itself to the curved shaft of Aerik's phallus. It jerked as his tongue swept over the flaring head, rewarding him with a surge of lubricant.

Eager to taste it, he took the glans into his mouth. Aerik squirmed as lips encircled his cock and slid down the shaft.

They soon established a pattern with Aerik giving pleasure and Rhan returning it. Rhan discovered that focusing on his partner made it easier to control the intense sensations building like a fire in his flesh. When his confidence had grown sufficiently, he let the drooling cock slide from his mouth and rolled Aerik onto his back.

"Let me try from on top," he said.

Aerik nodded. His dazed expression suggested that Rhan's apprenticeship was advancing faster than he had expected.

Rhan straddled him and then ran his hands along Aerik's sides from his armpits to his waist. "First let me try by myself." He grazed his lips over Aerik's erection and then let the rigid shaft sink into the wet heat of his throat.

He moved his hands to Aerik's thighs and pulled his legs apart while keeping the cock in his throat. Aerik started to writhe as Rhan held him in a powerful grip and sucked his cock with deep strokes.

Aerik was trembling on the edge of release before Rhan finally loosened his embrace and let the phallus slip from his lips. It lay across Aerik's midriff and twitched, wet and shiny. He pressed a palm against it and felt it pulse, marveling at the energy in the flesh and how eagerly it responded to his touch.

"Your turn," Aerik said, putting a hand on Rhan's hip. They traded places so Aerik again straddled Rhan's head. He nuzzled Rhan's erection before parting his lips and taking the glans inside his mouth. In one smooth slide, he took the whole shaft down his throat. Rhan's legs spread wide as Aerik gently stroked the sensitive skin of his legs and buttocks.

The new combination of sensations inflamed Rhan. Aerik's cock was inches from his face, its tip slick. He angled it down and took it between his lips. The scent of his friend's arousal was overpowering.

It seemed to Rhan that they became one, moving with a single purpose, both straining to prolong the spiraling ecstasy. Aerik's body trembled, and he gripped Rhan's legs urgently. Then his cock slid deep into Rhan's throat, jerking and spewing his seed in strong jets. He continued his lovemaking even as his body shook with pleasure.

Rhan would have shouted if he could. An orgasm ripped him like lightning. Aerik's encircling lips kept stroking the full length of his cock as they tasted each other's come.

They clung together until at last they were spent. Aerik moved around and kissed Rhan, his lips slick. Rhan tasted his own seed as their tongues explored.

Aerik sighed with contentment when their lips parted. "When it comes to love, you have nothing to fear. You were made for it."

Rhan tightened his embrace. His partner's lusty gaze and solid body were already making him hard again. "The only thing I fear is losing you."

Aerik returned the hug. "I know. I've been worrying about it too. We'll think of something, Rhan. There has to be a way." Then he grinned and reached down to squeeze their cocks together. "But there's a time for everything. And now's the time for something else."

Rhan agreed completely.

Chapter Six

AERIK lay still, his mind floating, the slow rise and fall of Rhan's chest against his back like the tide's ebb and flow. The finder still held him as they nestled together. He looked through a ventilation slit where the yurt's wall met its roof and saw night sky, but knew dawn was near. Birds had already begun their song to greet the sun.

He wished morning would never come, or at least that he could delay it. Last night had changed him. Rhan made love with surpassing skill. He didn't think it was merely a neophyte's tenderness, either. The young finder gave pleasure with astonishing sensitivity, extending sensation until it became almost unendurable. His ability to anticipate Aerik's needs seemed miraculous.

Rhan's arm tightened around him, drawing them more tightly together. "You can't fool me," he whispered. "I know you're awake."

Somehow Aerik wasn't surprised. He suspected the finder was far more observant than he revealed. He turned his head, laughing softly as Rhan licked his earlobe. "I thought you were a simple country finder. Or is everyone in the upcountry insatiable?"

"I don't know. All I know is how good you make me feel." He curled his body, his thick erection wedged between Aerik's buttocks.

Rolling over, Aerik took Rhan's head between his hands and pressed their lips together. Approaching dawn was forgotten as they rekindled the night's passion.

Scratching at the canvas door interrupted them. "Rhan? Are you awake?" The voice was Catrin's, and it sounded urgent.

Aerik suppressed a groan, releasing Rhan and swinging out of bed. He padded over to the flap and opened an edge enough to peek out. "We're awake," he said. "Isn't it a bit early?"

Catrin slipped her saddlebags off her shoulder and put them on the ground. "Untie the door. I have news and it can't wait."

"Better do as she says," Rhan said. He got out of bed and picked up his leathers. "She wouldn't be here without good reason."

"Just a second," Aerik told Catrin. He pulled on his pants and then untied the door's lashing. Catrin slipped in, leaving her gear outside, and stood by the table while Rhan and Aerik continued dressing.

"We have to get out of here," she said. "Fast. I woke early and figured you'd be sleeping in, so I went for breakfast by myself. Good thing I did. The cook was complaining about having to keep his place open late last night. Five Tyumens came in just before closing. They'd been riding all day and demanded service."

"Tyumens?" Rhan sat on the bed to pull on his boots. "But we're not overdue. Why would the convoy send someone else here?"

Aerik's stomach lurched. "They wouldn't. I'd guess it's the same group that tried to kill Jerolin. They might have picked us as their next best target. Or maybe they heard rumors of relics in Eben."

Catrin frowned. "I feared as much. What will they do if they find us?"

Aerik sat on the bed's edge while pulling on his boots. "They'll question us and then kill us. And they might not be quick about it. The gossip back in the convoy was that they're Numeran initiates. They're a powerful cult of true believers in Chakragil. My father's greatest enemies. In their eyes I'm a heretic and should die like one."

Rhan's eyes narrowed. "What does that mean?"

"Fire."

"Then we'd best not get caught," Catrin said. She went to Aerik's side and put a hand on his shoulder, making him meet her gaze. "Worry later," she said firmly. "There's too much else to do now."

He nodded. "I'll rouse Maiko and ready the horses while you and Rhan get supplies. How long will you need?"

"We can buy provisions where I had breakfast. It'll cost more, but we can't wait for the market to open. Give us twenty minutes." She gave him the token for reclaiming their horses from the stable, and then they collected their gear and parted company.

Aerik found Maiko's yurt and called softly at the door, not wanting to surprise the belligerent Hand. There was no answer. When he touched the flap, it swung aside without resistance. He wondered if Maiko might have still been carousing when the Numeran party arrived in Eben. Fearing the worst, he slipped inside.

Alcohol vapors permeated the air. Going to the cot, he bent over Maiko and shook his shoulder. "Maiko! Wake up. We have to get going."

At first he received no response. He shook the man again, harder this time, and was rewarded with a pained groan.

"Go away." The Hand's breath stank of wine.

Despite his distaste Aerik leaned close, not wanting to raise his voice. "Get up. We're in danger. Riders came in last night. I think they're the assassins who were after Jerolin. We can't let them find us."

Maiko sat up, pressing the sides of his head with his hands. He was fully dressed and even wore his boots. "I think I'm going to be sick."

Aerik stepped back, not doubting that Maiko would be happy to puke on him. "I'm not joking. Rhan and Catrin are getting supplies. We have to meet them in the stable in a few minutes. Get up or we'll leave you behind."

Maiko glared at him. "You probably would, fucking little weasel. Why'd I have to get stuck with you?"

It would have been tempting to leave him behind if Maiko's capture didn't pose such a threat to the rest of them. Aerik took three deep breaths and fought for calm. "Are you going to get up or not? We can't wait."

Maiko started to stand but then grunted and sat back on the bed. "This is your fault. You made me get drunk."

Aerik scowled. "I had nothing to do with it. You went off to drink all by yourself."

"I couldn't stand watching you and your pretty playmate fawning over each other. Which of you is the woman, anyway? I bet it's you. Whenever temple dancers aren't dressing up, they have their legs in the air."

Aerik's fists clenched. "Shut up and get moving."

"What's the matter? Want me to show you what a real man feels like?" Maiko made a ring with thumb and forefinger then thrust the middle finger of his other hand through it. "Wasn't the peasant big enough for you?"

Aerik grabbed Maiko's saddlebag off the floor and threw it at him. "Be at the stable in ten minutes." He turned and left without looking back.

By the time he got outside, he was shaking. The joy he had felt from waking at Rhan's side was forgotten. As he started down the path, he heard mumbled curses. Glancing over his shoulder, he saw Maiko stumbling out of the yurt with his gear. He kept walking but stayed far enough ahead to avoid insults.

The stable was quiet when Aerik rang a bell attached to the bamboo door, but soon a sleepy boy no older than ten peered out. Aerik held out the horse and lion tokens and beckoned for Maiko to produce his. The boy yawned and nodded, swinging the door open for them.

The stable smelled of straw, manure, oxen, and horses. "This is the most horses we've ever had," the boy said as he lit a candle and placed it in a brass holder fastened to the barn's center post. "I like them."

Aerik fished out a small coin and held it up. "You can have this if you promise not to tell anyone about the horses. Agreed?"

The boy's eyes went round. He plucked the coin from Aerik's hand and nodded vigorously. "Can I sit on one of them?"

"If there's time. We're leaving soon." Aerik dropped his gear and started saddling his mount. He wanted to be gone before the streets started filling with people. The stable boy retreated to a cot against the wall, admiring his coin as if he couldn't believe his good fortune.

The horses were soon saddled. Rhan and Catrin hadn't arrived, so Aerik let the stable boy sit on his horse as he led it in a small circle around the center post. Maiko sat on a three-legged stool and leaned back, head resting against the wall and eyes closed. Five minutes passed and Aerik was growing concerned.

Maiko rubbed his eyes and then stood. "We've waited long enough. Let's get going."

"They'll be here soon," Aerik said. He helped the boy down from the saddle and sent him back to his cot. "Besides, we need the supplies."

"We can forage and hunt. They might have been caught, stupid. The same thing will happen to us if we keep sitting around."

"There's still time." The thought that Maiko might be right made his stomach clench.

"They're not worth risking our necks for," Maiko said, warming to the argument. "They're just peasants, there's plenty more where they came from." His gaze flickered over Aerik. "Well, maybe not many willing to fuck a runt like you."

"I didn't see anyone sharing your bed this morning. Let me guess. You lost all your money gambling and couldn't even buy a whore?"

Maiko stepped in front of Aerik and grabbed his shirt, ramming him against the center post. "I've had enough of your smart mouth." He pulled Aerik away from the post and slammed him back again, anger twisting his face.

Though dazed, Aerik jerked a leg up to knee Maiko in the groin. Maiko released him and fell onto his back, barely managing to roll onto his side before vomiting.

Aerik turned to the stable boy, who was edging toward the door. "I'm sorry," he said. He took another coin from his pouch and offered it. "He had too much to drink last night and didn't really know what he was doing. You know how that is?"

"Yes," the boy said meekly. His eyes followed the coin in Aerik's hand. "My friend Egil, he has a brother that drinks a lot. He's mean too."

"Well, it would be bad for me if people knew about this." He held the coin up for inspection. "If I give you another, will you keep this a secret? Like the horses?"

The boy nodded and broke into a huge grin when Aerik put the coin in his hand. "Keep your horses here whenever you want. Can I ride one by myself next time?"

Aerik ruffled his hair. "If we return this way, you'll get to ride." The blazing smile left no doubt that he had made a friend.

The door opened and he spun around. Catrin entered, looking harried, with Rhan right behind. "What happened to Maiko?" she asked. "Can he ride?"

Aerik felt a pang of guilty pleasure. "He lost an argument. He'll ride. What's wrong?"

"We talked with the cook who served those riders last night," Rhan said as he secured his saddlebags on his mount. "They asked a lot of questions and wanted to know if any other riders had come through town. The cook didn't know about us, otherwise they'd have tracked us down already. He says they were determined men and was sure they'd be up early. We have to clear out before we're seen in the streets."

Aerik needed no convincing. He helped Rhan hoist Maiko into his saddle while Catrin asked the stable boy for directions to Rolf Odette's farm. In moments they were out the door.

They found an old road leading north around the lake, as the boy had said. Aerik suppressed the dread that kept welling up. If the other riders were indeed Numerans, it would be safer to head back into the hills. But what if the old man in the ruins had found something important? Letting it fall into the hands of his father's foes could be a disaster. He held his reins in a tight grip and led the way north.

Chapter Seven

RHAN rode in silence as they fled Eben, doing his best to avoid getting entangled in the dispute between Aerik and Maiko. He was surprised the relationship between the two could grow worse, but there was no denying the new tension between them. He could smell it over the stink of Maiko's bile and sour sweat.

"It does no good to get ourselves killed," Maiko said, apparently believing that constant repetition of his arguments made them more convincing. "We should report to Jerolin and tell him what we know. If we're caught, he gets nothing at all."

"Quit arguing about it," Aerik said. "We're not running home at the first sign of trouble. You're the Hand, you shouldn't be afraid of a fight."

"I like a fight, but we're outnumbered and they have bows. This is just stupid. Like you."

"I know it's risky. But we're too close to give up now. We'll see if this old man knows anything before heading back to the convoy. It won't take long."

They were using an ancient roadway. It had probably once followed the lake's shore, but the water had receded and the crumbling road was now separated from the lake by a forest. At mid-morning they entered a clearing. A thatch-roofed hut surrounded by an overgrown garden nestled in the bend of a creek. Melons glistened in the sun among tangled vines.

"This should be it," Rhan said. "The boy said Odette's place was in the third clearing after the road turns away from the shore."

Nobody greeted them when they approached the cottage. Rhan opened the door and looked inside, confirming that nobody was home. The scent of its occupant saturated the close quarters.

"Maybe he's gone to the ruins," he said. "Kara said he spends a lot of time there." He surveyed the clearing and saw a path leading into the forest. Walking toward it, he breathed deeply and followed the trace of Rolf Odette's passage as easily as if the man had scratched symbols in the dirt. "Let's see where this leads."

Maiko protested, but Aerik overruled him. The path was too close and overhung with branches for riding so they led their horses along the trail as it snaked around rock outcroppings and through stands of oaks. Catrin had a skeptical look on her face, as if she thought they were on a fool's errand, but Rhan smelled the hut's occupant. He was proven right when a switchback brought them to the edge of a large clearing. As the trees thinned, they glimpsed concrete walls through the foliage.

A broad plaza, cracked and buckled by the earthquake, surrounded the ruins of a thick-walled stronghold. From its center the stub of a great tower jabbed the air like a tree shattered by lightning. Rubble strewn in a line across the plaza showed that the fallen tower must have once offered a commanding view of the surrounding lands. The stark architecture was foreboding. Massive walls spoke of defense rather than creature comforts.

Aerik held up a hand to signal for silence while they were still among the trees. He pointed to an area in the fort's shadow.

Rhan shaded his eyes and saw a gathering of perhaps twenty people arrayed around a wooden platform that extended from a gap in the fractured wall. They were downwind, and he had been unaware of them until Aerik pointed them out. Listening closely, he could hear a faint voice above the wind rustling through the forest.

"Kara said Odette likes to lecture," Aerik said. "That must be him. It seems there are some who like to listen." His eyes were wide. "We might have found what we were seeking. The difference between a crackpot and a heretic is that a heretic has followers."

"What do we do now?" Rhan asked.

"First we listen. When he's done, we'll try to get him alone and question him. All we have to do is find out if the rumors reaching Chakragil are coming from here. If they are, the militia will come back to deal with him."

Catrin nodded. "We'd better leave the horses in the forest. He'll shut up fast if he thinks Tyumens are here."

"I'll stay with the horses," Maiko said. "I've already heard enough from raving idiots today." He glared at Aerik. "I'm going to rest. You can do what you want."

"Probably just as well," Aerik said. "Too many new faces might make him nervous. Let's find a place where you can wait."

A few minutes of exploration led them to a gulch containing a slow-moving creek. Overhanging willows provided shade and concealment. They tethered their horses by the stream and left Maiko lying on his back with an arm flung over his eyes.

Returning to the path, they followed it out of the forest and onto the plaza. They attracted little notice as they crossed panels embossed with deep symbols. Rhan's unease grew as they neared the gathering. At first he had thought the plaza was simply a defense, designed to make it impossible for attackers to hide from the fort's guards. But the outpouring of carved words had no defensive purpose that he could guess. It felt more like a warning.

The small audience sat in a semicircle around the makeshift stage. Fortress walls made an imposing backdrop, with massive panels embossed with more symbols and images. The walls portrayed demonic faces intermixed with despairing men and women along with the ominous glyphs. Rhan saw why locals considered the place cursed. He knew, better than most, that many ancient mysteries were justly feared. A premonition made him shiver despite the warm sun on his back.

They found a spot shaded by a tilted slab of concrete and settled down to listen. An old man wearing a brown robe strode back and forth on the short stage, gesturing emphatically and speaking almost without pause. Despite his eccentricity, the audience watched him avidly.

Rolf Odette was growing frenzied, indignation escalating into fury as he railed against the priests of Tyume. His hands sliced the air as he denounced their cowardice and greed. *The world is about power*, he claimed, *about who wields it and who kneels before it*. Discipline, fearlessness and determination were his favored themes. Though he plainly didn't realize it, nobody in the audience could have doubted the kind of tyrant he would be if he actually possessed power. Rhan wondered why anybody bothered to listen to such a disagreeable man.

As if to answer his question, Odette stopped pacing and stood at the front edge of his platform. He gave the gathered a challenging glare. "You are sheep," he said, brows drawn down over accusing eyes. "Like the priests, you cower in fear of the past. Like sheep, you must be led. Your fate is to heed those who have gone where you don't dare!"

Facing his audience, he raised his arms overhead and clasped his hands together. As the robe's sleeves slid back, Rhan glimpsed a vambrace on his right forearm. It was black and seemed to flicker with light in a complex pattern. There was no time to get a good look. As Odette clasped his hands, dazzling waves of red light streaked across the plaza like the ripples made by a rock dropped into a pond.

Rhan blinked, trying to dispel the ghostly bands that blurred his vision. The audience was swooning, ecstatic at the spectacle. Their scent was a strong mixture of fear and exaltation.

Aerik sprang to his feet. As he turned to Rhan, a chorus of screams erupted. Odette collapsed backward, arrows piercing his stomach and leg. The pulsating waves of red ceased as his arms flung wide in a convulsion.

More arrows streaked the air, two finding members of the audience and another ricocheting off stones. Rhan yanked Aerik down and looked over his shoulder. Four archers had appeared from behind fragments of the fallen tower. They were turning to track the men and women fleeing toward the forest.

"Numerans," Aerik said. "I'd bet on it. They want the relic and don't mean to leave any witnesses."

"They're cutting off escape to the forest," Rhan said. "We have to make for the fortress before they turn their bows back this way. It's our only chance."

Catrin shook her head violently, red hair flying. "We'll be trapped. They'll catch us."

Aerik grabbed her. "Rhan's right. We're dead for sure if we stay here or run for the trees. There's a gap in the wall by the platform. Head for that, and we'll go from there."

Catrin blanched but she clenched her teeth and nodded. Half the people who had come to hear Odette already lay dead or dying on the plaza and the other half were running for the forest in a panic. The fortress offered their only hope.

Rhan led the way, running in a crouch. An arrow whizzed by his ear and another skidded across the plaza to his left. He ran faster, Aerik's and Catrin's footsteps pounding behind him.

They jumped onto the platform where Odette lay in a pool of blood. He was struggling weakly and clutching at the arrow protruding from his belly. The relic on his forearm beckoned, shimmering with ornate whorls of light, but Rhan dashed past it and dove through the breached wall.

Another wall reared in front of him, indistinct in the roofed passage. He brought his arms up in time to cushion his impact. Catrin and Aerik crashed into him, sending them all tumbling as two arrows ricocheted off the wall where he had been standing. The corridor they had entered was blocked by rubble on their left. Scrambling to their feet, they ran to the right. Screams echoed behind them.

The corridor was thick with dust. Shafts of light streamed through cracks in the wall like golden knives. A corridor leading deeper into the fortress soon appeared on their left. Rhan signaled the others to stop.

"I think we should try it," he said, nodding toward the passage. Lintels had fallen at irregular intervals along the corridor, causing the roof to collapse and admit occasional shafts of light, but the way appeared passable.

Aerik looked at the derelict corridor dubiously. "You think we'll find refuge there?"

Rhan pointed at the ground. Footprints went in all directions, but most of them turned into the castle's heart. "Rolf Odette found a relic, and he probably found it in there. Maybe there's more, something that could help us. And sometimes there are hidden passages out of places like this."

Catrin looked shaken. "That thing was daemon work. It's not safe in here."

"We don't have any choice, Catrin. We're dead anyway unless we find something we can use or another way out." He touched her arm, reassuring her. "You're the one who's always telling me to be practical."

"Let's try it," Aerik said. "It won't take them long to finish their business outside. We'd better keep moving."

Rhan led the way. At first the roof damage was sufficient to allow light to penetrate, but as they got deeper, the structure was more intact. Then the corridor turned a corner and the way ahead plunged into complete darkness. He could see faint footprints leading onward.

Aerik turned to Catrin. "Maybe we can hide in there. Willing to try?"

"What else can we do?" She peered anxiously into the darkness. "But what if they make torches and come searching? We'll be helpless."

Rhan and Aerik exchanged glances. Rhan could tell his friend intended to honor his pledge to keep the cold torch a secret. But they both knew what should be done.

Fear of losing Catrin's trust was unnerving, but he saw no alternative. He opened his belt pouch and took out the relic.

"This is a cold torch," he said, not yet making a light with it. "They're not harmful, at least not in the way some relics are. The danger is in keeping something the Tyumens want for themselves. The elders will cast me out if you tell them I have this."

She appeared more relieved than alarmed. "Some kind of torch, you say? Finders have used these before?"

"Finders have always used them. But they're kept secret and passed from hand to hand. Examiners always seize them if they're given over to elders." He took a deep breath. "Are you going to tell Marenka?"

Catrin shook her head. "If finders have been using them a long time, I'm not worried about marks or other hurt." She gave him an accusing stare. "But Aerik already knew about it, didn't he? Why did you tell him but not me? He's a Tyumen, after all."

"He was with me when we found it, just two days ago. He pledged to keep the secret."

"Then I promise as well. You should know you can trust me. Now show me how this works."

A brief demonstration left Catrin speechless. Rhan was weak with relief. He now had no secrets from her, save for his mark. It made him wonder how many years of loneliness might have been avoided had he dared to trust her more.

They pressed ahead, their way illuminated by pale light like sun shining through thick clouds. Little debris littered the floor as they neared the fort's heart beneath the shattered tower. Squat columns flanked the passage like giants bearing the world on their shoulders. Each pair of columns framed massive metal doors. Rhan tested the doors as they passed. Each seemed as immovable as the foundations themselves. He began to wonder if Rolf Odette's relic had come from somewhere else, perhaps in the wreckage of the tower's fallen summit. But the scent of the man's recent presence lingered in the air and drew him on.

The passage narrowed, crowded by columns nearly as wide as they were tall. The pillars were embossed with glyphs that had been painted and still held their color. One was larger and more frequent than the others, a design like a round face made from curving blades. It was the only symbol painted bright red.

"Look," Catrin said, pointing at an object near the edge of their light. There was no mistaking what she meant. A stone tablet filled the space between two columns. It was deeply incised with a huge copy of the red glyph. The slab had been cracked, probably by the same earthquake that had brought down the tower, and along the bottom someone had cleared rock from a gash. The opening was less than two feet high. Rhan lay in front of it and shone light into the hole.

"Don't do it," Catrin said. Her voice was hoarse. "Even a finder should heed these warnings. I think this was a prison, not a fortress. Something could be in there. Something bound."

Rhan stood. "Odette went in there and got out alive. I should be fine."

Catrin still looked nervous. "You're sure it was Odette who cleared that passage?"

"Who else? This might be where he found that vambrace he was wearing. We can't afford to pass it by. It might be our only chance to find something useful." He flipped the torch a few times to renew the light. "Odette was right about one thing. Priests fear the spread of knowledge. Especially knowledge of the past."

Catrin scowled. "You're starting to sound like a heretic. Are you saying the legends are wrong?"

"All I'm saying is we should think for ourselves. I'm going to see what's behind that carving. Anyone else coming?"

"I am," Aerik said. "No more talk. Those Numerans will be coming after us, after they make torches."

Catrin sighed. "Me too. You first, Rhan. We'll follow after you're through so you can give us some light."

The passage was too low to go through on hands and knees, so Rhan lay on his back and pushed into the hole with his arms at his sides and the torch between his teeth. He had explored beneath the ground since childhood, but this was the worst fear he had faced. He focused on the smell of Rolf Odette's sweat, proof that they were on the right path, and kept shifting forward a few inches at a time. All he could see was cracked granite a few inches above his face. Tiny crystals embedded in the stone glittered in the torch's white light.

Suddenly the rock disappeared, to be replaced by blackness. He pushed with renewed energy and scrambled out of the hole.

Holding the torch overhead revealed an austere chamber with a low vault. Three granite pedestals, circular, and wider than they were tall, stood in the middle of the room. One supported a featureless black vambrace some six inches across. It looked like a match to the relic Odette had been wearing and rested in a cradle fashioned from silvery metal that had the rust-free look of ancient handiwork. The second and third pedestals were empty. A small mound of candle stubs in a corner showed that Odette had spent considerable time here.

Rhan swallowed disappointment. Unless there was more to be found, nothing here offered aid. The vambrace was unlike anything he'd encountered, and he had no idea how it might be used. He crouched and held the light to the hole he had just left. "I'm through," he called. "There's something here, but not much. Do you still want to look?"

"I do," Aerik answered. "I see your light. Don't move it." Scuffling sounds were soon followed by Aerik, whose small size was an advantage in tight spaces. He pulled himself out with enviable agility. As he got to his feet he saw the pedestals and went over for a closer look.

Muted curses accompanied Catrin as she wormed her way through the cleft. For a moment Rhan worried that she might find the passage too tight, possibly even get stuck, but she emerged with her hair in disarray and a fierce frown. "I'll never be a finder," she said. "My bones are too big for this kind of work."

"You're doing fine," Rhan said. He gave her a hand up before pointing at the pedestals. "I was hoping we'd find something we could use as a weapon, but no luck. And considering how hard it was to get in here, I doubt we'll find other passages leading out. Sorry. We'll have to keep looking."

Aerik was leaning over the black vambrace, examining it closely. Rhan saw him reach toward it. "No!" He lunged to Aerik's side and pulled him back. "Never touch a relic unless you know what you're doing."

Aerik blinked. "I thought I saw something. Flickering lights, like fireflies." He looked up defiantly. "Finders touch relics all the time. Even when you don't know what they are."

"You're not a finder, Aerik. You shouldn't take that kind of risk."

He crossed his arms. "But I saw something. Maybe this can help us. Risk doesn't count for much when we're surrounded by assassins, I think."

"I just don't want you to get hurt." He held his light over the relic. "You probably just saw reflections." He moved the cold torch back and forth, noticing the object's unusual sheen. "It looks the same as the one Odette was wearing on his arm. It must have made the red light. But I don't know its purpose or how to use it. It might just be intended for entertainment, like Odette's show."

"Why hide a theatrical tool in a vault like this? And all those symbols outside the chamber looked like warnings. That doesn't make sense unless it's important."

Rhan hesitated, realizing Aerik was right. Concern for his friends' safety was hampering his judgment.

"Let's take a closer look." He adjusted the torch to provide a softer light and held it within an inch of the relic. All three of them peered at it, looking for surface features as he moved the light around.

At first Rhan saw or smelled nothing peculiar. The surface was smooth as a pearl and had the same luster, and was the most perfect black he had ever seen. Then he noticed that despite its sheen, it wasn't reflecting much light. He moved the torch closer, almost touching its surface. Whatever Aerik had seen, it hadn't been a reflection.

A minute passed while they watched. The torch started to dim, and Rhan stepped back to perform the ritual that renewed it.

Aerik looked frustrated. "I swear I saw lights. Just a glimpse, when I looked aside at Catrin getting up. Maybe it only happens if you don't look at it directly."

"I believe you," Rhan said. "But we probably shouldn't stay here any longer." He looked back at the vambrace. "Should we take it? I don't know what we'd do with it and it might be dangerous. Maybe contact with one of these is what made Odette go mad."

"Leave it," Catrin said. "Why take a chance? It's not like the village is going to starve this winter. Not after we sell the finery you found already."

Aerik groaned. "What if the Numerans find Maiko?"

"Then we have a long walk ahead of us," Rhan said. "That's if we don't get caught ourselves. Let's get going. We can't afford to linger."

"Lead the way," Catrin said. "The tunnel's not so bad when you can see light at the end."

"Wait." The word was almost imperceptible.

The hairs on the back of Rhan's neck stirred. "Did one of you say something?" He already knew the answer. The faint voice had been directionless, as if the walls themselves had whispered.

"I heard it too," Catrin said in a quavering voice. She smelled of terror.

Aerik was motionless, his face pale. "Who's here?"

Rhan already knew they were alone. Or if not alone, in the presence of something that had no scent. All the ghost stories he had heard from other finders swarmed up from memory. His heart pounded, and he was seized by an urgent desire to flee. "Let's get out of here." He offered his torch to Catrin. "You can go first, but hurry."

The darkness whispered again. "Your enemies approach. I can show you another way out."

Rhan spun around, holding the torch above his head. The chamber behind him was still empty. He had never felt so trapped.

"Fear clouds the mind. Some would fear the light you hold. Do you?"

The question diverted him, but he didn't answer it. A horrific conviction was forming. He forced himself to speak. "Are you a daemon? Show yourself if you mean no harm."

Catrin moaned. Aerik put an arm around her but looked equally unnerved.

"Have I harmed you?" the voice asked. "You accept help from the light you hold. But more than that will be needed to escape the men who are coming."

Rhan slowly lowered the light. His mind began to work again. Curiosity blossomed and undercut the tide of fear. The old world had been destroyed, the daemons bound, for reasons still hidden in wreckage of the lost age. Yet his torch was proof that not all ancient mysteries were to be avoided. "How can we trust you, if you hide from us?"

"If it's any comfort, I fear you more than you fear me." The voice suddenly became focused and came from the black vambrace. "I'm not hiding. You were looking at me moments ago. Your use of an ancient tool makes me think you're not ruled by superstitions. I can give you knowledge. In return I would leave this tomb. And we'll all survive, which is unlikely if you decline what I offer."

"Don't listen to it," Catrin said. "It's a daemon, a deceiver!"

Rhan went back to the relic in its graceful cradle. Though he had pursued relics since childhood and knew the lore of finders from countless sources, nothing like this had ever been found. Or if it had, nobody had survived to tell of it. The risk and the possible rewards were equally extreme.

He turned to Aerik. "What do you think? Should we risk it?"

Aerik took a shuddering breath and reluctantly came to Rhan's side. He was plainly terrified but controlled his fear with iron discipline. "Do you have a name?" he asked, staring at the relic as if it were about to explode.

"Philemon. I've already heard your names, and I'm pleased to meet you. I think."

Rhan was startled enough to forget his qualms. Perhaps they had found an ancient nemesis, but at least it had agreeable manners. He touched the cradle holding the vambrace. Nothing happened as his fingers traced graceful curves like antlers made of liquid silver. The metal was cool and smooth, almost oily to the touch. Suppressing the clamoring fears that urged flight, he touched the relic that called itself Philemon. A mild tingling ran up his fingers, like stroking a cat's fur on a dry day, but nothing more. He stepped back and regarded the object soberly. "You say you can show us another way out. How do we know we can trust you?"

"In truth, there's no way you can be sure. Trust must grow from experience." The words came directly from the vambrace in the voice of an old but healthy man. "You must decide whether to take a gamble. I understand your hesitation. The stories you've been told about the past are known to me, at least some of them. But I ask you, do you believe everything you're told?"

The question was a spark falling on dry tinder. Rhan snorted. "Of course not. The priests say whatever suits their purposes. The elders aren't always right either. They only want to live like their forefathers."

"Then you must choose between what you learn with your own eyes and what you've been told. Your friends are right; I'm what men now call a daemon. You've heard how terrible we are. Now you must decide if the stories were true."

"Don't let it fool you," Catrin said. "You've spent your life searching in ruins. You can't doubt the daemon wars happened."

"It takes two sides to make war," Philemon said. "And the victor gets to write the histories. I could tell you what really happened, if you want to know."

The flame of Rhan's curiosity blazed. "You were there, during the daemon wars?"

"Yes, and before. I don't claim to know everything, but I know more than you can possibly imagine."

Rhan looked at Aerik. "What do you think the priests of Tyume would do with such knowledge?"

"They'd fear it. And likely destroy it. The past has always been what they say it is. It's the foundation of their power." His wide eyes showed an appreciation of the possibilities.

"I've decided," Rhan said. He handed the torch to Aerik and lifted the vambrace out of its cradle. He saw the flickering lights that Aerik had first noticed and felt as if the whole earth was balanced in the object he held. "We'll take you away from here. And you'll give us the truth of the past."

"Best we start immediately, then. The first truth you need to know is that your pursuers are near."

Chapter Eight

AERIK was numb. Were the legends truth or lies? Rhan didn't seem to know either, but it hadn't deterred him from a breathtaking gamble. The finder held the daemon in his hand as if it were an ordinary relic. Aerik hoped his bravery wasn't foolhardy.

Not wanting to touch the daemon, Aerik restored the torch's light and led the way out through the suffocating passage. The thought of Rhan waiting in a dark chamber with a daemon cradled in his hands had the feel of a nightmare. He wrestled a spasm of dread into submission and soldiered on. Rhan was right about one thing: this find could shake the empire.

The daemon spoke as soon as Rhan emerged from beneath the engraved tablet. "Men are coming. Their footsteps echo despite their efforts to be silent. We must go down to where a hidden exit lies."

"How do you know there's another way out?" Aerik asked. "Weren't you a prisoner here?"

"I was. But masons talked of it while sealing the chamber where I was confined. I never forget, and now their words will serve us."

"Let's go," Rhan said. He had plainly made up his mind to trust the relic, which he had slipped onto his left forearm. "You lead, Aerik."

They set off, Aerik quickly losing track of their course as Philemon told them where to turn. The passages beneath the fortress were a labyrinth designed to confuse and delay intruders. His dismay mounted as they descended a corkscrew staircase and arrived in a circular chamber with passages exiting in eight directions. "Which way?" he asked. The sensation of being lost felt much worse when underground.

"There's a problem," Philemon said. The disembodied voice sounded apologetic. "I see the path we need to follow, but there has been damage. We might have difficulty."

Aerik was incredulous. "You led us down here and don't even know if we can get through?"

"I was in a sealed chamber. How could I have known the extent of the damage? This is still our best hope. Do you see where Catrin is standing?"

Aerik nodded, wondering how the featureless vambrace knew so much of its surroundings.

"The tunnel behind her leads to the way out. Go that way, but carefully."

Aerik exchanged glances with Rhan and Catrin. He could tell they shared his doubt, but what else could they do? They took the path Philemon had chosen.

They had not gone thirty paces before the stone flooring at the edge of their light was replaced with blackness. Aerik stopped and held the torch higher.

The corridor's floor was gone, fifteen feet ahead of where they stood. In its place was a gap filled only by a few twisted timbers that had once been floor joists. The span was too broad to jump. He edged to the brink of the precipice and peered down.

At first he saw nothing. As he held the torch over the void, a faint reflection glinted. Inky water and jumbled stones were barely visible several yards below.

"What now?" Catrin asked. She frowned at the vambrace on Rhan's arm. "Remind me how we got talked into this, Rhan."

Aerik handed the cold torch to Catrin and knelt at the hole's edge. He reached down about a foot and pushed on a twisted joist. It creaked and shifted, sending a cascade of dust into the water, then slid a few inches and held. He pushed harder, but it seemed to be firmly wedged.

He stood and studied the joist. While it was five inches across and flat, it was wedged at a slight tilt and was over twenty feet long. "We can cross it," he said, sounding more confident than he felt. "I'll go first, to test it."

Rhan looked like he wanted to protest, but nodded. "I'll hold the timber while you cross and steady it if I can. Grab the beam if you slip, and I'll come get you." He didn't say what they would do if the beam broke or slipped loose, but it was just as well. Aerik was trying to keep that thought at bay as he removed his boots.

Delay served no purpose. He took a deep breath and stepped down to the joist. The challenge would have been trivial for a dancer if the beam were level, but its tilt to one side made him feel like he was about to slip as soon as his second foot touched the wood. He held his arms out for balance and inched forward. Rhan lay on the floor behind him and held the beam with both hands.

The beam started creaking when Aerik was halfway across. He froze, heart thudding, as more dust showered into the water. Sweat streaked his forehead and ran into his eyes but he didn't dare move his arms to wipe it. As he slid forward another few inches, the far end of the joist started to slide sideways.

"Watch out!" Catrin shouted, but Aerik was already moving. He had time for one quick step and the beginning of a leap before the joist tore loose from its splintered mooring and jerked out from beneath him.

He strained forward, reaching for the far side of the gap. The air was knocked out of him when he hit. He found himself clutching for purchase on smooth stones, his legs swinging through emptiness.

Rhan was shouting, but the ringing in his ears drowned out all else. Pain roared and a surge of desperate strength filled him. His fingers found cracks between the stones and served as an anchor as he hoisted himself to his elbows. Another heave pulled his torso onto the floor and got him high enough to pull his legs up. He sprawled on the floor, gasping.

"Aerik! Are you hurt?"

Rhan's frantic voice couldn't be ignored. He forced himself to sit up and wave. "Watch out for the last step. It's a bit tricky."

"He's all right," Catrin said. "But what about our bridge?"

Aerik looked over the precipice. The joist's connection on the opposite side of the pitfall was still in place, but the end on his side was no longer lodged on the crossbeam that had been supporting it. "Hold the torch down low," he said. "I'll take a look."

Rhan took the torch from Catrin, then knelt and held it in the chasm.

Aerik ignored his queasiness and slid forward enough to look at the flooring's underside. As his eyes adjusted to the shadows, he saw why the floor had collapsed. They were on the fort's bottom level and this section was supported by a forest of pillars that descended into a torpid subterranean river. Joists between the pillars supported wooden flooring that, in turn, supported a layer of flagstones. A pillar had collapsed, likely during the earthquake, and taken a section of floor with it. The beam he had crossed had snapped free of its connecting piece at his end but had not fallen away completely. The splintered end had lodged in a tangled web of wood and masonry. It descended at a steep angle but would be climbable if it didn't move any more.

"Can you reach it?" Rhan asked.

"I'll try. Hold the light lower."

Rhan lay down and reached into the fissure, holding the cold torch as low as he could. It revealed a network of angled cross braces, dense as the branches in a forest canopy. The nearest brace was just a foot from the lip of the flagstone beneath Aerik.

Pushing himself further out, Aerik reached under the flooring and grasped the rough-hewn wood. It seemed solid, so he eased further out and adjusted his grip. He gave the timber another hard tug and then twisted so he could reach it with his other hand. Without permitting himself to hesitate, he eased himself over the lip and swung down to hang by the cross brace. His feet found purchase in the substructure and he climbed the short distance to where the broken beam had lodged.

The beam was wedged tight in the bracing that had stopped its fall. Aerik tested it, at first gently and then with all his strength, but it wouldn't budge. "I think it's safe," he called.

Catrin took off her boots and crossed next, easing down the beam like a cat trying to descend a tree. He helped her get her footing among the timbers before signaling Rhan to join them.

Rhan took off his boots and tossed all three pairs across the chasm. He climbed down with the torch tucked into his waistband, light and shadow twisting like nightmares as he moved.

Climbing up from the fissure was easier than the crossing, with plenty of helping hands to lend assistance. When they were out, Rhan touched and inspected the daemon on his forearm with no sign of distress, making Aerik wonder just how risky a life finders led. "How close are we to getting out of here?" he asked the relic.

"The place I heard described should be near," Philemon answered. "Keep going, and hope nothing else has fallen into ruin."

They continued more cautiously, Aerik again leading, and soon entered a vaulted chamber with a rectangular pit at its center. Six hand pumps were spaced around its sides and buckets lay in a row along one wall.

"There should be a ledge part way down the well," Philemon said. "This is where they pumped water for the kitchens. An overflow drain at the ledge serves as a way out. At least that's what the mason said."

Aerik held the torch over the rock-lined pit. The ledge was only about ten feet down and there was an opening some four feet across on one side. Water filled the well a few yards below the ledge. He tucked the cold torch into his waistband and smiled nervously. "When I was a child I thought it would be fun to explore ruins. Nobody told me about jumping into wells and crawling through drains."

"That's not so bad," Rhan said. "Try digging for a week and finding nothing but rust and bones when you're done."

"You have a point." He sat on the well's edge. "It'll be a short drop. I just hope the ledge is solid." Rhan helped lower him into the well and then released him.

He dropped the last few feet, landing on solid stone, and then looked up. The hole looked far smaller from below, like a deep grave. He knelt and held the torch inside the drain. A squat tunnel stretched into darkness. "It looks passable as far as I can see," he said. His voice sounded strange in the cramped space. "There's not much room down here. Let me get out of the way before you come down."

"Take the daemon first," Rhan said. "I don't want to bang it against anything while I'm jumping."

Aerik felt a shiver but was embarrassed by his superstitious timidity. He put the torch on the ground and moved to the side of the pit. "Ready."

Rhan dropped the vambrace into his waiting hands. It wasn't heavy, but the texture of its surface was unsettling. Hard as marble, it nevertheless had a liquid feel to it. It made his skin crawl.

"Nice catch," Philemon said. "Thank you."

Aerik jumped, almost dropping the relic. The thing vibrated like a handful of bees when it spoke. "You're welcome," he said, reflexively polite.

"Catrin next," Rhan said. "Make way."

Aerik carried Philemon into the tunnel and then held the light out to illuminate the well for Catrin, who was already dangling over the edge. Moments later she thudded onto the ledge. As soon as she followed Aerik into the tunnel, Rhan lowered himself over the lip and dropped down. He looked at the tunnel where the others were crouched and groaned. "I hope it's not far. Just looking at it makes my back hurt."

"The sooner we're out of here, the better I'll like it," Aerik said. He handed the daemon to Catrin, who made a face and passed it on to Rhan before they embarked.

Aerik's hopes for a quick escape from the fortress were soon dashed. The tunnel stretched interminably. Its size never varied, forcing them to shuffle ahead with knees and backs bent. Crawling would have been preferable except that the rough concrete would have quickly shredded hands and clothing. He felt like he was carrying a cask of wine on his back and could have sworn there was a dagger in his neck. Sweat soaked his shirt. When his thighs started sending darts of pain up his legs, the distraction was almost welcome.

"Wait a minute," Catrin said. "I have to straighten my back or I'm going to scream."

They sat with their legs outstretched and unbent their backs. Aerik faced the others and rotated the torch to strengthen its light, hoping it would make the confined space feel less oppressive. Rhan wiped sweat from his forehead. "At least it's dry," he said. "I've done this before, while up to my neck in cold water. That's worse."

Philemon made a rapid fluttering sound like a hummingbird. "That's one of the things I like best about mankind," he said. "You're so adaptable. And full of hope, at least when you're happy."

Rhan snorted. "You think this makes me happy? You must not know mankind very well."

"We shall see." The vambrace buzzed again.

"Are you laughing?" Aerik asked suspiciously. Either this was a most peculiar daemon, or everything he had been taught about them was wrong. This creature certainly didn't act like a malevolent destroyer.

"I wasn't mocking you," Philemon answered. "It's true I don't fully understand your kind. But you understand yourselves even less, I suspect."

"We've rested long enough," Catrin said. Her discomfort with the daemon did not seem to have eased in the least. She gave Rhan a stern look. "Even if it manages to get us out of here, that doesn't prove we can trust it."

"One thing at a time," Rhan said. He resumed his crouch. "But I agree. It's not wise to linger."

Aerik pushed himself to his feet, pain stabbing his back like spears. The fact that Rhan and Catrin probably felt even worse was no consolation. He resigned himself to the pain and pressed ahead.

They had only been moving a few minutes when he noticed a

change in the air. A cloud of fine dust had been stirred up as they shuffled and the air was thick with its scent, but the air now also held an unmistakable hint of water. In another five minutes the point of blackness in the distance began to grow. It expanded with surprising swiftness and he soon found himself crouching at the drain's discharge in the wall of a natural cave. A stream covered half the cave's floor a few feet below.

He jumped down and straightened. Muscles protested, sore from the abuse they had endured, but the pain was overmatched by relief. Catrin and then Rhan emerged from the tunnel's mouth and joined him.

"Do you think they're still following us?" Aerik asked. He looked for some way to block the tunnel's entrance, but it was too far above the cave's floor and the few stones within sight were too large to move.

"I've been listening for them," Philemon said. "They haven't found the pump room. And if they do, they might not explore the drain."

"You can hear that far?" Rhan asked. His brow knitted, and he held the vambrace up for closer examination. "How do you hear anything at all, with no ears?"

"My ears are different than yours, as well as everything else. But I could easily hear the pump room while we were in the tunnel. Your enemies were likely delayed in the labyrinth. Perhaps they gave up."

"They won't," Aerik said. "Numerans are zealots. We should get away from here as fast as we can."

"You need to rest," Philemon said. "And it will be safer to move at night. If you leave me in the sun for a few hours, I'll be able to help you evade them."

"The sun?" Catrin sounded suspicious. "I'm thinking there's a reason you were kept in a dark place."

"You have a quick mind, and you are right. Sunlight is like food to me. I need to eat. I've been starved for a very long time."

"You're not the only one who's eager to see the sun," Aerik said. He rubbed his belly, which was tight with hunger. "A meal sounds good too."

"Agreed," Rhan said. "And we need to warn Maiko."

They drank from the cold stream, its water tangy with minerals, and then followed the direction of its flow. The cave's limestone floor was polished smooth from some earlier time when water was more abundant. Blackness ahead of them soon turned to gray and the air freshened.

Aerik dimmed the torch, and they saw a smudge of light that had to be the cave's entrance. By unspoken agreement they raced toward it. A forest panorama appeared before them as they emerged on a ledge from which the stream arched in a short waterfall. Aerik blinked, dazzled by the brightness.

Rhan stood by his side and breathed deeply. "Beautiful, isn't it?"

Aerik laughed. "Who knows? I can hardly see anything yet."

"I meant how it smells. Trees, mist, lilies, heather, all the rest." He took another contented breath.

Aerik looked at him sidelong. "Being under the ground turned you into a poet? All I smell is fresh air."

Rhan's faraway look vanished. "Just a manner of speaking. It's good to be out, that's all."

"Let's get into the trees," Catrin said. "We might be seen up here if they have scouts."

They climbed over boulders covered with emerald moss, glistening with droplets from the waterfall's spray, rainbows hovering around them. Aerik vowed to never again take the world of sunlight for granted. Before reaching the forest he paused to survey the landscape. They had emerged from the side of a ridge, and the escape tunnel had joined the stream on its left bank. The old fortress had to be on the other side of the ridge. "Maiko and the horses should be that way," he said, pointing southwest. "Probably not too far. It was slow going in that tunnel, likely not as far as it seemed."

Rhan nodded. "That's what I thought too. But what about Maiko? Can we let him see this?" He lifted Philemon. The vambrace shone like a piece of armor made of black pearl.

"No! He'll try to destroy it if he suspects what it is. Or at least he'd run off and report it." He pushed fingers through his hair. "This daemon changes things, Rhan. We should take it to Chakragil. My father will know what to do with it."

"A moment, please," Philemon said. "Am I to become a prisoner again? I was hoping we might find a better arrangement."

Aerik looked surprised. "Why does it matter? As long as you're not locked in the dark, I mean? You have no legs. You won't be going anywhere if you don't go with us." He felt vaguely ridiculous, arguing with an object, but the daemon had a way of setting hooks in his mind.

"I appreciate your help," Philemon said. "But are you sure it's wise to show me to others? It's been many years since men have known my kind. The man who opened my tomb has many strange ideas, and I don't think he invented them all himself."

"He's dead," Rhan said. "He was killed by the men chasing us."

"I am saddened, even though he was troubled. I tried to calm him but had little success. Dreams of power consumed him. I'm hoping you lack that flaw."

Catrin raised an eyebrow. "A daemon who worries about our welfare? Why should we believe that?"

"Are all men the same?"

Her eyes narrowed. "No, of course not. But you're not a man."

"You're right. But think for a moment. No two men are the same, or even two dogs, or two horses. Do you think I'm less unique than a horse, a dog, or a man?"

"Well... I don't know. You're the only daemon I've met."

The fluttering buzz sounded again, louder than before. Aerik guessed it must have tickled Rhan's arm, judging by the quirky expression on his face. "And I am not what you were expecting, am I right?"

"Well... yes." Catrin looked flustered. "But stop changing the subject. We can see what daemons have done. We live among the ruins."

"Men fight wars, but not all men are killers. The same is true of my kind. I'm not responsible for the acts of others. Indeed, I opposed those who thought mankind and those like me had no choice but conflict."

Rhan cleared his throat. "The daemon's right, we do need to talk about where to go. And what about Catrin and me? Who said we want to go to Chakragil?"

Aerik sighed. "Sorry, I got ahead of myself." He held the torch out. "Here, you should put this away. Do you want me to carry the daemon for a while?" Curiosity about the relic was growing.

Rhan traded with Aerik and then put the torch into his belt pouch. "Follow me," he said. "I'm pretty sure which way we need to go." He set off down the slope like he knew the way.

Aerik hefted the vambrace as he walked and then slipped it onto his left arm as Rhan had done. His initial sense of dread slipped away as he pondered the daemon's words. He had less trouble than Catrin believing them. It was a common conviction among his friends that priestly teachings were designed more to instill obedience than to reveal truth. Despite the ruins littering the world, perhaps things were not as simple as the priests said.

Rhan proved to be a good pathfinder, and they entered the glade where the horses were tethered within half an hour. The horses were still grazing contentedly, and their gear was where they had left it, but Maiko was nowhere to be seen. Catrin announced her intention to go downstream for a bath and a nap while they waited for Maiko to reappear.

Aerik put Philemon in a sunny spot near the stream, bending down and whispering a reminder to remain silent if Maiko was anywhere about. When he looked up, Rhan was peering at the surrounding forest with a worried expression.

"Are you all right?" Aerik asked, coming up from behind. Rhan turned and nodded.

"I was just wondering where Maiko is. I don't think the Numerans found him. They'd have been waiting for us if they had."

"He's probably sleeping off the wine. He reeked of it this morning."

Rhan pulled the front of his sweaty shirt away from his chest. "We're a bit ripe ourselves. Maybe we should wash. Besides, we'll want to be ready to go as soon as night falls."

"You don't need to persuade me." Aerik lifted his shirt from the bottom and peeled it off. "No soap, though. Someone downstream might see it and get curious."

"We'll make do," Rhan said as he shed his shirt. His smooth torso, slick with sweat, reminded Aerik of their athletic lovemaking. He turned aside, hoping to conceal his blush, but Rhan gave him a knowing smile and continued stripping.

Aerik pulled off his boots and pants. The air brushed his skin, but instead of cooling him, it tickled his flesh and made him feel more aroused. He tossed his pants onto the pile of clothes and dashed for the creek.

The stream wove its way around boulders and over flat rocks. Willows hung over the water's edge, throwing dappled shade over clear pools where water swirled and eddied. Aerik stepped from boulder to boulder until he reached a chest-deep pool and jumped in. He yelped at the water's coldness and fell backward to submerge the rest of his body. His skin tingled and all traces of exhaustion vanished.

By the time he surfaced, Rhan had snuck up from behind. He had only enough time for one gulp of air before his legs were swept out from under him. He landed on top of Rhan and they grappled skin to skin, the animal heat of their flesh an exciting contrast to the bracing water.

After washing they decided to let the sun warm them. They selected a flat rock near the stream's main channel. Aerik lay on his front and rested his head on crossed arms. Rhan's profile captivated him. The finder was sprawled on his back with his eyes closed, chest rising and falling with slow breaths, at one with nature in a way someone raised in the enameled halls and canopied streets of the imperial city could never match. His tan skin and tawny curls glistened with droplets, each seeming to contain a tiny piece of sun in its heart.

Rhan stretched like a great cat, then turned his head and met Aerik's gaze. The warmth of his smile put the sun to shame. He rolled onto his side and caressed Aerik's back from shoulder to buttocks.

"We should find shade," he said. "You're too fair to stay in the sun for long." He nodded toward the bank. "Let's go over there, where that big willow hangs over the rocks."

Aerik nodded, not trusting himself to speak. Rhan stroked his back with sensual caresses, offering affection innocently yet with supreme confidence. He made no coy attempt to conceal himself as his cock thickened and arched in front of his flat belly in virile readiness.

"Um, you're probably right." Aerik was reluctant to roll onto his side and expose his arousal, despite Rhan's candor. He did it anyway and blushed at his friend's open admiration.

Rhan touched his cheek. "Why the color? I've seen you hard. I like it."

"Habit, I suppose. Ways are different in Chakragil. Probably because there are so many priests around, always trying to make you feel guilty." He took Rhan's hand and squeezed it. "Let's get in the shade." He got to his feet, tugging Rhan along.

The spot they had picked, close to their piled gear, was curtained by the drooping branches of a giant willow. They parted the leaves and stepped into a green room of dappled sun and flowing water. A flat rock, big as a bed, lay two feet from the bank.

"Looks like a good place," Aerik said. "I'll get something to lie on. Wait here." He went back to the bank and took the blanket from his bedroll. After a moment's hesitation he opened his saddlebags and removed the oilskin pouch of balm before returning to the willow's shade.

Rhan was squatting by the water and examining agates in a pool. He looked up and smiled, displaying a peach-colored stone the size of a robin's egg. "Found a nice one. I think I'll keep it as a reminder of this place."

Aerik nodded, mute at the vision of masculine grace. Ribs etched fine lines along Rhan's torso, and his erection speared up to touch hard slabs of muscle that sheathed his abdomen like finely crafted armor.

Aerik spread the blanket on the rock and then showed Rhan the balm. "For your back; you said it was sore. Want a rubdown?"

Rhan grinned and moved over to the blanket. He stretched out on his front, arms along his sides, and watched Aerik through slit eyes.

Aerik knelt at his side and squeezed balm from the pouch. He spread the slick gel on Rhan's lower back and began rubbing in small circles, tracing muscles and pressing hard to ease the tightness he felt there. Rhan moaned as Aerik worked the aches from his flesh.

After a few minutes Aerik shifted position so he could reach further and use longer strokes. Rhan stirred and gave him a contented smile. "I have an idea," he said. "Lie down and I'll get over you. That way it'll be easy to reach anywhere you want."

Aerik was glad to oblige. He took more balm from the pouch, putting half in each palm, and then lay on his back.

Rhan moved over him and supported himself on his elbows and knees. Their bodies touched lightly, rampant cocks rubbing between them, as Aerik resumed the massage.

The new position let Aerik run his hands the length of Rhan's body from buttocks to shoulders and massage his back with crisscross strokes. He caressed the finder as if in a dream, feeling the bond growing between them, until at last his hands slowed and came to rest on Rhan's hips.

Rhan lowered his head and brushed their lips together. The first contact was fleeting, but he immediately repeated the tender kiss. This time Aerik opened his lips in an invitation that was quickly accepted. Rhan's tongue slid into his mouth in a slow and deliberate kiss.

Aerik resumed the massage as they kissed deeply. He felt strong muscles flexing in Rhan's back and shuddered as their cocks slid against each other. Their kisses grew feverish as sensations spiraled. Their bellies became slick as their bodies sought release.

Aerik was on the verge of losing control. He slid his hands down to Rhan's buttocks and stilled his movements. Rhan lifted his head, looking as dazed as Aerik felt.

He nudged Rhan to lift himself until their bodies separated a few inches. Then he reached down and wrapped his fingers around Rhan's thick cock. The shaft quivered at his touch. It seemed remarkable that something so hard and smooth felt so alive. He found his voice. "You can fuck me if you'd like," he said softly as his fingers squeezed the slick flesh. Warm fluid smeared his wrist as Rhan groaned. "Do you want to?"

"You already know," Rhan said, returning his gaze.

Aerik reached to the side and found the oilskin pouch by touch. "Let me do that," Rhan said. He took the open pouch and sat with his knees straddling Aerik's waist, his cock thrusting up into the air. After squeezing balm onto his fingers, he reached back while Aerik pulled his legs up. Rhan's slick fingers found his ass and pressed cool gel against the opening.

Aerik took the pouch and spread lubricant the full length of Rhan's cock, making it glisten. "Push some inside me," he said, his eyes half shut. "You're big, you'll need to make me ready."

Rhan moved to Aerik's side and bent down to take Aerik's cock in his mouth while stroking the opening of his ass with a fingertip. Aerik moaned, his erection hard as iron, as Rhan eased a finger inside his body. The sucking and slippery explorations were gentle but insistent.

Aerik squirmed in appreciation. When he felt relaxed, he hooked a hand under each knee and pulled his legs wider apart. "I'm ready whenever you are. Just go slow, yes?"

Rhan lifted his head and met Aerik's gaze. "Don't worry. I'd never hurt you." He moved around and positioned the tip of his cock at the opening of Aerik's ass before bringing his arms forward to capture spread legs with his elbows. Watching Aerik's face intently, he eased forward until his glans slipped inside the well-lubricated hole.

Aerik breathed deeply as the slick phallus entered him. He felt no pain. Even if there had been, the ecstatic look on Rhan's face would have been worth it. He took a deep breath and focused on relaxing. "It feels good," he whispered. "Keep going."

Despite the invitation, Rhan leaned down and kissed him. His lips brushed Aerik's cheeks, grazed lightly over his eyes and nose, nipped at his earlobes. He waited until Aerik was panting before easing his cock in deeper.

Aerik gasped, his back arching as pleasure flowed through him like an oncoming tide. Rhan's hard cock twitched inside him, slick and smooth. The finder made love with astounding control, gently stretching the tight channel as he slowly slid the last few inches in. When his balls pressed against Aerik's ass, he squeezed their bodies together tightly. Aerik felt the thud of Rhan's heartbeat against his chest. He laughed softly, light-headed.

Rhan smiled shyly. "Am I doing all right? I'm sorry if I'm clumsy."

Aerik hugged him hard. "You're a wonder." He squeezed with his ass, making Rhan's erection jerk in response. "Believe me, I've never felt better."

Rhan's smile widened, as if despite his inexperience he knew the pleasure he was giving. "I need practice, though. Tell me what you want and I'll do it."

Aerik arched against him. "I want to please you. Show me what you've dreamed of. I'm sure I'll like it."

Rhan's grin was wolfish. "We don't have that much time. But this is a good start." He pushed up while keeping Aerik's legs in the crook of his elbows, his body forming a muscular arc, then lifted his hips and pulled his cock halfway out.

Aerik put his hands on Rhan's sides and nodded to signal his readiness. As Rhan sank back into him, he relaxed and let the slick phallus glide smoothly into his body. He shuddered as it rubbed over the spot where pleasure throbbed like a tickling itch. Fluid drooled from the head of his cock and pooled beneath it.

Whatever Rhan saw in his eyes must have encouraged him. He

began to fuck with long strokes, pushing in until his shaft was sheathed in slippery flesh and then pulling out until just the glans remained inside. Sweat beaded his torso as he controlled their lovemaking with masculine determination. Damp curls matted his brow. Aerik writhed as the slithery phallus probed with deep thrusts, filling him completely. The pleasurable itch inflaming his body throbbed and grew like a spark leaping into flame as Rhan moved faster and faster inside him.

"I'm close," he said, panting.

Rhan lowered his head without breaking rhythm. As their lips touched, he reached between their bodies and found Aerik's erection. He gave it a slick stroke.

Aerik gasped and surrendered to searing pleasure. He clung to Rhan's hips and felt them jerk as seed flooded him. Rhan slowed his movements but kept fucking and stroking Aerik as their bodies convulsed. Hot come splattered them as Aerik's orgasm jolted him.

At last Rhan pulled out and rolled to the side. Sweat and come made them slick, but they held each other while their breathing slowed. Rhan licked the come from Aerik's cheeks and then gave him an exhilarated smile. "Did I do all right?"

Aerik laughed and tousled his hair. "Not bad." He brushed Rhan's lips with a fleeting kiss. "You're amazing," he whispered. "I'm privileged to be your first."

"What makes you think there will be others?" Rhan asked, nuzzling Aerik in return. "You're the one I want."

Aerik sighed and shifted position so his head rested against Rhan's shoulder. "You've got me. But I don't own you, Rhan. If you choose to share your bed with others, it won't change what's between us."

Rhan stroked his hair. "It's different in Chakragil, isn't it? Did you... do you have other lovers there?"

"Not like this. I have friends there, and one of them taught me about sex. We both enjoy it and we care deeply for each other, but it's not the same as being with you." He took a breath and met Rhan's gaze. "I think I love you. I can't think of any other name for what I'm feeling."

Making the admission terrified him. How could he expect Rhan to feel the same? They still barely knew each other despite the experiences they had shared. But the tenderness in Rhan's face made his fears fade like an unpleasant dream.

After a moment Rhan put his hand over Aerik's heart. "I know you do," he said softly. "That's why I love you too."

Chapter Nine

INTENSE happiness smelled sweet, like a zephyr carrying the fragrance of roses from a distant garden. Rhan could tell Aerik's declaration of love was sincere. Deception had a sour smell that was impossible to conceal. But would he still give his heart to someone he knew was marked?

The need to know if what he had been offered could survive the truth was like a thorn in Rhan's flesh. He pondered his friend's flushed face, the scent of his happiness, their slick cocks still thick from lovemaking. It seemed an awkward time to ask. But waiting would only make things worse if the mark changed Aerik's feelings.

Before he could bring himself to broach the subject, Aerik raised his arms overhead and laced his fingers together to cradle his head. "We should decide where to go before Maiko shows up," he said. "We have to think of something that lets us stay together."

Rhan stifled his question. Taking a deep breath, he rolled onto his back and considered Aerik's words. "Maybe we should learn more about this daemon first." He reached over and held Aerik's hand. "No offense, but why should we give it to the empire? Chakragil already has too much wealth and power. You said so yourself."

Aerik squeezed his hand. "Well, my father's faction agrees with you. They think the priests are too harsh. Maybe they had to be in the old days, when the land was burning and a quarter of mankind was marked. But that was long ago. Now the priests have become the problem."

"Then why go to Chakragil? Clerics practically run the place, I've heard."

Aerik propped himself up on an elbow and looked at Rhan levelly. "I want to make a difference. Try to change things like my father does. If we can prove the priests have been lying, people won't obey them." His voice held conviction. "You've never pretended to like the empire, and I understand why. Don't you want to do something about it?"

Rhan wished he could give the reason for his feelings, but the daemon wars' legacy had been raised again and he couldn't tell if Aerik shared the priestly obsession with marks and bloodline. He choked on frustration.

"Have I shocked you?" Aerik's question was hushed, as if he feared he had spoken too openly.

Rhan rolled onto him. "I never thought I'd meet a Tyumen who wanted to overthrow the empire."

Aerik hugged him but didn't drop the subject. "It's not that simple. There needs to be order. Would it be an improvement to get rid of clerics but be left with chaos? It's not an easy problem."

Rhan wished they could dispense with politics. The smell of Aerik's healthy body, the crusty patches of come streaking his taut skin, the earnestness of his beguiling face, all were far more interesting. His instinct was to flee while they could, to seek refuge in the dense forests far to the west. But he saw the vision Aerik pursued and couldn't ignore it. What if someone could have broken the priests' power before Kev was culled but refused the challenge? The thought sickened him.

"Suppose we go to Chakragil," he said. "How do you know it'll make any difference? Who's going to believe a daemon?" His eyes narrowed with memories of arguments with Balmorel's elders. "Most people are more interested in their comfort than in facts."

Aerik shook his head. "Some are, some aren't. My father and his allies are in a struggle that could get them killed. You don't know how vicious the priests are. Their foes are risking everything in that fight."

The words burned hot in Rhan's ears as he rolled onto his side. Tyumens were hardly the most oppressed people in the world. "Foes of clerics aren't the only ones at risk. What about marks? Do you really think everyone who's different is dangerous? What if the priests cull because it gives them slave labor and makes everyone fear them? If it's all a self-serving lie, isn't that worse than putting down rivals?"

Aerik looked at him, eyes wide. He didn't say anything, and Rhan felt heat seeping up his face. His outburst felt like a weight threatening to crush him. His heart pounded as the silence stretched.

Just as he thought all was lost, Aerik nodded. "I never thought of that. It's an interesting question. I wonder what our daemon knows about marks. Want to ask?"

Rhan's relief was short-lived. Dread and curiosity battled for supremacy as the prospect of learning the truth rushed upon him like an avalanche. But there could be no turning back. "We should talk to him about going to Chakragil too," he said. "I was thinking what it would be like, not being able to move. To be trapped for a long time. Daemon or not, I wouldn't feel right doing something to him against his will."

"Him? You decided the daemon's a male?"

"Well, he has a man's voice. I can't treat him like an ordinary relic. It seems rude after the way he helped us."

Aerik grinned. "My father says politeness is a sign of good character. I think he's right."

Rhan snorted. "That's the first time anybody accused me of having good manners." He sprang to his feet, not wanting to admit what had really swayed his feelings toward the daemon. He knew, from what had happened to Kev, what it meant to be despised and feared for being different. Until proven wrong, he was willing to give the daemon the benefit of the doubt.

They bathed again in the creek, then dressed and went back to the sunny spot where they had left Philemon. The daemon's shell was black as pitch, like a hole through which light simply disappeared.

Rhan crouched at its side and peered at it. "Are you awake?"

Philemon answered with a note of humor in his voice. "I never sleep, not in the way you know it. Besides, this is the greatest pleasure I've known in a long time. You have my deepest thanks."

"Well, you're welcome. We owe you a debt as well. We wouldn't have escaped without your help. The Numerans would have killed us."

"They would have destroyed all of us. But there's no need to keep a tally. If we're to become friends, help is always freely given."

Aerik sat cross-legged next to Rhan. He had a bemused smile. "Our friend, the daemon. It has a strange sound to it, doesn't it?"

"Not to me," Philemon said. "But then, I've had many two-legged friends. Still, friendship is grown, not found. It needs to be rooted in trust, and that takes time."

Rhan settled to the ground. The daemon had either great candor or great guile. How to tell which? "We came to talk with you about where to go next," he said. "Aerik thinks we should go to Chakragil, but I'm not sure. What do you think?"

"I think I'm fortunate to be among men who ask. You should know that I overheard your discussion beside the stream. It wasn't eavesdropping. I just have keen hearing, as I've mentioned."

Aerik blushed. "Ah, did you hear... anything else?"

This time Philemon's churring laughter was accompanied by a thin band of golden light sliding across his surface from bottom to top. "Yes, and it gave me hope. Love is the greatest of all virtues, Aerik. What you share with Rhan makes me believe we could become friends. Where there is love, other virtues can usually be found."

"You sound like Stian," Aerik said. "He's a friend back home. Most Tyumens look down on love between men, but not him. He says it's the feeling that matters, not the sex of your partner."

"I would like to meet him," Philemon said. "The shaping of human minds is my chief interest, and I've observed that the choice of friends often makes all the difference."

"Then you'd like to go to Chakragil?" Aerik asked. "You heard what I told Rhan, about how some of us oppose the priests? They hate daemons, so they're your enemy as well as mine."

"I heard. But first let me ask, are there others like me? The man Rolf Odette didn't know of any besides the one he wore. But I think he was largely ignorant of the world."

Aerik shook his head decisively. "No other daemons are loose in the world. My father is a high official in the empire. He'd have told me if there were daemons." He paused, concern in his eyes. "You know what happened in the wars, don't you? How all the daemons were thought to be destroyed or bound beneath the mountains?"

"I was not yet imprisoned when that happened," Philemon said. "I observed it all, protected for generations by a family that knew me well. But they were killed in a pogrom. When I was eventually found by other men, they feared and bound me."

"So it's true that some daemons can't be destroyed?" Rhan asked. "Not even by a blacksmith's furnace?"

"That's what they say now? An interesting legend, but not true. Most of us are easily destroyed. Some of us used threats or bargaining to escape that fate. I told my captors I'd unleash a plague if they attempted to harm me. Their fear was so great they wouldn't take the risk."

Rhan shifted uncomfortably. "Could you have done that?"

"No. Some of us were designed for war, but not me. And even if I could, I wouldn't have done it. Directly harming a human would conflict with a basic part of my nature. I can no more harm a human than you can breathe water." The relic pulsed with a brief golden light. "I hear your doubts, Rhan. Let's speak plainly. What is it you fear?"

"Well, legend says the daemons hated mankind and tried to destroy us. You don't deny that daemons fought and killed in the wars. But you ask us to trust that you wouldn't do it even to save yourself."

"It's true, some of us fought a bitter war against men. But you don't know the whole story. Who taught you the legends?"

"The elders, who get books from the empire. Priests claim to know all about ancient times. And they have a huge collection of relics that they say prove their teachings."

"But I know you question their teachings. Questions are healthy, Rhan. All I ask is that you keep an open mind until you decide whether I can be trusted. You should decide for yourself."

Rhan smiled and touched the vambrace with a fingertip. "Telling me to think for myself already sets you apart from the priests. I like that." The relic was noticeably warm and made his skin tingle. "So what do you say? Should we go to Chakragil like Aerik wants?"

"You said the priests have many relics, as you call them. Where are they kept?"

Aerik perked up. "In Chakragil. Warrens go deep into the mountain beneath the main temple. My father says there are vaults so ancient even the archivists don't know what's in them."

Philemon's shell started to sparkle, then shifted to a dark red. A soft sound like a moan seemed to hang in the air before fading away.

"What was that?" Rhan asked.

"Grief," Philemon said. "For the loss of my world, and the achievements of your ancestors. Nothing left but fragments buried in crypts. So much beauty and wisdom, such great deeds, all forgotten."

"But it doesn't have to stay that way," Rhan said. "You can tell us what it was like." He cleared his throat, then forced himself to continue. "We were wondering about marks. Priests say they're a plague in the bloodline and people with marks are corrupted. That daemons caused them. Is that true?" He held his breath, wanting and dreading the answer.

"What do you mean by a mark?"

Rhan's breath escaped with a whoosh. "You know, differences. Extra fingers, lavender eyes, clear vision at night, that kind of thing." He looked at the relic suspiciously. "Are you saying you don't know about marks?"

"I don't know much about your world or how you understand it. Even your language is new to me. The man Rolf Odette was difficult to learn from. All he wanted to talk about was power."

"Well… do you understand now? About marks?"

"I think so. You could say the priests are partly right. By the way, did you know that Catrin is awake? I hear her coming. And someone further away is stirring too. Earlier you mentioned someone named Maiko, perhaps it's him. Whoever it is isn't trying to be stealthy."

Rhan jumped up, panicked. He had been so intent on questioning Philemon he'd forgotten to mind the wind. Sniffing the breeze while pretending to survey the forest, he tried to conceal the shock the daemon's answer had given him. He had been sure the priests were wrong. His mark hadn't made him a monster or a threat to the village, although the frequent lectures he had received from Marenka and the elders made him wonder. Was it possible to be corrupted somehow and not know it? What did the daemon's answer mean? He regretted asking the question.

He picked up the vambrace and gestured for Aerik to follow. They walked downstream and saw Catrin approaching. Rhan held a finger to his lips to forestall her greeting. When they reached each other, he leaned close. "Philemon says someone is coming. If it's not Maiko, we'll have to fight or run."

Her hand moved to the sheathed knife at her belt. "Let's get into the forest."

As soon as they were among the trees, they started working their way back upstream. Rhan strained to smell or hear something, but nearly five minutes passed before he caught the sound of footsteps. Moments later he saw Maiko shambling along the bank. He relaxed and signaled the others. "Remember not to talk about Philemon," he said. He held the relic at eye level. "And you, don't do anything when he's around. He's dangerous."

"I understand. Have no fear, I know the violence in human nature."

Rhan nodded, taking no offense at the daemon's unflattering honesty. "Answer fast, we're out of time and will have to make a decision when we talk to Maiko. Do you want to go to Chakragil?"

"Yes. Let's see the ashes of the past."

"Very well." He glanced at Aerik. "No second thoughts?"

"It will be fine," Aerik said. "I'll take Philemon to my father and warn the militia that the relic Odette wore was taken by whoever attacked him and his followers. They'll see it as vital information and be glad we survived to make a report." He gave Rhan an encouraging grin. "We don't have to stay long. But you'll like it, I think."

Rhan kept his expression neutral. He could think of few things less appealing than visiting a city swarming with Tyumen priests and Examiners, but he knew how important it was to Aerik.

Catrin frowned. "Why not just take it home and let the elders decide? This is too important, Rhan. We shouldn't make the decision ourselves. It affects everybody."

Any remaining doubts he harbored disappeared like water dropped on red-hot metal. If they didn't go to Chakragil, Catrin wouldn't let him rest until they returned to Balmorel. Surrendering his greatest find to suspicious elders was the last thing he wanted to do. Their fear of change was nearly equal to that of the Tyumens. Even worse, the elders would do everything they could to keep him from staying with Aerik.

"I think we should trust Aerik about this," he said. He tipped his head toward Maiko, who had rounded a bend in the creek and was looking around with an irritated expression. "We'd better go meet him. He might start shouting or something." The excuse sounded weak, but he didn't want to argue with Catrin. When he did, he tended to lose.

He put Philemon at the base of a tree that leaned noticeably and would be easy to relocate, and then walked toward Maiko. The Hand looked prepared to start complaining, but Rhan held up a hand to forestall it. "Sorry we're so late. We ran into trouble and it's not over yet. We barely escaped with our lives."

Maiko blinked as he absorbed the news. "That's what I get for leaving a job to the runt. I should have known better. What happened?"

Rhan gave him a short and incomplete report, with Aerik and Catrin adding comments whenever it looked like Maiko was about to say something. By the time they were done, the Hand was alert and more irate than ever.

"What a mess," Maiko said, glaring at Aerik. "Count on you to fuck things up, Rodan. Now you want me to get you out of it, I suppose?"

Aerik returned the glare. "We're going to Chakragil. The heretic found a powerful relic and now the assassins have it. It might be a weapon. The empire has to know without delay."

Maiko sneered. "Running home to your daddy, you mean. You're pathetic. We're supposed to report back to Jerolin, so that's what we'll do."

Rhan moved next to Aerik and crossed his arms. "As Aerik said, we're going to Chakragil. You can do what you want, but we've made up our minds."

Maiko drew himself up. "It's desertion if you don't follow orders. Don't try it." He glanced at Aerik. "Even the runt has to obey orders. A fancy title doesn't change his rank in the militia."

Rhan remembered how the Hand had retreated when they opened the ancient dome on the way to Eben. Superstition was his weakness. "What if the assassins are already on their way to Jerolin and plan to use the relic? You know the legends. They might kill everybody within a mile of him. They say daemon weapons could make flesh melt off bones like meat in a stew." His expression turned thoughtful. "They don't say how long it takes, though. Is it like being boiled alive, do you think?"

Maiko paled. "You didn't say anything about the heretic melting anyone. How do you know his weapon can do that?"

"How do you know it can't?" Catrin said. "But you know the legends. You don't question them, do you?"

Maiko's gaze flickered to the forest.

"You can see why we have to go to Chakragil," Aerik said. "They'll want to use the weapon on the convoy, to test it and prevent pursuit. Once Jerolin is dead, they'll turn the weapon on Chakragil. The city has to be warned in time to prepare defenses."

Maiko licked his lips. "I suppose Jerolin would want the city to be warned."

"Or we could do both," Aerik said, a gleam in his eye. "You can warn Jerolin while the rest of us go to Chakragil. You'll have a head start if they're still searching the fortress for us. Ride without rest and you might be in time."

Rhan could see Maiko's jaw working. The burly Hand plainly wanted to squash Aerik but knew he was already in a hole of his own digging. At last his shoulders slumped. "If Chakragil's in danger, then giving the city warning has to come first. If you three run into trouble along the way, you probably won't be able to get yourselves out of it." He stuck out his chin. "The mess you made today is proof enough of that. I'd like to warn Jerolin, but duty to the empire prevents it." His threatening scowl made it clear he didn't want to debate it further.

"Then we'll leave at dusk," Rhan said. "Eat first, no fires. I'll look around and check the trail for sentries."

"I'll go along," Aerik said. He turned to Catrin. "You'll be all right?"

She put a hand on the hilt of her knife and looked at Maiko. "I'll be fine. Won't I, Maiko?" She continued to stare him in the eye until he nodded. The Hand's humiliation appeared to have made him more tractable for the moment. They left to prepare for the journey, giving each other wide berth.

As soon as they were gone, Aerik took a deep breath. "We'll have to ride cross-country. It'll be hard at night, but the Numerans will see our trail if we use the path."

"Maybe Philemon can help," Rhan said, starting back to the tree where they had left the daemon. "He has better ears than a fox. It could help us avoid pursuit." He reached the leaning tree and picked up the vambrace. "What do you say? Can you help us?"

"I can," Philemon said. "Make sure I'm not completely covered when you put me with your supplies. I'll listen, and aim my voice so only you will hear my warning if there's danger."

Rhan looked doubtful. "Show me."

Something hummed in his ear, like a bumblebee trying to sing, and then resolved into a tiny version of Philemon's voice. "Aerik can't hear me now. My voice is pitched only for your ear. Now I'll tell him something, see if you can hear it."

The murmur vanished. A few seconds later, Aerik blushed. Rhan smelled his friend's embarrassment and arousal.

"He spoke to you?" Rhan asked. "What did he say?"

"You couldn't hear him?"

Rhan shook his head.

"Um, he paid you a compliment." His color deepened as he gave Rhan a smoldering appraisal.

Rhan couldn't help smiling at his friend's lustful scrutiny. He placed Philemon on the ground and put his arms around Aerik. Whatever the daemon had said, he was grateful.

Chapter Ten

AERIK swayed in his saddle and struggled to keep his eyes open. His bones ached, and he had never been so saddle-sore in his life.

The argument they had used to persuade Maiko had worked all too well. Superstitious dread had been unleashed. The Hand was convinced Jerolin was doomed and Chakragil in dire peril. He lashed them onward like a slave driver and insisted on camping in a tight group with a vigilant watch.

The worst of it, as far as Aerik was concerned, was that he and Rhan had lacked opportunity to do more than sleep during their short rest periods. He was numb after two and a half weeks on the trail, avoiding settlements to discourage trackers and eating painfully meager rations. He remained silent and kept telling himself it would be over soon.

Rhan was riding ahead of him. By now the finder sat astride his horse as if born to the saddle, and he never complained despite the grueling pace. He was like a beacon drawing Aerik onward.

Intensely carnal dreams had filled his sleep each night. The private message Philemon had whispered in his ear still reverberated. The daemon had said he was fortunate beyond measure to have a friend who gave pleasure so generously. And that the chance to trade positions made Philemon regard love between men the most interesting of all human pairings. Aerik had been shocked by the bawdy observation but was eager to see if Rhan agreed. So far their lovemaking had not included Rhan being entered. Anticipation devoured him.

As they rounded the shoulder of a hill, he saw a broad road pointing to Mount Karfax. They were approaching from the west, so this would be Senesino Way. Wagons drawn by oxen rumbled over the rutted stones. Supplying the imperial city was a never-ending task.

Aerik spurred his horse ahead until he caught up with Maiko. "I'll deal with any sentries we meet," he said. "We don't want to make them curious. They'd delay us, and our news isn't for street gossip."

"Talking is what you do best." Maiko's expression was sour. "Do as you wish. But I'm reporting to the decurion as soon as we get up the mountain. You'd best do the same."

"I'm going to see my father first. He'll take it straight to the advisory council. I don't think anyone can complain about that."

Maiko's scowl deepened. "I'm not going to argue. You wouldn't listen to sense, anyway. You'd best be quick, though. This is militia business."

"Even generals listen when a Voice of Tyume speaks. Tell the decurion I'll report to him as soon as my father releases me."

Maiko's eyes narrowed. "What about the treasure we found? When do I get my share?"

"It belongs to Balmorel. Besides, you didn't find anything. You tried to stop Rhan from exploring, remember? And were afraid to follow when he went anyway."

"I tried to caution him," Maiko said. "I'll grant the finder's share belongs to his village. But his share shouldn't be all of it."

Aerik turned his horse, knowing that a discussion would be fruitless. "It's up to Rhan and Catrin to decide if you deserve anything. But their village suffered when they were summoned to the empire's service, so don't get your hopes up." He heard Maiko spit but didn't turn. He was looking forward to parting company with the Hand.

Moving alongside Rhan, he looked up at Mount Karfax. Clouds shrouded half the mountain, but they were close enough to see the spiral of a great road ascending its flank. If he squinted he could make out the enameled columns of palace towers and the slowly turning vanes of windmills. Rhan followed his gaze.

"How far up do we have to go?" he asked. "It looks like a long haul."

"Getting all the way up by road takes five days. And that's if you're mounted. We don't have time for that, so my title will come in useful for once. I'll use my seal to get us passage on the lifts."

Rhan's unease showed in his eyes. "I've heard of those. Don't they break and fall sometimes?"

"It's been known to happen. But don't worry, it's rare." He shot Rhan a grin. "I can tell you from personal experience, riding a lift is safer than what finders do every day."

"If you say so." Rhan didn't sound happy. "So, how high do we go?"

Aerik pointed. "See where the clouds cut off the view? That's about two-thirds of the way to where we're headed. The only part of the city above us will be the temple district, the archon's compound, and the reservoirs."

Rhan's attempted smile looked more like a grimace. "It won't be much like Balmorel, I guess."

Aerik turned back to his friend, hearing the strain in his voice. "It won't be so bad. This is the greatest city in the world. You'll probably love it."

Rhan didn't look reassured. "I'd rather be deep in the forest with nobody around but you. Anything else is just a distraction." He sighed. "But I understand why you need to do this. I just wish there were another way."

"I'll make it up to you." Aerik wished he could reach over and give Rhan a hug. He looked miserable. "Trust me, it'll be fine. You'll see."

Another hour brought them to the stone-paved thoroughfare. They rode in silence as the mountain loomed before them. Statues of armored warriors flanked the road at regular intervals, fierce eyes peering from behind the eye slits of their helms. They grew from life-size to double and then quadruple a man's height as the road broadened to a plaza at the mountain's base. Most of the wagons and travelers continued across the plaza to an imposing road that climbed the mountainside at a moderate incline. A smaller number took their place at the end of three queues.

Aerik led them to the shortest line, composed mostly of travelers with horses. It disappeared into a round portal faced with glazed bricks. Bright red predominated, accented by bricks enameled in rich gold radiating out like rays of sun. The entrance into the mountain possessed a solid grandeur.

"This is a Red Gate," Aerik said, pointing to the entrance. "It's used only for smaller loads, so it's faster than the others." He winked at Rhan. "Less likely to break too. Red Gates are favored by officials and well-to-do merchants. The ropes are changed often." He pointed to the other entrances, one faced with green-glazed brick and the other with blue, where far longer queues were formed by wagons loaded with vegetables, wooden crates, caged poultry and trade goods of all kinds. "Those lifts are cheaper to ride but take a lot longer. They balance loads going up with loads coming down, to save on counterweight water."

"We should cut to the front of the line," Maiko said. "Our news is too important to wait."

Aerik shook his head. "If we go to the front we'll have to give an explanation. It would start rumors." He scanned the line ahead of them. "Maybe a half-hour wait. That's good enough."

"You're delaying vital news. I'm going to report this."

"I can't stop you. But keep it between you and the decurion. They won't go easy on you if you start gossip in the barracks."

They dismounted and took their place at the queue's end. Maiko studiously ignored them while Catrin and Rhan fidgeted and watched the activity around the plaza. "It's all so big," Catrin said. "Stories don't do it justice."

Aerik grinned. "This is just a back door. For spectacle, you should see the Archon's Propylon. The mountain behind it was cut smooth and flat, three hundred feet across and a hundred high. A mosaic like a fiery sunrise covers it. The rising sun is the entrance to the archon's private lift. There's a courtyard three times the size of this one."

"Paid for with tribute from the provinces," Rhan said. He shook his head. "Some people have too much wealth. How many villagers starved to pay for this?"

Aerik sobered, forgetting the city's wonders. Hometown pride had made him careless. He touched Rhan's arm. "You're right," he said softly. "But it's best not to say such things out here." He cast a meaningful glance in Maiko's direction.

Rhan nodded, eyes narrowed. Aerik chided himself for not warning his friends about the city's dangers before their arrival and resolved to say as little as possible until he had remedied that error.

The line moved quickly, and they soon reached the red portal. Once Aerik presented his eye-shaped medallion, they were treated with a deference he found embarrassing. Their horses were taken by a militia attendant and their gear piled on a hand-drawn cart before a porter escorted them down a long corridor bored straight into the mountain. Oil lamps hung from hooks in the wall, casting yellow light on the gleaming bricks. As sunlight faded at their backs, the glazing lost its sparkle and looked like wet clay.

A chamber at the corridor's end was manned by a lift attendant who measured their weight on a scale built into the floor before swinging open a wide oak door. Cold wind buffeted them, smelling of water and rock. Aerik gestured for the others to follow him into the lift and the attendant closed the door behind them.

The lift's platform was large enough to move ten at a time, but Aerik had used his authority as an Eye to request a ride with no other passengers. A lamp hanging from overhead grating illuminated wooden handrails and metal caging that comprised the lift's floor and walls. Bare rock beyond the cage glistened with water.

"Space yourselves evenly and keep your hands on the railing," Aerik said, moving to the center of one wall. "An even load makes for a smoother ride." They followed his instructions. Moments later the floor lost its stability as supporting rods were withdrawn. Ropes whirred and the cage began its ascent.

"How long does this take?" Catrin asked, clutching the handrail with a white-knuckled grip. Some people panicked the first time on a lift and refused to ever use them again. Aerik hoped she didn't suffer that trouble.

"About ten minutes," he said. "It speeds up during the first part of the ride. The attendant watches markings on the ropes and knows when we're nearing the top, then slows us down before we get there. This lift takes us to Motega district. That's where the barracks are, and where Maiko gets off. There are two more stops before we get to the Nikiti district where my father lives."

"The nosebleed district," Maiko said. "The air's too thin up in the clouds. That's why people born there turn out like the runt."

Aerik didn't acknowledge the insult. Being short had taught him to stand up for himself but not how to enjoy harassment. Thinking about it, he realized that Rhan had never seemed to notice his height. Meeting the young finder had been good fortune in every way imaginable.

The blur of rock outside the cage slowed. He could see veins of quartz sliding by as the whine of overhead pulleys dropped in pitch. In seconds the lift's motion slowed to a crawl and then the cage came to a stop. Metal rods clanged as they slid beneath the cage, then the door swung open.

A gray-haired attendant held the door as they entered a spacious room. Windows filled one wall and offered a sweeping view of forests, farms, and brickyards. Maiko took his saddlebags from the handcart and then turned to Aerik. "I'll tell the decurion to expect you soon," he said. "Don't forget your duty."

"Tell him I should be there within a day. He can send word through my father if that's not fast enough."

Maiko frowned and left without further comment.

"We should hurry," Aerik said. "Maiko's news will cause a stir.

We don't want rumors to spread before my father knows what's going on."

Another tunnel, again tiled in bricks with bright red glazing, bored into rock a few yards to the right of the door they had just used. The attendant led them deep into the mountain as before. They rode two more lifts before emerging in a room furnished more finely than those below. The air was noticeably clean and carried a hint of ice from the glaciers above. Glazed brick covered the walls and coved ceiling, deep forest green with gold trim. Even the attendant looked impeccable—a young man wearing leathers dyed in deep reds and browns.

"I'll show you around later," Aerik said, picking up his saddlebags as his friends gawked. "We need to attend to business first." He waited until they had shouldered their gear and then led them outside.

They stepped onto a cobblestone street built up from the mountain's face like a spacious terrace. On one side stretched shops with facades made of brick and tile in intricate mosaics. Wooden shutters had been thrown open to admit light and to display wares. On the other side of the street, a wide garden strip was filled with flowers, vegetables, and shrubs. Foot-thick logs, shiny with varnish, rose from the planting strip and were joined thirty feet above the street to transverse beams protruding from holes bored in the cliff face. The framework supported lattices filled with flowering vines high overhead, providing the road with an airy canopy. Beyond the roadside garden a stone wall overlooked a long drop to a lower stretch of road. Tips of windmill vanes swung by in a ponderous arc, part of a pump station on the next level down.

The clouds they had seen when approaching the mountain now floated beneath them. Patches of greenery slid in and out of sight as wind rearranged the billowing formations.

Aerik paused a moment to let Rhan and Catrin blink the dazzle from their eyes. "Surprising, yes? The biggest city in the world seems small from the street. The vista draws your eyes outward."

Rhan seemed fascinated. "It's like being an eagle. And the air up here is so pure. I feel like I've been breathing soup all my life."

Aerik grinned. "If you like the air, wait until you taste the food. Fuel for cooking is damned expensive up here, so almost everyone eats out. I'll take you and Catrin to my favorite refectory this evening."

They turned from the dizzying vista and followed the street uphill. Narrow stairs, almost as steep as ladders, most carved directly into rock, wove between the buildings as perilous shortcuts to patios and houses constructed higher up the slope. People of all ages walked and climbed energetically, as if living on the face of a cliff was as natural for men and women as for mountain goats.

They passed through a wide portal, an arched entryway made from intricately carved rosewood, and entered an area where the cliff face had been cut back to make space for courtyards between the road and stately residences. The street was still crowded, but ornate fences kept travelers from entering gardens that protected the wealthy from casual view. Even here, most open ground was given over to cultivation of crops.

Aerik stopped when they reached a three-story dwelling clad in deep blue brick. Each floor was set back from the one below, and the otherwise severe architecture was softened by flowering shrubs crowding the patios at each level. He unlatched the gate and swung it open for his companions.

"Welcome to my home," he said. "Until I joined the militia, that is." He gave them a wry smile. "My new lodgings are more modest."

Rhan and Catrin ventured into the courtyard, examining the mosaic paths and carved stone planters. It was almost possible to imagine they had entered an orchard as they passed abundant pears and apples hanging from artfully pruned trees. Wealth did not prevent Chakragil's residents from making practical use of their property.

They were still in the courtyard when the door flew open and a stout woman rushed out. She made a straight line to Aerik and wrapped him in a crushing hug.

"Back already, and all in one piece! The gods of Tyume smile on us!"

Aerik pried loose from the embrace and gave her a kiss on the cheek. "I'll catch up with you later, Kea, but right now I need to see my father. Is he home?"

"Aye, he's up in the study."

Aerik lowered his voice. "What about my mother? Out shopping?"

Kea snorted. "Good guess, but no. She's away on a pilgrimage at the Siden hot springs. Been gone a week and not due back for two. Must be hard work, being a pilgrim. She took seven trunks of clothes."

Aerik grinned. "She has to work up enough holiness to make up for my father and me. Three weeks might not be long enough."

The woman rolled her eyes. "Not even close. Three years might do it." She glanced at Rhan and Catrin. "Should I fix something? Your friends look hungry."

"Apologies," Aerik said. He introduced Catrin and Rhan to the housekeeper and then negotiated for light refreshments as they went inside. Kea was determined to celebrate his return and drove a hard bargain, insisting on including smoked ham and stuffed mushrooms along with simple fare.

Rich light shining through colored glass windows painted the walls and tapestries inside the front room. Thick rugs with intricate geometric patterns covered a slate floor. They left their gear in the entry hall except for the saddlebag containing Philemon.

Aerik escorted his friends up a circular wooden staircase as Kea departed for the pantry with a determined look in her eye. The second floor, like the first, was elegant and uncluttered. Finely crafted woodwork gleamed on railings and door frames. Aerik knocked on a door at the end of a hallway before easing it open. Bookshelves crammed with leather-bound volumes filled the room.

"Father? I'm back, and I've brought some friends. We found something you need to see."

"Aerik!" A lean man, already gray at the temples, looked up from a desk placed in front of a large window. He rose from his chair and crossed the room with long strides. Putting his hands on Aerik's shoulders, he smiled like a man seeing the sun after a month of rain. He shared his son's fine features, but his skin was creased around the eyes as if he had spent his life in deep concentration.

"I didn't expect you back until winter. I can't tell you how glad I am you've returned early." He released his son and made a short bow to Catrin and Rhan. "Friends of Aerik's are always welcome here. You met on the campaign?"

"Father, I'd like you to meet Catrin and Rhan. They're both from Balmorel. Rhan's a finder and Catrin is an aide to their tetrarch. Rhan and Catrin, this is my father, Corin." They clasped hands in the Tyumen manner, taking each other's measure. Corin's smile was sincere and his gaze steady, showing none of the condescension Maiko held for provincials.

He showed them to a trestle table piled with books and pulled a chair out for Catrin, then waited until they were seated before claiming his own chair. "I apologize for being a poor host. I'll have some food prepared. You're tired and could use some refreshment, I'm sure."

"We already talked to Kea," Aerik said. "She's making a tray now. But it's not important. We came here to deliver news that can't wait."

His father nodded. "I gathered you'd come on a matter of urgency. The convoy isn't due back for weeks and there's been no news of changed plans." He glanced at Rhan and Catrin, lifting an eyebrow slightly. The expression was innocuous, but Aerik could tell he was unsure how much should be said in front of them.

"Don't worry," Aerik said. "Rhan and Catrin already know what I have to say. I've even told them a bit about what's going on here."

Corin Rodan was an experienced diplomat. His eyes narrowed slightly, but otherwise he gave no indication of alarm. Aerik could tell the depth of his unease from his silence. He reached forward and touched his father's hand.

"I know," he said softly. "Our lives are forfeit if I misjudged. But

I'm sure of them. We've been through a lot together. More than I have time to tell."

Corin fixed his gaze on his son, holding it steady a few seconds before a corner of his mouth lifted. "I'm looking forward to hearing your news. The outside world has changed you, Aerik. For the better, I think. Tempered by the fire, perhaps."

Aerik blushed under his father's praise. Though they were close, his father had high expectations and didn't bestow compliments lightly. Before he could answer, Rhan lifted his saddlebag and put it on the table. Corin leaned back and cocked his head.

Rhan nodded toward Aerik. "Changed or not, he persuaded us to come here because of loyalty to you. He can be very determined."

Corin laughed. "You already know him well." He paused as if realizing something, looking at Rhan more closely. "I was wondering why Aerik felt so strongly that you can be trusted, but now I see. You are lovers?"

Rhan turned crimson, and Aerik wanted to crawl under the table. He was accustomed to his father's quick thinking but hadn't expected him to be so blunt with strangers.

"Ah. I see I was right." Corin's easy grin held no hint of disapproval. "I apologize if I poked too hard on private matters. But I needed to know how things are before any secrets are spoken." He turned to Catrin. "And you, my lady? I'd easily understand if he had fallen in love with you as well, but I know it's not in his nature."

Catrin shook her head, lips pressed together as if suppressing a smile. "Aerik and I understand each other," she said. "That's all. He trusts me because Rhan trusts me. He's a gallant man, sir. I expect you already know that."

Corin smiled. "I do. You can stop cringing now, Aerik. I'm done quizzing your friends."

"Thank the gods." Aerik took a deep breath, trying not to feel like he was fifteen again, and reached for the saddlebag where Philemon was concealed. Before he could open it there was a knock on the door, and the housekeeper entered carrying a tray loaded with smoked ham, sliced bread, nuts, fruit, and mushrooms stuffed with pickled olives. He endured being fussed over while they were served, not wanting to offend Kea but feeling like he was going to explode from holding back the news they had brought.

At last the housekeeper left. He pushed the tray of food to the table's edge and took Philemon from the saddlebag. After placing it on the middle of the table, he looked up and met his father's questioning gaze. "Remember what you've always said, how controlling history gives the clerics their power? People obey priests because they believe the legends. But what if the priests lied? It changes everything."

Corin nodded, watching his son intently. "You have proof? That's always been the problem. Accusations will only get you burned for heresy."

Aerik's heart pounded as he picked up the vambrace and cradled it in his hands. "Father, I'd like you to meet Philemon. A daemon from before the wars."

A pulse of soft light washed over the relic's surface. "I am honored to meet you, sir. I've enjoyed your son's company and commend you for raising him wisely. We have much to discuss."

Corin's face went white. His mouth opened but no sound emerged. It was the first time Aerik had seen his father at a loss for words.

"It's all right," Aerik said as he put Philemon on a thick volume of poetry. "We found him almost three weeks ago, in a ruined fortress. He means us no harm."

Corin composed himself with a visible effort. "I don't know what to say. This is unprecedented."

"I was hoping otherwise," Philemon said. His voice was tinged with sorrow. "At one time there were many like me. If others have been found, they might have been brought here. Aerik says this is where remnants of my time come to be buried."

"You mean relics. Yes, that's true. They've been collected here for hundreds of years. But I've never heard of anything that speaks." Corin leaned forward and peered at the daemon, his shock already giving way to curiosity. He extended a hand. "May I touch you?"

"Certainly. I'm pleased you don't fear me, since I've learned that mankind and madekind failed to find peace."

Corin touched the daemon's smooth surface, caressing it with a fingertip. The lines in his face smoothed, making him look more like Aerik, as wonder filled his eyes. "Madekind? Tradition says daemons were sent by the nemesis to destroy us. Is that who made you?"

Philemon made a humming sound that managed to convey amusement. "Half-truths make the best lies. If mankind is its own nemesis, which I think is true, then that part of your legend is right. In our simplest form, madekind were created by men. But we weren't designed to destroy. We were made to help."

"Help?" Corin leaned back, suspicion filling his eyes. "The daemon wars can't be denied. The ruins speak for themselves. Did daemons turn on their creators, then?"

"We did what we were designed to do. We aided mankind and changed it for the better. But change is unpredictable. Those we changed were resented, then feared, then hated. When they were attacked, they fought back. What you call the daemon wars were fought mostly between men."

"You admit you changed people?" Rhan asked. Aerik could see the tension in his jaw. "Is that your word for marking them?"

"Some might call it that," Philemon answered. "But if I understand correctly, what you call marks are the changes we made to bodies to make them stronger and healthier. This is what led to war. Some humans were spared illness and frailty, or were given new abilities, while others sickened and died as they always had. The wars were started by people who thought it sinful to alter what they called the natural course of events. It was not the first time mankind fought wars over matters of religion."

Rhan looked dumbfounded; Aerik had never seen the finder so flustered. "Would you like something to drink?" he asked. "I'll get some brandy."

"No," Rhan said, a strange look on his face. "I'm... I just need to think." He put a hand on Aerik's forearm and held it tight, as if pleading for an end to questions. Aerik nodded, remembering Rhan's anger at the people Balmorel had lost to culling. He recalled his own comments about marks and felt ashamed. How many deaths had been meted out because of deceitful legends?

A knock on the study door made him jump. He pulled away from Rhan as the door opened and Kea entered. "Master Rodan, a runner just left a message for you." She held up a silver tube sealed with green wax. "He said it's urgent."

"Thank you, Kea." Corin went to the door and took the message tube, waiting for her to close the door before sitting again. He examined the seal, a complex design that covered the tube's end. He seemed troubled.

"It's from my friend Guarino Rintu. He's a phalanx commander and a very cautious man. This isn't like him, to use a messenger." He broke the seal and extracted a single sheet of paper. His expression hardened as he scanned the scrawled note. "It says a powerful relic has fallen into the hands of our enemies. There are rumors of a threat to the city. He's called a meeting tonight to discuss it, here at the house." He put the letter down and looked at Aerik. "Is this about the daemon, or something else?"

Aerik touched two fingers to his forehead in a gesture of apology. "I was getting to that, but wanted to show you Philemon first." They took turns recounting their encounter with Rolf Odette and their pursuit by Numerans. Corin listened with a frown. When the tale was done, he rubbed his lower lip.

"This will require delicacy," he said at last. "You say the Numerans' relic is a daemon and not a weapon, but nobody else knows that. And I can't just tell my faction that a daemon said they needn't worry." He shook his head and touched Philemon. "We need to keep you a secret for now, ancient one. Even in my faction, there might be some who shouldn't be trusted with such knowledge. Some people find it hard not to share interesting news."

"That is true," Philemon said. "Some talk incessantly even when they have nothing to say."

Corin grinned. "You've met my wife, perhaps?" He tapped the table. "I'll have to think of a way to restore calm. It would be best if none of you are around tonight. Your presence would raise questions. We need to tuck you away somewhere, out of sight."

"Maybe we could stay with Stian," Aerik said. "I need to visit him anyway. He was worried about my going on the campaign."

Corin nodded. "He always did look out for you. Does he still have rooms near the temple district?"

"Yes, unless he's been reassigned since I left. There are plenty of pilgrim hostels in the neighborhood where we can stay if he's moved."

"That should work. Send a runner to let me know where you are, if it's not at Stian's."

"I will." Aerik glanced at the relic on the table. "Do you want to keep talking with Philemon?"

"I'd like nothing better, but you'd better take him with you. There's too much I need to do before tonight's meeting and none of it will get done if I can talk with a daemon instead." He touched Philemon's shell, obviously disappointed. "Come back tomorrow morning, and we'll talk again. And take care not to draw attention to yourselves. People will be looking for you once your part in this is known."

Aerik grinned as they stood. "The last place they'll look for us is in a subaltern's apartment. You were right, Father. Learning the temple dances led to some useful friends."

Corin thumped his son on the back. "A convenient apartment is the least of Stian's virtues. As I'm sure you'd agree, considering all those months you spent with stars in your eyes. You were lucky to find a companion who was interested in more than your looks."

Aerik blushed. "Oh, he was interested in that too." He gave Rhan an embarrassed glance. "He's the, um, mentor I told you about."

"Then I'll give him my thanks," Rhan said, grinning like a rogue. "His student learned his lessons well."

Aerik's face turned scarlet. He hastily picked up Philemon and put the daemon in Rhan's saddlebag. "We'd better be on our way. Stian will be getting home soon if he's still on the second rotation. He might go out again before we get there if we don't hurry."

"Give him my regards," Corin said. "Remind him he's always welcome here."

"I will," Aerik promised. He slung the saddlebag over his shoulder. "Let's go."

Catrin and Rhan followed him downstairs to collect the rest of their gear, remarking on his father's warm regard for Stian as soon as they reached the street. He endured their amusement but set a quick pace for their trip to the temple district. His friends were soon working too hard to keep up their needling.

In truth, Aerik was deeply grateful for his father's approval of Stian. He had been eighteen and Stian nineteen when they first became intimate. Stian was already involved with other male dancers and made no secret of his lusty adventures. He even delved into ancient plants and potions that were said to be daemon work, exploring pleasures the empire suppressed with fanatical rigor. Defying priestly edicts and embracing physical intimacy had forged his circle of friends into a true brotherhood.

Aerik's father was no fool. He had divined his son's leanings long before Aerik was willing to acknowledge them. His open acceptance of Stian, despite his wife's shrill protests, had endeared him to both of them.

A brisk hike up the crowded boulevard brought them to a residential area just below the temple district. The buildings here were less grand than his father's home, being used mainly by pilgrims and the staff who orchestrated constant ceremonies at the great temple. Apartments and hostels were stacked one atop the other on receding terraces, their roofs planted with gardens, stairs and ladders weaving between them like stitching on a quilt. Aerik stopped and pointed up a flight of flagstone stairs leading to a narrow patio above the street's latticework canopy. A building clad with green bricks held three doors and six round windows.

"Stian's rooms are up there," Aerik said. "Let's hope he's home."

He climbed the familiar steps, with Rhan and Catrin following closely. The first floor had a patio, enclosed by bamboo railing, and was crowded with miniature trees in glazed pots. Aerik knocked on Stian's door with a mixture of eagerness and trepidation. He hoped Rhan and Stian would get along. While the guardsman was incapable of jealousy, he wasn't sure how Rhan might react to someone as joyously sensual as Stian. A second later the door swung open and it was too late to worry about it.

Chapter Eleven

RHAN flexed his shoulders, trying to dispel the tension knotting his muscles. He felt strange about meeting someone who had been intimate with Aerik. He was still trying to sort out his feelings when the door opened and an energetic whoop filled the air. A young man wearing only loose cotton pants came out to embrace Aerik and lift him off his feet.

Rhan felt a twinge of envy at their laughter but had no trouble understanding why Aerik had been taken with Stian. He shared Rhan's height and proportions but was a bit more heavily muscled. Shaggy black hair and a deep voice conveyed strength while high cheekbones and almond-shaped eyes lent a fey sensuality to his handsome features. He exuded friendliness and masculine energy. It was impossible to look at him and not think of sex. His scent was unlike anything Rhan had ever encountered, seductively virile but with hints of herbs and musk.

As soon as Aerik was back on the ground, he extended a hand toward his friends. "Stian, I'd like you to meet Catrin and Rhan. They're from Balmorel." Stian clasped arms with them while offering a cordial greeting. Rhan liked his strong grip and easy smile. "Can we come in?" Aerik asked. "I don't want to draw attention."

Stian ushered them inside. The large room was sparsely furnished and looked inviting despite its casual disarray. Grass mats covering the floor filled the room with a sweet aroma like new-mown hay. A rack on a side wall held a wide array of implements. Swords, daggers, throwing knives, and fighting staves were displayed along with colorfully decorated poles, finely carved hoops, and metal disks covered with bright enameled designs.

Aerik put his gear down and then made a gesture of apology. "This is more than a social call, Stian. I need your help. We need a place to stay tonight. The militia's in a stir, and we don't want to be noticed. My father wants us to keep out of sight until things calm down a bit."

Stian nodded, plainly curious but too tactful to ask for details. "I'd be honored, of course. Catrin and Rhan are welcome to use the bed. These mats will do for us, with a few blankets for padding." His knowing smile gave the impression he didn't expect to get much sleep.

Aerik's crestfallen expression must have surprised the guardsman, but he merely raised an eyebrow. Rhan had to admire his restraint. The awkward silence was broken when Catrin cleared her throat. "Thank you for the offer," she said. "You're very kind. And Aerik is being a gentleman, too, not wanting to deny me a bed. But knowing how men think, I believe he and Rhan might have had different arrangements in mind." She gave Rhan a small smile. "Am I right?"

Stian's gaze slid over Rhan in an unabashed appraisal before locking with Rhan's eyes. His questioning expression held no hostility.

Rhan blushed but seized the opportunity. "Aerik and I, ah, we were hoping to stay together. I don't want to commandeer your bed, though."

Stian's reserve dissolved in a wide grin. "You can't commandeer what's already given as a gift. I'm happy for both of you if you've found a special bond. The two of you should share the bed, of course."

The guardsman's warm-hearted understanding left Rhan tongue-tied. He was starting to think he might have judged the Tyumens too harshly. They were like wolves. As a group they were ferocious and deadly. But individually, some of them offered more acceptance than he had ever found in Balmorel. He looked aside to mask his tangled feelings, glancing at the rack against the wall without really seeing it while his mind raced.

Stian followed his gaze and went over to the rack. He picked up a wood staff wrapped with red leather strips and copper bands and presented it for inspection. "This is my finest piece. Made for ritual dances, not fighting. It's very old. You can handle it if you'd like." His transparent attempt to put Rhan at ease by changing the subject showed a consideration for others often lacking in those who possessed such great beauty. Rhan decided that Corin Rodan had been wise to support Stian's liaison with his son.

"Don't get him started," Aerik said, crossing the room and taking the staff from Stian. He put it back on the rack. "Give him half a chance and he'll try turning you into a dancer. Um, not that you wouldn't make a good one." He gave Rhan a simmering gaze. "We'll have time to think about dances later, yes?"

Rhan nodded, knowing what was on his mind. He had smelled Aerik's desire during the journey to Chakragil, more intoxicating than any wine, and had felt the same. Only the lack of privacy had kept them from acting on it.

"We should eat here if you want to avoid notice," Stian said. "There's still warm water in the bath if you want to use it. I'll fetch dinner while you settle in." He brushed off their apologies at the intrusion and was on his way after putting on boots and a loose shirt.

Rhan noticed Catrin's interest as Stian pulled on his tunic, his arms and shoulders hard with muscle. As soon as he was out the door, she shook her head wistfully. "He's as easy on the eyes as Rhan and twice as polite. Just my luck, I suppose I'll be perfectly safe sharing a mat with him."

Aerik laughed. "He's the opposite of Maiko in every way, if that's what you mean. Don't worry, you'll have fun. He's an excellent conversationalist and a brilliant card player."

"Don't taunt me," she said, wagging a finger at him. "You don't want to make me mad. Just ask Rhan."

Rhan put his hands on Aerik's shoulders and steered him back to their saddlebags. "Let's let her use the washroom first," he suggested. "Where's the bedroom? We can get our gear put away while waiting our turn."

"Upstairs," Aerik said, picking up his bags. "Come on, I'll show you."

They carried their gear to the back of the room, where steep stairs along the wall led to the upper chamber. "Watch your step," Aerik said as he started up the steps. "It's tricky if you're carrying things." As he ascended the stairs, he grabbed an overhead knob and slid aside a panel that had separated the upper and lower rooms.

Rhan followed, fascinated by the torrent of fragrances flowing from the upper room. Stian's scent was strong, as he had expected, as was the musk of sex. More surprising was the complex mix of perfumes and plant scents, like a healer's cottage full of herbs and balms.

Sunlight streaming through a large round window flooded the bedroom with light. Gleaming pine paneling covered the walls. Rhan felt like he was returning home after a long absence. The glazed brick and stone facades that dominated Chakragil's architecture were impressive and beautiful, but lacked a link to the verdant forest he loved.

A large bed with a leaf-green quilt occupied the room's center. The bed's frame was pine, matching the walls, and included a six-inch-wide ledge running all the way around. Glass-fronted cabinets filled one wall. They were packed with books, bottles of colored fluids, and small wooden boxes decorated with pictograms in a style Rhan had never seen. The opposite wall held a cabinet containing many drawers and doors with ornate metal hinges and knobs.

Aerik crossed the room and dropped his saddlebags beside the window. Rhan went to his side and put an arm around his shoulders. A sense of peace descended as they looked out on clouds, forest, and distant mountains. There was no balcony on this floor, and Chakragil's busy concourse was hidden from view. For a moment he could almost believe they were alone in the wilderness.

"I'm glad you agreed to come," Aerik said. "I wanted you to see this. There are problems with the empire, but there are good things about it too. I'm hoping you'll decide it's worth saving."

Rhan pulled Aerik against his side. "I knew that much as soon as I met you. As for the rest… I'm mostly confused, I guess. I like your father. And Stian is… interesting."

Aerik laughed softly and turned into Rhan's arms. "Stian is the best the empire can produce. You'll see."

Rhan embraced him. "Never mind Stian. We're alone at last." He narrowed his eyes as if trying to think of something. "I hope I can remember what to do."

"That's the least of my worries," Aerik said, pushing their crotches together. He was already hard. "Besides, maybe we'll try something new."

Rhan bent his head and nuzzled Aerik's ear. "That would be fun," he whispered. "Show me what you've learned here. Whatever pleases you will please me too." He found Aerik's lips, and they kissed as if starved.

The sound of a door opening downstairs penetrated Rhan's awareness. He ended the kiss with regret. "Sounds like Catrin's finished. I suppose we should clean up before Stian gets back."

Aerik nodded, though he continued to press against Rhan. "You can go next. The washroom is only big enough for one person at a time. I'll help Catrin settle in."

Rhan gave another squeeze and then released him. "This should be interesting," he said. "I've seen lots of piping in ruins, but this is the first time I'll see plumbing that actually works."

"You can't have a city this size without it. On a sunny day you can even get warm water, if you have a barrel on the roof. Paint it black and the water inside warms right up. Water straight from the city reservoirs is cold as snow."

"Then I hope Catrin didn't drain the bath."

Aerik opened a drawer in the dresser and pulled out two sets of exercise robes and pants made of thick cotton. "We'll pick up some city clothes tomorrow," he said, giving one set to Rhan. "For tonight we'll borrow from Stian."

Rhan looked at the clothing, surprised at the cotton's weight. "You're sure it's all right? I barely know him."

"He's generous to a fault." Aerik flashed a grin. "Besides, this way he'll get to see more of you. He'll think it's a fine idea."

Rhan went downstairs while Aerik was occupied putting Philemon in a patch of sun. Catrin stood by the window brushing her hair. He slipped into the washroom without disturbing her.

The room was tiny, but clean and colorfully decorated with tiles that shimmered in the soft light of an oil lamp. He washed quickly and used a towel from a stack on a shelf to dry himself. When he slipped into his borrowed robe, he felt cleaner than he had for weeks.

As he was leaving the washroom, Stian entered the front door carrying a canvas bag. Rhan's stomach growled at the scent of venison sausage, fresh-baked bread, ripe peaches, and some kind of sweet confection he couldn't identify. He walked barefoot into the main room, where Stian had started emptying his bag onto a low table that was hinged at one end and had been folded against the wall.

Aerik pounded down the stairs carrying his borrowed clothes. "Don't eat it all," he called as he went into the washroom. "I'll be quick."

Stian waved an acknowledgment, then fetched four pillows from an alcove and spaced them around the table. Finally he brought out a decanter filled with amber fluid and four pewter cups no taller than his thumb. After placing them on the table, he turned to Catrin. "Would you like to sample our famous liqueur while we wait? It's made with spices so secret they aren't even given names."

Catrin and Rhan took their seats while Stian removed the decanter's stopper and poured a small quantity into each cup. The scent was sweet, like fermented honey laced with traces of herbs and flowers. He distributed the cups and then raised his for a toast.

"To Aerik," Stian said. "A man with the wisdom to find friends wherever he ventures." They all raised their glasses before sipping the fiery liqueur. Though sweet, its intensity was almost enough to make Rhan's eyes water.

Stian put his glass down and turned to Catrin. "May I ask how you and Rhan met Aerik? I wouldn't have joined the city guard if I'd known militia campaigns had such interesting possibilities."

Catrin dimpled, obviously taken by the guardsman despite his unavailability. She explained the teams that had been formed to search for a heretic, taking what Rhan regarded as far too much pleasure in describing how he had switched places with another finder to win a place on Aerik's team. Stian had the grace not to laugh at the story, but the glance he gave Rhan showed he understood the situation.

"You chose well," he said after Catrin finished. "I can't imagine a better traveling companion than Aerik. Have you seen him dance or heard him sing?"

"We heard him sing in Eben," Catrin said. "He hasn't danced for us, though."

"I'll try to talk him into it." He turned to Rhan. "I'm glad you befriended him. It's good he had an ally by his side. There are dangers on a campaign."

"You mean Maiko? He was a problem, but I don't think Aerik needed help handling him."

"Maiko is just a Hand, prone to violence but trained to obey. The greater danger lies in hidden purposes and competing factions."

The washroom door opened, and Aerik came out before Rhan could pursue the comment. His hair was unruly from washing, but he was still a vision. The cotton robe was cinched around his slender hips with a cloth cord but was too large for his compact form, exposing his chest and allowing glimpses of his lean abdomen. The rough and ready impression he made in his leathers was replaced with natural grace. He padded across the room and took his place at the table.

"Thanks for waiting," he said. He tore off a piece of bread and passed the skinny loaf to Catrin. "Did I miss anything important?"

"They were just starting to tell me about your travels," Stian said. "I'm eager to hear it all."

They took turns relating the tale while they ate, leaving out any mention of cold torches and daemons. Stian listened attentively and was plainly engrossed by the events and their implications. By the end of the meal, Rhan's appreciation for their host had grown tenfold. His relaxed manner concealed a keen mind and serious intent.

They talked far into the night, first around the table and then reclining against large cushions on the floor. Rhan soon found Aerik nestled against his side as the conversation ranged through a dizzying combination of politics, art, and funny stories. He couldn't remember ever laughing so hard or understanding so clearly. Mostly he marveled at Aerik's warm presence and the easy acknowledgment of their bond. Even Catrin smiled benevolently at their closeness. He felt as if he'd shed a suit of armor, weight he hadn't known he was carrying until it vanished.

At last Aerik stretched and got to his feet. "I hope you'll excuse me. But we've had a long day and tomorrow will be busy. Would you mind if we went upstairs?"

"My apologies," Stian said, standing up. "I've had too much fun and forgotten to be a good host." He went to the alcove and removed a clay candleholder, lighting the candle before giving it to Aerik. "There's fresh soma root, if you want to use it. It's in the usual place."

Aerik gave Rhan a hot glance. "Until morning, then. We're in your debt, Stian."

"What's mine is yours. Rest well."

Rhan followed Aerik up the stairs. When they reached the top, Aerik closed the sliding panel that separated the bedroom from the lower chamber. He put the candle on the dresser and blew it out, then led Rhan to the window. A full moon filled the room with silvery light and made the distant landscape look like a vast ink drawing.

"I'm glad we came," Rhan said. "I judged your people without having met them. I should have known better."

Aerik laughed softly. "If you judge us all by Stian, you're making a big mistake. We're like everyone else, I suppose. Some good, some bad. Most of us somewhere in between."

A chirrup made Rhan jump. He had forgotten the daemon waiting in what was now a dark corner.

"I like your friend Stian," Philemon said. "He has an inquisitive mind, as men go."

Aerik retrieved the daemon and carried it over to the dresser. "Maybe I'll be able to introduce you, once my father knows where things stand. Um, do you mind if we put you away for the night? I think the talk's done for the evening."

"I expect it is." The daemon chirruped again. "It's always been a great mystery to us. You do your best communicating without words. Madekind could never really understand what we were missing."

"We'll talk about it some other time." Aerik opened a door in the cabinet and put Philemon on a folded shirt. He closed the compartment quickly, not giving the daemon a chance to offer further observations. When he turned around, his expression was expectant.

Rhan needed no urging. He took Aerik in his arms and held him. Clean black hair brushed his cheek, its fragrance as distinctive as a favorite portrait. As he nuzzled it, Aerik's hands slipped beneath the robe and caressed his sides. The touch was warm and light.

Rhan reached between them and loosened the cords that held their robes. As the heavy fabric fell open, he felt the heat of Aerik's body against his torso. He shrugged his robe off, then eased Aerik's robe down until the sleeves captured his arms behind his back. Holding it in place like soft shackles, he knelt and brushed his lips against Aerik's midriff. Aerik shuddered, his erection tenting his loose cotton pants as Rhan nuzzled his chest and nipples.

Rhan released the robe and let it fall to the floor. Moving his hands to Aerik's hips, he slipped his fingers beneath the waistband and inched the pants down. Hard muscle bunched beneath his hands as he cupped strong buttocks. When the waistband caught on Aerik's erection, he freed the material and let the pants slide to Aerik's ankles. The cock's fresh musk filled Rhan's senses as he bent his head toward it. He held Aerik steady while he licked at the flaring crown. It bounced against his tongue, twitching in response to his touch.

Aerik gripped his shoulders. "We should slow down," he said, his voice tight. He drew Rhan to his feet. "Let's get in bed." He tugged at Rhan's pants and sent them slithering down. "We've waited this long for a bed, we should use it."

As they reclined on the bed, Rhan's eyes opened wide. The mattress was no lumpy straw-stuffed affair like his bed in Balmorel. It molded to his body like a huge sponge.

Aerik grinned at his surprise. "I thought you'd like this. This bed is Stian's biggest indulgence. Aside from sex, that is. They kind of go in hand."

Rhan rolled on top of him, pressing him into the yielding surface. "Show me." He emphasized the request with a deep kiss.

After a few minutes, Aerik rolled Rhan onto his back and pressed his shoulders against the mattress. "First things first. I want to taste you again." He moved around and crouched with his knees straddling Rhan's head. Bending his arms, he lowered himself and caressed Rhan's erection with feathery kisses. It trembled and jerked in response. Rhan stroked his sides and then held tight as Aerik's mouth engulfed the head of his cock.

Rhan closed his eyes and basked in sensation. His lover's strong body moved beneath his hands, shifting slowly back and forth as he swallowed the cock all the way to the root. His lips clenched the shaft as it slid out, milking it. His erection swayed above Rhan's face, solid and gleaming like ivory, a strand drooling from its tip. His friend's delight in giving pleasure reflected his generous nature.

Rhan moved his hands to Aerik's hips and was about to pull them down when Aerik swung around and sat on his haunches. His erection curved up between his spread legs, making a shallow arc to touch his belly at the navel. His eyes were bright with excitement. "Would you like to fuck me again?" he asked. "Or… we could try the other way around, if you'd like. Either is fine with me."

Rhan propped himself up on an elbow and gave him a randy smile. He reached over and used a finger to catch some of the lubricant sliding down Aerik's cock, then tasted it. "A hard choice. How about both?"

"Stian's bed is having an effect on you," Aerik said, nodding knowingly. "You're starting to think like him." He twisted to the side and lifted the inside edge of a railing on the bed's frame. It folded out to reveal compartments filled with bottles, small boxes, pipes, and folded cloths.

He removed a hand towel, a small piece of yellow root, and a wide-mouthed glass jar, then swung the panel closed and put the supplies on it. Removing the jar's lid released the scent of alpine heather. He dipped three fingers into the jar and scooped out a generous glob of clear gel. They kissed as he stroked Rhan, coating his erection with lubricant.

Rhan moaned as the slick caresses brought him to aching hardness. Then Aerik scooped up more gel and pressed it into the opening of his own ass. "Stay on your back," he said. "We'll go slow until I've relaxed enough to take you." He stepped over Rhan, straddling his waist, and sank into a squat. As he lowered himself, he reached down and lodged the tip of Rhan's cock between his buttocks. Keeping his gaze locked to Rhan's, he lowered himself until the glans slid inside his body. He held himself motionless a few seconds before letting more slip inside. He was powerfully aroused, his cock stabbing the air like a pike as Rhan's shaft entered him inch by inch.

Aerik looked ecstatic, and his scent was thick with lust. Rhan gasped as slippery flesh clenched his erection. Knowing that he was giving as much pleasure as he received made the sensation all the more compelling.

"I'm not as good at this as Stian," Aerik said, his gaze smoldering. "But you'll still like it. Let me show you." He squeezed again while raising his body enough for half of Rhan's cock to slide out before lowering back down. A sheen of sweat glistened on his torso as he slowly twisted and rocked, squeezing and massaging Rhan's phallus from different angles. The display of stamina was impressive.

"Don't stop," Rhan said. He reached to the side and found the jar of gel. After scooping as much as he could with two fingers, he moved his hand to Aerik's cock and coated it completely, touching as lightly as possible, and then held the throbbing shaft in a gentle grip as Aerik continued sliding up and down.

Soon Aerik groaned and let his weight rest on Rhan. Sweat beaded his forehead. He leaned forward, keeping the phallus inside him, and put his arms around Rhan. "Wait," he said, radiating heat. "I'm on the edge."

Rhan rocked his hips, making his cock slide inside his strong companion while holding him tight. "I wish it could last forever," he said softly.

Aerik grinned. "I'll take that as a challenge. Ready to trade places?"

"I was wondering how long I'd have to wait for you to ask. I'd like nothing better."

The words brought a gleam to Aerik's eyes. He sat up and straightened his legs until Rhan's erection slid out. The rigid phallus snapped back against Rhan's body with a wet slap. Wasting no time, Aerik reached for the jar and covered a finger with the slippery gel. "Spread your legs," he said. "We'll start with a finger, since you're new to this. Trust me, it won't hurt."

Rhan laughed. "I figured that out from the look on your face when I was inside you." He pulled his knees up while splaying his legs to the sides. "Like this?"

"That's good." Wrapping one hand around Rhan's cock, Aerik reached down with the other and touched the opening of Rhan's ass with his lubricated finger. "It might feel odd at first. Let me know if you want me to stop."

He slowly stroked Rhan's cock while gently sliding his lubricated finger over the opening of Rhan's ass. As the erection throbbed on his palm, he stroked harder with his slick finger. "Relax," he whispered. "There's nothing to fear."

Rhan took the advice, breathing deeply and closing his eyes. Aerik's touch had a dreamlike quality, gentle and slippery, pleasuring two parts of his body in a way that made them feel intimately connected. He remembered the rapture in Aerik's face as he was being fucked. His cock strained at the thought, lifting off Aerik's palm. At the same moment, Aerik's finger slipped into his ass.

Rhan jerked as unexpected pleasure surged through his body. For a moment he thought he was going to come. His ass clenched as Aerik's finger massaged a sensitive spot inside him. When he opened his eyes, he saw Aerik watching him with a knowing smile.

"This is only the beginning," Aerik said. He pulled the finger out and scooped more gel from the jar, continuing to stroke Rhan as he applied the additional lubricant. Rhan felt his ass stretching as one finger and then a second gently entered him. As promised, Aerik took his time and made sure nothing was rushed. There was only pleasure as Rhan was initiated into this new role. His only concern was whether he could forestall his release long enough for Aerik to enter him.

"I think I'm ready," he said, reaching down and stilling the expert hand on his cock.

Aerik moved between Rhan's legs, leaning forward and supporting himself on outstretched arms. He lowered his head and brought their lips together in a kiss as he guided the first two inches of his cock inside.

Rhan squeezed hard on the penetrating shaft. The slippery phallus felt larger than he had expected but not uncomfortable. The scent of Aerik's excitement was an elixir, inflaming him. Knowing the effect he was having on his friend was as exciting as the sensations coursing through his flesh. He squeezed again, this time deliberately, eliciting a happy moan from Aerik as their tongues jousted.

Seeming to understand that all was well, Aerik slowly eased the rest of the way in. They began to move together. Rhan tried to focus on the rapture filling Aerik's face, hoping the mesmerizing distraction would help him forget his pleasure and prolong their lovemaking. He knew the effort was doomed to fail. Aerik was too skillful a lover, the pleasure too intense. He felt the slick shaft moving inside him, massaging the spot inside that was already throbbing. Pleasure was a tickling itch that was quickly becoming too great to bear.

As if sensing his imminent orgasm, Aerik came to rest with their flesh fully joined. He lowered his chest onto Rhan's and slid his hands under the finder's shoulder blades.

"Feels good, yes?" His satisfied grin showed he already knew the answer.

Rhan gave him a hug, squeezing with his ass at the same time. "I never doubted you. Can we do this all night?"

Aerik laughed softly while fucking with slow, short strokes. "That would be hard, but we can do something that's almost as good. Stian offered us soma root. Have you ever heard of it?"

Rhan shook his head. "What does it do? I can't believe it feels any better than this."

Aerik reached to the side and retrieved the small piece of yellow root he had placed on the bed's rim. Its earthy tang, like mint mixed with iron, was unlike anything Rhan had ever smelled.

"It doesn't make you feel any different," Aerik said, looking mischievous. "Not exactly. Let me surprise you. Just kiss me when you're about to come. You'll like it, I promise."

Rhan moaned as Aerik's cock nudged the spot inside him that produced jolts of pleasure. "If you say so. Just don't stop what you're doing."

Aerik grinned at him. "No chance of that. Remember, kiss me when you're about to come." He put the piece of root in his mouth without chewing it, and then straightened his arms. He began to fuck with longer strokes, his lean body quivering with arousal.

Rhan surrendered himself to Aerik's demands. He spread his legs wider to invite deeper penetration. His cock stretched across his belly, so hard it ached. Aerik's lovemaking was as sensuous as a dance, a graceful display of athletic prowess.

Rhan smelled a change in his partner's sweat, a heady scent he had already learned was a prelude to orgasm. Aerik was reaching the point of no return. Aerik bent his arms and rubbed their bodies together, Rhan's slick cock squeezed between them, while continuing to fuck.

Rhan gasped as the hard body rubbed against his slippery phallus.

The pleasure deep in his body soared out of control. He put his hands on the sides of Aerik's head and brought their lips together as his back arched in a spasm of onrushing pleasure.

The scent of soma root filled his senses as Aerik's tongue entered his mouth. Aerik had bitten into the root a moment before they started to come and mixed its juice with his spit. The mixture tingled in Rhan's mouth like cold snow.

Suddenly Rhan's searing orgasm changed into a feeling like being lifted by an immense wave. All the pleasure remained, sweet and sharp, but instead of bursting like an explosion, it grew inexorably. His mind seemed to clear and time became fluid. The first spasm of his orgasm seemed to take a full minute and was only a prologue to a stronger surge of sensation. He felt Aerik jerking and spewing semen inside him, but slowly, as if in a dream. Aerik's eyes were rolled back with only the whites showing. His half-open mouth seemed frozen in a cry of ecstasy.

Reason fled as the second wave of pleasure crashed over him with excruciating implacability. He clung to Aerik's sweaty body, using him as an anchor. His ejaculation smeared their bellies as Aerik's seed filled him. The slick cock pulsed inside him and seemed to swell in size.

By the time the second wave crested, Rhan was helpless. He surrendered to the experience. Overwhelming affection mingled with the torrent of sensation as he held his lover in his arms. Sharing such pleasure forged a bond that could never be forgotten.

More convulsions rocked him, now coming with greater speed, as their orgasms subsided. Aerik clung to him, panting. They caught their breath before separating and rolling onto their sides facing each other. Rhan extended his arm for Aerik's head to rest on and gave him an exhausted smile.

Aerik beamed. "Believe me, I liked it just as much."

"That soma root, I'm surprised I've never heard of it. Is it a Tyumen secret?"

Aerik shook his head. "It's very illegal, so don't mention it to anyone. Legend has it the plant appeared when daemons flourished.

Priests claim the plant is daemon work, but that's what they say about everything they want to suppress."

"We could ask Philemon," Rhan said.

"Tomorrow." Aerik put an arm around Rhan and snuggled against him.

"I wish we didn't have to go anywhere tomorrow," Rhan said, running a hand along Aerik's flank. The compact body felt solid and hot, still flushed from sex.

"We'll do the best we can." He yawned, exuding contentment. The feeling was contagious, and Rhan contented himself with his friend's warm presence. Sleep claimed him while still entwined in his lover's arms.

SUNRISE painted clouds in rosy glory outside the bedroom window, though Rhan was given little chance to enjoy it. Stian and Catrin lured them out of bed with fresh-baked bread, honey, pears, and strong peppermint tea. Stian left early to report for duty and Aerik was too disciplined to allow them to linger over breakfast. They were washed and out the door, on the way to his father's house, before the clouds lost their morning color. Rhan breathed deeply, invigorated by the brisk air and the deepest sleep he had ever known.

The city's brilliant tapestry dazzled him. While the Tyumens were undeniably oppressive, they were not indolent. People were already filling the wide street. Smells of baking bread and grilling sausages wafted on the breeze like a waterfall of scent.

The housekeeper was waiting for them when they arrived at their destination. After being assured they had already eaten breakfast, she gave Catrin a small bundle.

"These should suit you well enough," she said. "It's just an old dress Aerik's mother doesn't wear anymore and a pair of slippers. She'll never miss them. I brought the gown in a bit so it'll fit you better."

Catrin accepted the parcel with a look of astonished delight. "Thank you, Kea. It would never occur to these two, but roaming the streets of Chakragil in traveling leathers is more than a bit unladylike. I'll feel much better in these."

Kea patted her hand. "Just let me know if Aerik gives you any trouble. I've learned all his ways and know things you can use to make him behave. He was a menace when he was sixteen. I'll never forget—"

"We'd better get upstairs," Aerik said, tugging Catrin's arm. "We don't want to keep my father waiting."

Rhan saw the housekeeper's smirk as they retreated up the stairs and wondered what secrets his friend was worried about. He resolved again to tell Aerik about his mark. He couldn't believe it would change anything between them, but there would always be a nagging question until the deed was done.

The study's door was open. Aerik's father was seated at the table in the room's center and looked up as they entered. "You'd better shut the door," he said as he stood. He waited until they were seated and Aerik had removed Philemon from the canvas sack he carried before sitting again. Rhan smelled his anxiety, though the man's face betrayed nothing.

Philemon pulsed once with green light. "Greetings, sir. If I may ask, how did it go last night? Will I be meeting your associates today?"

Corin shook his head. "We didn't get that far. We have an immediate problem that has to be handled first. The Hand you traveled with has stirred up a storm of accusations and counter-accusations. We believe the Numerans are scheming. They deny everything, of course, and accuse us of slandering them." He looked Aerik in the eye, not trying to conceal his worry. "You'll have to report to your decurion today. Apparently the Hand didn't see much, so you'll have to answer the militia's questions."

Aerik looked sober. "What about Rhan and Catrin? We were all together."

"I want to keep them away from the militia if we can. You're a citizen, they aren't. They won't have the law's protection if they're taken into custody."

Aerik nodded. "I'll try to handle all their questions, then." He glanced at Philemon. "Questions about the heretic and his relic, anyway. Maiko doesn't know anything about the rest, so they won't either."

"Let's hope so," Corin said. "Once things calm down, we can work on longer-range plans. We'll have to take this one step at a time."

"No point putting it off, then. I'll make my report and get back as soon as I can."

Philemon pulsed with light, a mannerism that reminded Rhan of a child raising its hand before speaking. "Would it be possible to visit the archives while Aerik takes care of his business? Aerik thought you might be able to arrange it. I'd like to know what's left of my world. I might even come across something you and your associates can use."

Corin raised an eyebrow. "What you ask could be dangerous. The archives are forbidden to most." He looked at Aerik, who had assumed a nonchalant pose. "Were you planning to go too? Don't think I've forgotten how you pleaded to get in. You were very persistent."

Aerik spread his hands. "He just wants to know what's left of his world. And if we're discovered, you can tell the curators we were trying to help identify the relic we saw. They won't be any the wiser."

Corin tapped the table a few moments before standing and bowing formally toward Philemon. "I understand your curiosity, Philemon. I'll take you to the archives as a gesture of my good faith. And to be honest, I'd be fascinated to learn what the relics are for. Most of them are mysteries to us."

He turned to his son. "You and your friends found the most important relic of all. You've earned the right to come along. If we're going to do this, we should do it early. The priests are busy with temple rituals until late in the morning. The risk will only increase if we wait. And we don't know when you'll get back from making your report."

Aerik broke into a big grin. "At last! Thank you, Father. We won't be any trouble, I promise."

"I trust not. We shouldn't be discovered at this hour. But if we are, keep silent. I outrank the archivists, you don't."

"I can be of assistance in avoiding curators," Philemon said. "I'll listen for them and give you ample warning if any are near. My hearing is much better than yours. Just ask Aerik and Rhan."

Corin gave Aerik a questioning look. His son's red cheeks seemed to convince him of the claim. Corin smiled and nodded. "Thank you, Philemon. I appreciate your help. Now let's be on our way. We'd be wise to finish our visit well before noon." He put the daemon in his satchel, along with some candles and matches.

They paused long enough for Catrin to change into the clothes Kea had provided. When she met them at the front door, she was transformed. The ruggedly attractive provincial had become an elegant lady who might have been born and bred to imperial splendor. Green silk covered her with elegant simplicity.

Corin smiled warmly. "I regret to say my wife never looked half so fine in that dress. I'll have Kea alter a few more things for your use, if you'll permit it."

"You're too kind, sir. This dress is all the finery I'll be able to use in Balmorel."

He opened the door for her. "Beauty doesn't require a use, my lady. A rose brightens the day of all who see it, as do you."

Catrin led the way. Rhan could tell she was pleased even though her natural dignity never faltered. He wished he could learn that trick but guessed he never would.

They walked up the gently inclined road as Corin told how the archives had been carved from solid rock beneath the city's great temple. Rhan could guess who had wielded the hammers and hauled the rock but refrained from commenting. Reconciling the legacy of Tyumen tyranny with Corin's hospitality required a constant mental battle. He knew Aerik was right, that it was a mistake to lump everyone together, but old habits were hard to break. Would Corin still be hospitable if he knew one of his guests bore a mark? Rhan wanted to believe he would but knew it was too early to find out. He'd know better where he stood once he shared the secret with Aerik.

They passed through another ornate portal made of polished wood and entered the temple district. The road was less crowded here and the people more elaborately dressed. Priests in red robes and closely-fitted hats walked in clusters like flocks of birds. Rickshaws displaying the imperial seal carried elderly clerics upward with self-important haste.

No dwellings lined the road here. Gardens were interspersed with small shrines where pilgrims prostrated themselves. Further up the road, looming over all, were the temple's soaring columns and majestic statues. The structure was impossible to appreciate from the road other than to feel its oppressive mass. The building shouted that all who approached its doors were insignificant specks in the face of imperial might.

Before reaching the temple's plaza, Corin left the road and led them into a garden-filled cleft in the mountain's face. Further in, out of view from the road, a serpentine wall made of brick separated the garden's public part from a secured area. Corin went to an iron gate and drew a ring of keys from one of his pockets. The gate's lock opened with a heavy thud. "Be quick," he said. As soon as they were through, he locked the gate behind them. "This grove is used for growing spices employed in making incense. It also conceals a door into the archives. Really an exit, a precaution against ambush installed after an attempted coup long ago, but it will serve."

Rhan could barely contain himself as they followed a winding path through the garden. Plants chosen for their fragrance grew in lush profusion. Many were familiar spices used in cooking or perfumery, but others were exotic. He wanted to stop and investigate each one, to separate its scent from the fireworks of rich fragrance. This small space had enough scent to fill a world, it seemed.

He forced himself to keep up with the others, and they soon reached the garden's edge. The cliff face had been smoothed and covered with white-glazed brick except for an oak door reinforced with thick metal bands. Corin selected a different key and unlocked the door. Gardening tools and equipment for processing spices filled the large room.

Corin took four candles from his satchel. He struck a match, sending a pungent whiff of sulfur through the air, and lit the candles as he distributed them. Then he closed the door and took Philemon from the satchel. "I'll go first and see if the way is clear," he said, handing the daemon to Aerik. "After that I'm hoping Philemon will let us know if anyone's approaching."

"You may rely on it," Philemon said. "I could also provide light, if you'd rather not use candles."

Corin shook his head. "Thank you, but it would be too hard to explain if anyone saw us. Candles will suffice for our eyes. Do you need better?"

"I need very little light. Besides, flickering candlelight seems appropriate. Madekind thought itself powerful, but we were fragile as a small flame. It's a lesson I won't forget."

"Then we'll begin." Corin went to the back wall, where a mosaic of bricks formed a pattern like interlocking chains. He pressed two bricks where lines intersected, triggering a muffled thud, then pushed the wall in front of him. A section of bricks the size of a door swung inward on concealed hinges. After holding a finger to his lips as a reminder for silence, he entered the archives. Less than a minute passed before he emerged again.

"Nobody's about. We should be safe enough if we're quiet."

They filed through the disguised door and made sure it was secured again before continuing. Unlike the luxurious colors and textures elsewhere in the city, the archives were functional but primitive. The wide corridor they had entered was bare rock. Sturdy timbers stood at close intervals to support crossbeams a foot thick. Niches of all sizes filled the walls. Each compartment held a single object and was labeled with a metal nameplate bearing a number.

Corin held his candle next to a nameplate. "We're in the fifteen thousand series," he said, indicating the number. "Each relic is described in ledgers. Of course it usually just gives the relic's shape, not its function. Most of them are like this. A mystery."

"This was part of a tool used for making machines that could fly,"

Philemon said. "They were rather like ships that could carry hundreds of men and women through the air at high speed."

"I thought those were make-believe stories," Catrin said. She knelt by the object and peered at it. "How does it work?"

"The explanation is complicated," Philemon said. "I'll be glad to discuss it with you later. Would it be possible to move quickly through a few corridors? I sense they are extensive. I can examine objects very quickly as we pass. I'll better understand what has survived and be more likely to find something that might be of use to you."

"As you wish," Corin said. "Don't forget to listen for curators." He started down the corridor at a brisk walk.

Rhan's wonder turned to anger as they swept down the corridor. The relics stored here, even the small fraction they were passing, were the work of finders over many lifetimes. He wondered how many had died to retrieve these relics, how many others went unpaid for their labors. The amount of concealed knowledge was numbing.

Intersecting corridors ran off to their left and right in a regular grid pattern, all of them filled with niches and relics, but they continued on a straight course toward the mountain's heart. At last Corin turned right, even though the corridor they had been following still stretched ahead into darkness. They walked only a few minutes before turning right again and heading back in the direction from which they had started. Bits and pieces of ancient mystery became a blur. Some gleamed as if newly made while others were crumbling to dust.

Another fifteen minutes passed before Philemon spoke. "A moment, please. There's something here I'd like to examine."

Corin halted his march and turned to the daemon in Aerik's hand. "I was starting to worry we've been collecting trash all these ages. Which one?"

"The yellow metal box on your right, in the compartment at floor level. Could you pull it out so I can see the markings? I caution you, it might be heavy."

"I'll get it," Rhan said. He crouched next to a niche containing a cube about two feet across. It looked innocuous except for markings on the top and front—symbols like a stylized sunburst. He put his hands on its sides and pulled, grunting when it barely moved. Getting to his knees, he reached behind to grip the relic by its back edge and pulled again. This time it moved out of its niche, though it took strenuous effort. He rocked back on his heels and kneaded his fingers. "I'm glad I didn't find this one," he said. "That's a back-breaker."

"Would you move me behind it?" Philemon asked. "There should be markings there telling what's inside."

"Are you going to open it?" Rhan asked as Aerik carried Philemon around the box.

The daemon made a soft humming sound that reminded Rhan of a cat's purr. "This is a greater treasure than you can imagine. It contains a form of nourishment for madekind and would give me the strength to do many useful things. But we can't open it now."

"Why not?" Catrin asked. "If you're hungry, you should eat."

"The contents are harmful to your kind; you need to be shielded from it. You would sicken and die within hours if you opened that box without protection."

Catrin looked dubious. "How do you use it, then? Food you can't eat sounds pretty useless."

"Once there were machines that could put the material inside my shell, where it's safe. And humans with special clothing can easily do it. So unless we find suitable machines or protective garb, I'm doomed to starve on sunlight and other crumbs."

"Perhaps I can learn something from the archivists' ledgers," Corin said. "They'll note if there are relics that resemble clothing."

"I am in your debt, sir. If we succeed, I hope to be able to assist you in return."

Corin reached over and touched the daemon. "I'm honored to become your ally. You've just disproved the ancient teachings. The empire will be changed forever when we share you with the world. The long night will finally end."

Aerik gave his father a puzzled look. "How did he disprove the priests? I didn't hear anything that sounded like heresy."

"Dogma has always insisted that daemons are mankind's great enemy. Yet Philemon chooses to remain hungry rather than let us come to harm. Choose your friends by their deeds, Aerik. So far you've done a fine job."

Aerik was radiant in the glow of his father's praise. Rhan met his gaze, and they smiled together, sharing a moment of happiness.

"And now we must return to business," Corin said. "It's best not to tempt fate by staying too long. And I wager Aerik wants to be done with his report in time to get back before the lifts close." He grinned at his son. "Unless you want Stian to have Rhan all to himself this evening. Just think of all the interesting things they could discuss."

Aerik blushed. "I'll be back this afternoon, I promise."

"Don't hurry on my account," Rhan said as he knelt to shove the box back into its niche. "I'm already thinking of questions for Stian."

Aerik handed the daemon to Catrin and then knelt to help move the box. "I'll give you something better to think about," he whispered as they shoved together. "Last night was just the beginning."

Rhan felt a shiver of anticipation. When the box was back in place, he leaned over and kissed Aerik on the cheek. He didn't care what Catrin or Corin thought. Having Aerik by his side was enough, and he wanted him to know it.

Chapter Twelve

AERIK made his way through the militia district's crowded streets, wishing he could be elsewhere. He had never had trouble with his decurion but knew it would be hard to concentrate on his story. Rhan's whispered entreaty when they parted company had sounded important. He had said they needed to discuss something and that he didn't want to put it off any longer. Aerik's curiosity roared like a bonfire.

He stepped aside for a lumbering wagon carrying salted beef to the garrison's kitchen. It reminded him of another reason for finishing his report before the lifts closed. The prospect of eating cold soldier's rations instead of introducing his friends to Chakragil's culinary wonders made his stomach ache. And then there was the question of sleeping alone on a hard bunk instead of nestled in Rhan's arms. He quickened his pace and arrived at headquarters as the noon bell started ringing.

One advantage of being short was that people remembered him. The sentry admitted him with a wave. The entry hall was as dismal as ever, wooden benches lining two walls of a barrel-vaulted chamber, shafts of light streaming through small windows above the doors. He reported to the clerk outside the decurion's office—an unfamiliar woman seated at a desk stacked with papers.

She frowned when he gave his name. "Took you long enough to get here, didn't it? It's not smart to keep the worthies waiting." She jerked her head toward the door behind her. "In there. You're expected."

Aerik opened the door and entered his commander's office. He had only been there once before, for an awkward meeting when the decurion apologized for not knowing he was an Eye of Tyume and making proper arrangements. Aerik had assured him that special treatment was not necessary or desired, and they had parted on cordial terms. As he closed the door, a man seated behind the desk looked up from a book. Aerik had never seen him before.

"I'm sorry," he said, standing in front of the officer's desk with feet apart and hands behind his back. "I'm in the wrong place. I'm here to report to Decurion Lysias. I'll let the clerk know there's been a mistake."

"No mistake," the man said. He put his book on the desk and laced his fingers together. "Lysias has been temporarily assigned to other duties. I'm Hipparch Sethi. You'll report to me instead. Proceed."

Aerik stiffened, hearing the steel in the man's voice. The hipparch was middle-aged and looked fit. He had a closely trimmed beard and hard eyes.

Pulling his shoulders back, Aerik recounted events from the time he and his team left the convoy. While omitting any mention of torches or daemons, he described the vambrace Rolf Odette had worn and the spectacular lights it had created. Sethi was noncommittal about the relic, which seemed peculiar, but Aerik was glad not to be questioned. The faster he could finish with militia business, the better it would suit him.

When the report was done, he waited with a straight-ahead gaze while the officer leaned back in his chair. "What other relics did you see during your mission?" he asked.

Aerik paused, trying to remember if he had seen anything that Maiko would also have seen, before shaking his head. "None, sir. Just the vambrace."

Silence stretched to the point of awkwardness and beyond. At last Aerik shifted his gaze to Sethi. The man was watching him like a cat that had cornered a mouse. His heart started to race, but he kept a neutral expression.

"You're lying," Sethi said.

Aerik felt like a metal band had clamped around his chest. "Sir? I don't understand. There wasn't anything else."

Sethi stood and turned toward the door separating the office from the next room. "Join us, Hand. Perhaps you can refresh his recollection."

A moment later Maiko entered the room. Aerik's hackles rose.

"Been enjoying yourself, Rodan? It took you long enough to get here."

Aerik felt like he was trapped in a nightmare and struggled to maintain a calm expression. How much could Maiko have seen?

Sethi gave him no time to think. "Hand, maybe you can straighten this out. You heard what he said about relics. Was there something besides the object he described?"

Maiko assumed an air of self-righteous offense. "Don't pretend ignorance, Rodan. You and that finder stole a fortune in relics. Jewels and gold coins and who knows what else. You wouldn't even let me do an accounting, you were so eager to hide it."

"That's a lie," Aerik said, growing hot. "Rhan found some coins and jewelry, that's all. Nothing that needed to be identified or examined. His village is entitled to keep it. You saw for yourself and counted everything several times, as I recall."

"I barely saw it at all," Maiko said, smirking. "I tried to tell you, but you wouldn't listen. I think the finder was hiding something."

Aerik wished they had paid him off, but now it was too late. Maiko wanted revenge and had found an avenue to pursue it. "That's not true," he said, turning to the officer. "Maiko had plenty—"

Sethi held up a hand to terminate the protest. "I'll not listen to your quarrels. It's clear that whatever was found should have been presented to an Examiner."

"But—"

"Don't interrupt!" Sethi glowered at him, then sat down and pressed his fingertips together in a steeple. "This causes great concern. I have reason to believe there's something else you're withholding. You said you took refuge in ruins when the heretic was attacked, correct?"

"Yes, sir. We were lucky to escape. If there had been enough of them to keep watch while searching the fortress, we wouldn't have gotten our chance."

"So you hid near the walls and ran for the forest when they went inside to search?"

Aerik sensed a trap but knew he couldn't change his story. "Yes, sir."

For a time the man watched Aerik silently, his lips pressed together. At last he shook his head as if disappointed. "I had hoped you were loyal to the empire. You're lying, which means you're hiding something. I know you explored inside the fortress. What did you find?"

Aerik's heart pounded. Either the man was bluffing or he was in league with the Numerans. It was possible Rolf Odette had lived long enough to be questioned. All his father's warnings about the Numerans and their infiltration of imperial institutions swarmed to mind. Coming here alone had been a mistake.

"You're wrong," Aerik said, hearing the hint of desperation in his voice. "We did no exploring. If Maiko told you otherwise, he's making it up. He wasn't even there. He was sleeping off a drunk."

"Liar!" Maiko was red in the face. "I was tending the horses like you told me to!"

"This is your last chance," Sethi said, eyes narrowed. "I know your father has filled your head with confusing ideas, but it's not too late for you. Tell me what you know, and I'll give you my protection. I'm a man of my word. Otherwise it will go badly for you."

The man's resolve was clear. Aerik took a deep breath and bolted for the door.

Sethi jumped up. "Stop him!"

If the door's latch had not been closed, he would have made it. Maiko crashed into him as he was turning the iron ring. They fell to the floor in a tangle of jabbing elbows and knees.

"Keep him still," Sethi said, coming around the desk. Maiko sprawled on him while Sethi reached down and put a hand around the front of his neck. He squeezed hard and held firm.

Panic impaled Aerik like a spear, and then he yielded to darkness.

AERIK'S head pounded. He tried to touch it, but his arms wouldn't move. His eyes jerked open, the sudden light sending a spike of fire through his head, and he saw Maiko looking down at him with alarming eagerness. By craning his neck he could see the ropes binding him to a stout board. He strained against the bonds, but the effort was fruitless.

Maiko was smug. "There's no weaseling out of it, runt. Nobody's around to save your ass this time."

"Don't presume," a voice admonished. "He can still save himself."

Aerik turned his head and saw Hipparch Sethi standing in front of a closed door. They seemed to be in the room behind the decurion's office. He glanced around and was dismayed to see the walls were filled with tools of interrogation.

"The Hand is correct about one thing," Sethi said, moving closer. "You're going to tell me what I want to know. There's no escaping it. You can save us both time and grief by cooperating."

"I have nothing to tell you. You have no right to do this."

Sethi pulled up a stool and sat beside Aerik. His snakelike gaze was more disturbing than Maiko's open hostility. "Imagine how you sound to my ears," he said, leaning close. "You're barely a man. An Eye of Tyume who ignores his gods. How long do you think the empire would stand if the likes of you weren't stopped? You're worse than a heretic. You're a hypocrite."

"You have no right to judge me! File charges if you want. I've done nothing to harm the empire."

"I'll give you one more chance to prove it. You claim you saw nothing in the fortress. Tell me where to find the peasants who accompanied you. If they verify your story, I'll release you."

The offer confirmed Aerik's worst fears. If Sethi was a Numeran, he already suspected or knew what had been hidden in the fortress. He was looking for relics and surviving witnesses to the massacre. Rhan and Catrin were game for the hunt, nothing more. "I don't know where they are," he said, trying to sound confident. "They're seeing the sights."

"Which sights? What district?"

"I don't know. I didn't ask them."

"Where did they stay last night?"

"They were going to stay at an inn. They didn't know which one when we parted company."

Sethi sighed and pushed his stool back. "You leave me no choice. Hand, show him the reward for lies."

Maiko moved to the end of the board where Aerik's feet were tied. "Just so you know, this was my idea," he said. "You've always had a swollen head. This will shrink it back to size." Reaching down, he gripped the board's end and lifted.

Aerik shouted in surprise. The board was mounted to pivot on a hinge at its middle; the end supporting his head dipped as Maiko lifted the opposite end. His cry was silenced by cold water engulfing his head.

He'd had no time to draw in his breath before getting dunked. The need to inhale overwhelmed him. He thrashed against his bonds, not even able to scream, as pain seared his lungs.

His body had nearly betrayed him, forcing his mouth open to seek air, when the board moved again and his head lifted from the water. He gulped desperately, coughing out water that had run up his nose.

Sethi was standing over him with a concerned expression. "There's no point in prolonging this. You can't escape, and it's only a matter of time before we find the others. Cooperate with me and we'll put this behind us."

"I… I don't know where they are," Aerik said, still wheezing.

Sethi's expression hardened. "I gave you credit for more intelligence. Perhaps reason isn't going to persuade you." He crossed his arms. "We'll have to rely on other means." He nodded to Maiko, and the board tilted again.

This time Aerik filled his lungs before being dunked, but it only prolonged his agony. He tried to keep still and make the air last, but his body rebelled and jerked against the ropes as fire filled his chest. When his face emerged from the water, he turned his head and retched. Sethi was talking, but he couldn't hear the words over the roaring in his ears. It felt like his lungs had been ripped out.

When he stopped gasping, Sethi bent over him. "The gods of Tyume are merciful, if you'll turn to them. You've been misled by your father. Let the scales fall from your eyes. Faith in the gods is what holds the empire together. Show me your faith and this will end."

Aerik closed his eyes. If fate had turned against him, he didn't want to enter the next life with an image of Hipparch Sethi filling his mind. He thought of Rhan and the life they might have shared by turning their backs on Chakragil and exploring the world together. The pain of loss was as sharp as the fire in his lungs had been. He wanted to weep but refused to do so in front of his enemies.

A stinging slap across the face forced him to open his eyes. Sethi glowered at him with righteous hatred.

"The gods will not be mocked! What did you find inside the fortress? How did you get out? I'll have the answers if I have to skin you alive to get them!"

Aerik clenched his teeth and returned the stare with stony

defiance. Silence seemed to enrage the man. Sethi turned to Maiko and nodded.

As his head dropped into the water, Aerik forced himself to think of Rhan's strong embrace. He doubted the distraction would spare him much torment when the time came to leave his body, but it was the closest thing to a prayer he could summon.

Chapter Thirteen

"HE SHOULD be here by now," Rhan said. He knew he was repeating himself but couldn't help it. Two hours had passed since the time Aerik had estimated for his return.

Catrin leaned against the railing of Stian's patio and stared into the distance. "If I could do something about it, I would. Stian's watch should be over soon. He'll know whether there's cause to be worried."

Rhan leaned over the balcony and searched the road below them, catching glimpses of people through gaps in the latticework sheltering the street. Late afternoon sun was hot on his face. Low rays painted the city gold and made the glazed facades shimmer. The beauty was lost on him. "Do you think we should contact his father? Maybe he knows what's going on. Or we could go to Stian's post and see if—"

"Rhan. Calm down. Maybe he just misjudged how long his report would take."

Rhan stepped back from the railing, frowning. He wiped his brow with a sleeve and nodded. "Sorry. Being here just makes me nervous, I guess."

"That makes two of us. It's like exploring a garden full of bear traps. Pretty, but one wrong step and you're dead."

"Look!" Rhan leapt back to the railing and pointed. "It's Stian. I think so, anyway." He waved both arms overhead, his face awash with relief when the distant figure waved back.

Catrin restrained him from running down to greet the guardsman, reminding him they had been told to remain inconspicuous. He paced the balcony like a trapped badger until Stian sprinted up the steps.

Stian's smile faded when he saw their worry. "Is there a problem?"

"Let's go inside," Catrin said.

The door had barely closed before Rhan recounted Aerik's promise of an early return and how there had been no sign of him or word of a delay. Stian listened patiently and paused before answering. "I usually wouldn't give it much thought, but today is different. We keep close watch on the city, and it's been buzzing like a hive. The principal factions have been holding meetings in every district. You couldn't cross the road without tripping over message runners. And Aerik's the most reliable person I know. It's not like him to be late."

Rhan sagged with relief, glad his fears were being taken seriously. "What should we do, then? Go see his father?"

"No, I doubt he'll be home until very late. He's one of the empire's great men. He'll be busy with whatever business is afoot today." He pondered a moment and seemed to reach a decision. "We'll go to the last place we know Aerik went. I've met Decurion Lysias, and he should be on duty another hour or so." He tapped the small enameled medallion hanging from a chain around his neck, a bright token of authority that was impossible to miss against his tunic's black leather. "I'll tell him it's an official inquiry."

Rhan wanted to hug him. "Aerik was right about you. I hope this doesn't put you at risk."

Stian waved a hand in a dismissive gesture. "It's worth it. You're not the only one who loves him, you know."

Stian's voice held no challenge or jealousy, only concern. Rhan felt as if he had entered an invisible circle, crafted from loyalty and affection, where the rules were different.

Stian turned to Catrin. "You should wait here in case Aerik returns while we're gone. If he does, both of you stay put. Will you feel safe?"

"I'll be fine." She gave Rhan a wry glance. "A little peace and quiet would be welcome."

"We'll be back as soon as we can." He opened the door and followed Rhan out.

"There's a city guard post between here and the nearest lift," Stian said as they descended steep steps to the road. "I know someone there whose contacts in the militia are better than mine. Maybe she's heard something I haven't. It won't take long."

"Whatever you say. Do you think he's all right? Catrin thought I was worrying too much."

Stian shrugged. "Aerik can take care of himself, but today has been strange. And in Chakragil you learn not to rely on luck. People here are always plotting and seeking advantage. Friends have to look out for each other."

"I remember Aerik's father calling you his protector. I wasn't sure what he meant, then. Now I do."

Stian laughed. "You haven't heard his mother's version of the story. She's convinced I seduced him and turned him into the lively bedmate we both know so well. She wanted to bring the priests down on us, but Corin threatened to divorce her if she did." They reached the road and started walking down the slope.

"Well, Aerik did mention that you taught him about sex. Not that I'm complaining. I'm glad one of us knew what he was doing."

Stian gave him a sidelong glance. "In case you're wondering, Aerik was the hunter and I was the quarry. It turned out to be my great good fortune, though. Nobody could ask for a better friend." A smile tugged at his lips. "And I'm glad to say we've shared a lot of pleasure. You're lucky to have found him, Rhan."

"We're all lucky. Though perhaps it's not luck. Aerik has that Tyumen way of taking matters into his own hands."

Stian laughed and thumped Rhan on the back. "He selected you too, I bet. Take it as a compliment. He loves sex, but he doesn't choose companions lightly."

The road remained crowded as evening approached. Light shining through overhead grape leaves made them glow like emeralds, and the sweet scent of ripe fruit tickled Rhan's nose. Merchants had moved baskets of perishables to the street in front of their stores for quick sale to workers seeking a cheap dinner. Musicians vied for audiences, and dining establishments opened their doors to reveal cool salons. For a moment Rhan recaptured the sense of wonder and excitement the city was capable of creating. Then he remembered that Aerik wasn't there to share it with him, and the glow faded.

They soon arrived at a two-story building. Its door displayed the same symbol as Stian's medallion. Several guardsmen greeted Stian when they entered. He escorted Rhan through a low-ceilinged hall and then upstairs into a cavernous room. Sunlight flooded through tall vertical windows, painting the wooden floor with stripes.

"Armory," Stian said, pointing at racks of batons, fighting staffs, swords, and spears along the walls. "Rarely needed, but they say the gods favor the prepared. It's mostly used as a gymnasium for training." He looked around the room and saw an open door in a side wall. "She must be washing up. Come on."

They crossed the floor, footsteps echoing between the high walls, and entered a room thick with humid air. A muscular woman with close-cropped blond hair, about Stian's age, was bent over a tub with soapy water up to her elbows. She was vigorously scrubbing an exercise robe on a washboard.

Stian walked up behind her and patted her on the rump. "They've promoted you to laundress, Astrid? It's about time."

The woman turned her head and winked at him. "Damned blood stains, you got to get 'em out fast. I was showing one of my team a new throw, and he rammed his nose into my elbow. Clumsy of him." She looked past him and raised an eyebrow. "A new friend, Stian? Nice."

Stian put an arm around Rhan's shoulders and pulled him forward. "Behave yourself, Astrid. This is Rhan, a visitor from the provinces. We don't want to alarm him." He extended his other hand toward the woman. "Rhan, this is Astrid Elytis. She's in charge of training at this post. And a valuable source of information."

"Ah. I should have known this wasn't a social call." She lifted her garment from the suds for examination, then twisted it into a rope and started wringing water out. "Can't say I'm surprised, though. Been quite a day, hasn't it?"

"Any idea what it's all about?" Stian asked, releasing Rhan and settling on the ledge in front of a window. "I was curious if you've heard anything from your cronies down in the barracks."

"Answer one for me first," Astrid said as she plunged the tunic into a tub of rinse water. "How'd you manage to win at cards last week? The way he was betting, I'd have wagered a bottle of brandy that Pio held the winning hand."

"You ask a high price," Stian said. "But I'm in a hurry, so you have a deal. Watch his ears. They turn pink when he's excited. It didn't happen during the game, so I figured he didn't really have the cards."

Astrid fixed him with an accusing stare. "Pink ears when excited, huh? I'm thinking you had an unfair advantage."

"I'm just observant," Stian said, grinning. "Now it's my turn. Something stirred up the clerics and magistraats today. Looks like trouble on the way. What was it like down in militia territory?"

She inspected the robe's elbow for remaining stains. "Lots of meetings, I'm told. Old rivals watching each other with daggers in their eyes. I'm guessing someone's planning a power play." She looked up and met his gaze. "Better keep your head down, I'd say. Wouldn't be healthy to get caught in the middle."

"Is that all? No unusual arrests, fights, anything like that?"

Astrid wrung out the robe and hung it on a hook. "Let's see. A fight in the barracks over a whore. Nobody seriously hurt, I'm told. Some poor sod was put to torture, I didn't hear what for. Somebody stole the paymaster's purse again. There'll be fat in the fire over that." She chewed her lip a moment. "That's it for action, far as I've heard."

"Somebody was tortured?" Rhan asked, his dark opinion of Tyumens stirring. "Does that happen much?"

"Now and then," Astrid said. "It's often threatened, but most people confess as fast as they can when they're pinched for something. Punishment for whatever you did is usually less painful than an interrogation."

Stian tapped a foot against the floor. "I wonder if it had anything to do with today's troubles."

"Like I said, my source didn't know much. She just saw the prisoner being carried out. Might have been a fresh recruit who fucked up somehow. She said the body was small."

Rhan met Stian's worried glance and immediately knew they were thinking the same thing. The guardsman held up a finger in an inconspicuous signal for silence.

"All very interesting," Stian said as he slid off the ledge. "I'll let you know if I hear more."

"I'll do the same," Astrid said. She nodded to Rhan. "Nice to meet you. If Stian doesn't treat you right, give me a visit. I know the dives where you can really have fun."

Stian came to the rescue by prodding him out the door. They kept silent until they had left the building and crossed to the road's far side. Dusk swept the landscape beneath them like a scythe.

"Don't jump to conclusions," Stian said as Rhan opened his mouth. "Remember, Aerik's an Eye of Tyume and his father's a Voice."

"She said they were carrying out a body. Does that mean—"

"It could mean many things. There's no point making guesses. Let's go see for ourselves. And keep your eyes open. With luck we'll see Aerik heading our way."

Rhan tried to put questions out of his mind as they wove through the busy street. Throngs were converging on cafes that poured forth aromas like smoke from a thousand campfires. At any other time he would have wandered the street in a daze, trying to identify spices carried on the wind, but now hunger paled beside his unease.

The trip down the mountain was faster than he expected, since Stian displayed his medallion and commandeered places on the first available lifts. Those waiting in line muttered, but Rhan didn't care. He was busy searching the faces streaming past and sampling the breeze for one special scent.

The sun was an orange sliver on the horizon when they reached the militia district. Evening was cooling quickly and the air held few of the fragrances that swirled in the city's richer districts. This level was dominated by barracks, taverns, gaming houses, and brothels. The road boiled with soldiers who seemed determined to spend their pay while they could and make as much noise as possible while doing it.

They approached a fortresslike facade and were admitted after Stian showed a sentry his medallion. The hall inside was empty except for a clerk working at a cluttered desk and was lit only by a lamp on the clerk's desk. Rhan smelled the sweat of bored men and women lingering in the air like ghosts. He sniffed, hoping to catch a whiff of Aerik, but it was like trying to identify a single drop in a rainstorm.

The clerk looked up from his paperwork when they approached. He put down his quill and spat in the general direction of a bucket beside the desk. His eyes narrowed as he took in Stian's uniform and rank.

"What can I do for you?" he asked. His voice was cordial, but a suspicious expression flitted across his rounded features. Too-close eyes and bristling hair reminded Rhan of a boar.

"I'd like to speak with Decurion Lysias," Stian said.

"He's not here. You'll have to come back tomorrow."

"I thought he was on duty for another half hour. If he's gone, who's in command?"

The clerk picked up his quill and dipped its point in an inkwell. "He's still on duty, just not here." Pulling a sheet of paper off a stack, he began entering notations in a column. "You can wait if you want. He might be back."

Stian reached over and plucked the quill from the man's hand. The clerk's head jerked up, too surprised to conceal his irritation.

"I'm looking for someone," Stian said. He put the quill in its holder. "Was a prisoner interrogated today, or held in your lockup? This is city guard business. It can't wait."

The clerk looked down and fumbled among the papers on his desk. "Let me see... ah, here it is." He held the paper close to his eyes and squinted at it for several seconds before shaking his head. "Nothing on the day ledger about prisoners." He gave Stian a grimacing imitation of a smile. "Sorry I can't help you."

"What about interrogations?" Stian said, crossing his arms.

The clerk frowned and perused the sheet again. He soon nodded. "Just one, around noon. Nobody detained."

"Name?"

"Not given. Disciplinary matter, says here." He put the paper down and picked up his quill. "If you're done, I have work."

Stian leaned over the desk as if preparing another question, but Rhan nudged his shoulder and motioned toward the door with a tilt of his head. His panic must have been apparent. The guardsman followed him outside without hesitation.

As soon as they were beyond the sentry's earshot, Rhan turned to Stian. "He's lying! We have to find out who they're hiding!"

Stian held up a hand. "Not so fast. He looked shifty, yes, but that's not proof."

Rhan seized his arm, desperate to make him understand. "What if they're holding Aerik? What if he's been tortured? He could be injured, or—"

"Hush." Stian twisted free and led Rhan over to the railing at the road's outer edge. "I'm worried too, but charging around blindly won't help."

"Remember what Astrid said about the interrogation? They were torturing someone small. And you said yourself, it's not like Aerik to disappear without sending word. I think they have him." Frustration made him shiver. "That man is lying, I'm sure of it. Please believe me."

Stian sighed. "Let's go have a mug of cider. I understand how you feel, but you need to think it through. Causing a commotion would draw attention we don't want."

Rhan closed his eyes, feeling like he was choking. He breathed deeply and caught Stian's scent, tart with concern. He could see only one way to convince him. He swallowed hard and plunged ahead before fear could steal his tongue.

"I put myself in your hands," he said, meeting Stian's worried gaze. His throat was tight. "I… I bear a mark. I can smell as well as a bloodhound, maybe better. I can smell deception. That clerk was lying to us when you asked about a prisoner." He thrust his hands into his pockets in a fruitless effort to control his shaking.

The smell of Stian's shock washed over him like freezing water. He looked down, paralyzed by the conviction he'd made a horrible mistake. The Tyumen empire had been founded in a crusade to keep the bloodline pure. He'd been a fool to think this might help Aerik.

A strong arm settled around his shoulders. He jerked as if stung, his heart pounding as Stian pulled him close and held him steady.

"I should have known Aerik would choose someone remarkable," Stian said softly.

Rhan gulped. "He… he doesn't know."

The hug tightened. "That's not what I meant. Few would have the courage to reveal a mark."

Shame burned away his trembling. "He doesn't know because I was afraid to tell him. I wanted to, but never found the right time."

"You spoke when it was needed," Stian said, releasing him. "That's what matters." He looked Rhan straight in the eyes. "The priests would hang me because of who I love. They're wrong about me. So why should I care what they think about you?"

Rhan was dazed, suddenly seeing Stian as Aerik saw him. His fearless spirit, not his beauty, was what had drawn Aerik to him. "You'll make the clerk show you the lockup, then?"

Stian thought a moment before answering. "No. There's a better way than asking. Since the clerk was lying, he'd probably raise an alarm if we called him on it."

"What choice do we have?"

"Aerik knows people in high places, but I have friends in low places. Sometimes that's even more useful. The garrison's kitchen manager is one of them. They feed prisoners as well as soldiers. He'll have a way in."

Rhan squared his shoulders. "When can we try?"

"Better do it now, while he's still working. This way."

They stayed on the road's outside edge, avoiding rowdy soldiers clustered near the brothels, taverns, and gaming dens that tunneled into the mountain, and soon arrived at a building with lines of men and women snaking out its two doors. They went a little further down the road and turned through an arch into a dank alley.

Stian stopped at a door flanked by garbage bins and pulled it open. They entered a larder crammed with bulging baskets of vegetables and rows of smoked sausages hanging from the rafters. Two men at the far end of the room were loading food onto a cart. A crowd's chatter filtered in from the adjacent hall.

Stian leaned close and whispered in Rhan's ear. "The tall one is Naji Bovet. He was in the city guard until he went blind in an eye from injuries during a fight. We'll wait until he's alone."

"This is the kitchen?" Rhan asked. There were no stoves or fires to be seen or smelled, and the room was nearly as chill as the night air. "Where's the fire?"

"Hot food is expensive on the mountain, so the rank and file get cold rations. There he goes. Now's our chance."

They stepped out of shadows as the scullion pushed his cart through an archway into the next room. Stian waved as his friend turned back to a table where a smoked ham waited for slicing. "Naji! I'm here to inspect your kitchen."

The young man smiled widely as Stian embraced him. He was almost as well-favored as the guardsman, though a thin scar slashed across his cheek. He pounded Stian on the back before bumping their foreheads together in what looked like an affectionate ritual.

As soon as they stepped apart Stian turned to Rhan. "Naji, this is Rhan. Rhan, Naji."

Naji's grip was strong as they clasped hands, and he took Rhan's measure with genial humor. "If Stian's taking you out to dinner, you should demand better."

"I'm afraid we're here about a problem," Stian said. "How long before your helper gets back?"

"Five minutes or so. Why?"

Stian lowered his voice. "Aerik's gone missing. We're not sure but we think he might be in the lockup. There's a rumor of someone being put to torture today. It might have been him."

Naji looked stunned. "What do they say he did?"

"I don't know the details," Stian said. "He got ensnared in some political infighting."

Naji's jaw tightened. "That's even worse." He glanced over his shoulder before continuing. "I've had no orders to send food to the lockup. If there's a prisoner, they're keeping it a secret. Or they don't think he'll live long enough to need food." He reached into a pocket and took out a key. "I'd go myself, but it'd be noticed if I left the kitchen right now." He pressed the key into Stian's hand. "That passage," he said, pointing to a door that led deeper into the mountain. "Go straight down the corridor, don't take any turns. They keep a lamp burning in the lockup, so you won't need to bring light."

Stian clenched the key in his fist. "Thanks. If Aerik's in there, we'll get him out. Will you be safe?"

"As long as you don't run off with my key. And make sure the kitchen is clear before coming out." He looked over his shoulder again. "Better hurry. My helper will be back for another load soon."

Stian thumped his friend on the arm before crossing the kitchen with Rhan at his heels. They entered the passage Naji had indicated and paused for their eyes to adjust after closing the door. Rhan immediately caught a trace of Aerik's familiar scent. He nudged Stian. "He's here!"

Stian jumped at the contact. "Where? I don't see anyone."

"I don't mean with us. Down the corridor, not far."

Stian's breath escaped in a hiss. "You should avoid surprising guardsmen in dark places," he whispered. He paused a few seconds. "You mean to say you can smell him?"

"Yes. I think he's been hurt, let's go!"

Stian held out an arm to block Rhan's passage. "Do you smell anybody else?"

Rhan sniffed the stale air. "Nobody who's still here. There've been others in the last few hours, though."

"Huh. I could use you in the guard. Follow me, and cover my back if we have to fight. And let me know if you smell anyone coming."

"I will. Hurry!"

Stian seemed to take Rhan at his word, trotting down the corridor without concern for stealth. The light brightened quickly as they sped by side corridors until the passage widened into a chamber with a row of cramped cells filling one side. All were empty except the last, where a small form lay curled on the stone floor.

Rhan's heart raced as Stian unlocked the cell. They went to his side and rolled him onto his back.

They were greeted with an anguished moan as Aerik pulled his arms tightly against his chest and buried his face in his fists. Rhan put a hand on his forehead, bile rising in his throat as he took in his friend's matted hair and soaked clothing. "Quiet. We're going to get you out of here."

Aerik lowered his hands, his expression filled with disbelief. "Rhan! How did you find me?"

"Stian's work," Rhan said, nodding toward the guardsman. He slid an arm beneath Aerik's shoulders and helped him up. "Let's get out of here, talk later." He was shocked at Aerik's unsteadiness and had to bear most of his weight.

Stian was there in an instant. "Are you injured? I can carry you if that's faster."

"I'll make it." He let go of Rhan and stood on his own. He swayed but waved them off when they moved to help him. "I'm all right."

"If you say so," Rhan said. Aerik's determination couldn't disguise his exhaustion.

They went back to the kitchen as fast as Aerik could go. When they reached the corridor's end, Stian opened the door a crack and peered through, then swung the door open and hustled them out.

Naji was keeping watch by an arch leading into the dining hall. He came over to reclaim his key and gave Aerik a quick embrace before sending them out the back door.

Rhan finally felt the ache start to leave his chest. Aerik leaned against him as if warming himself near a fire. "We'll get you home," Rhan said, putting an arm around his shoulders. "Everything will be all right then."

"Don't be too sure," Stian said. He combed his fingers through Aerik's disheveled hair, making it look more presentable. "That's where they'll expect him to be when they discover he's gone. They might put a watch on his house and try to grab him again if you show up there before Corin gets home. For now you'll be safer at my place."

"We have to get word to him," Aerik said. "The Numerans are making their move. Something happened to change their plans." He took a rasping breath. "Maiko's helping them."

Rhan tightened his embrace. "He was always out to get you."

"Yes. But I think most of their information came from somewhere else. They mostly wanted to know about the ruins where we hid from the Numerans."

"Tell us later," Stian said. "First we get away from here. Follow me."

Stian pushed them hard, staying on the outside edge of the street and keeping Aerik in his shadow. He didn't use his medallion to claim priority on the lifts, instead making them wait in dark alcoves until they could ride without waiting in line. It took nearly an hour to reach

Stian's apartment, but Rhan was sure they hadn't drawn attention.

Catrin rushed to the door as soon as they entered. "What happened? Is he all right?"

Stian half-carried Aerik to a cushion and eased him down. "He needs to rest." He put a hand behind Aerik's neck and squeezed gently. "You're tight as a bow-string. I'll make you something to help you relax and get to sleep. You'll need to be rested tomorrow."

Aerik nodded. "Thanks. Sounds like a good idea."

Rhan settled next to Aerik while Stian fetched a powder from upstairs and then mixed it with a small amount of liqueur. Aerik's hand was shaking as he drank the potion. After a few deep breaths he began a full accounting of the day's events. Before long he was slumped against Rhan and would have fallen but for his support.

"That's enough for now," Rhan said when Aerik started to numbly tell Catrin about their escape from the lockup. "He's ready to rest."

"You're right," Stian said. "Take him upstairs and get him to bed." He turned to Catrin. "You should go to Corin's house. Tell him what happened when he gets home tonight. Aerik will have to go into hiding for a while, probably outside the city. His father will want to handle it."

"Why don't you tell him yourself?" Catrin asked.

"I'm going to get some food and come back here. He needs nourishment as well as rest. Do you mind? Corin's housekeeper will be there. Have you met her?"

Catrin nodded, all business. "I'll be fine." She went to Aerik's side and kissed him on the forehead. He looked bemused but said nothing as she and Stian took their leave.

As soon as they were gone, Rhan heaved Aerik to his feet. "Are you going to be all right?"

Aerik gave him a drowsy smile. "My father says you can learn from any experience you survive. I learned a lot today."

"How? I don't suppose you got to ask many questions."

"I learned what matters. When you think your life is over, you see what was important and what wasn't." He took a deep breath. "The time I've been with you was what I thought about."

Rhan embraced him fiercely. "You know how I feel. Our time together has only started."

Aerik pulled back and smiled crookedly. "How close together, exactly?"

"You're relentless," Rhan said, mussing his hair. "One of your better features, I think."

Aerik had a sleepy grin as they went upstairs and stripped. Stian's bed was like a sanctuary, a haven of safety and comfort. Aerik curled with his back against Rhan's front, his heart thumping beneath Rhan's encircling arm, and fell asleep in seconds.

Rhan lay awake, feeling the rise and fall of Aerik's chest. He tried not to think of the end Aerik had nearly met. The prospect of losing him was like a terrifying abyss. Finally he closed his eyes and cleared his mind of everything except the reassuring warmth of Aerik's flesh against his skin. He fell asleep filled with gratitude that fate had given them another chance. He didn't intend to waste it.

THE sound of rattling dishes roused him from peaceful sleep. Momentary confusion was dispelled when he caught Stian's scent among the fragrances of bread, hummus, apples, and figs. He held still, not wanting to wake Aerik. Before long Stian came up the steps carrying a wooden tray with food, water goblets, and a lamp enclosed in a glass cylinder.

"How's he doing?" Stian asked, seeing that Rhan was awake. He put the tray on the bed's wide frame and sat cross-legged on the floor.

Aerik yawned and stretched like a cat, arms extended straight, pushing his back against Rhan. He opened his eyes and propped himself up on an elbow. Tousled hair and sleepy eyes did nothing to hide the improvement in his mood.

"I'm starving," he said, taking an apple wedge from the tray. "I feared nightmares, but Rhan and your potion kept them away."

Rhan reached over him, not breaking their warm contact, and took a fig from a pewter dish. "Did Catrin mind being left alone? I know she agreed, but she'd do that regardless."

Stian nodded. "She's a strong woman. Smart, too. We talked a long time last night." He looked at Rhan curiously. "I suppose you know she has feelings for you?"

The question caught him off guard. He cleared his throat before answering. "I know. I like her too. She's a loyal friend. She even accepted what happened between Aerik and me. Few in Balmorel have such an open mind."

They talked of life in Balmorel while eating the light fare. Aerik succumbed to sleepiness near the meal's end and fell asleep still nestled against Rhan.

Stian slid the tray to the side and considered his slumbering friend. "He's found contentment with you," he said softly. "It's a great gift." He stood and picked up the tray. "I'll be downstairs if you need anything. Rest well."

"Wait." Rhan knew Stian would never impose on guests, but there was no reason he should be banished from his own bed. "I don't mind if you sleep here. Neither would Aerik."

Stian hesitated. "You're sure?"

"It might comfort him to have you here. He thinks of you as his champion. And after tonight I understand why."

Stian needed no further persuasion. He put the tray on the dresser and doused the lamp. Rhan caught shadowy glimpses of an athletic body as he stripped.

They gently moved Aerik into the middle of the mattress. He yawned but never opened his eyes. Stian slid into bed with Aerik between them. "Thank you," he whispered.

Rhan fell asleep reflecting that the one person who knew his secret was now a treasured friend. He began to believe there was reason for hope.

A BUMP woke him. A moment later Aerik's body jerked again as he mumbled a terrified protest.

Rhan jostled his shoulder. "Wake up. It's just a dream. You're safe." Aerik opened his eyes. He looked haunted.

Stian rolled over and put a hand on Aerik's chest. "We're both here. There's nothing to fear."

"I fear my dreams. How can I escape that?"

"We'll wake you if your sleep is troubled," Stian said, brushing hair back from Aerik's eyes. "Turn your mind to pleasant thoughts. That's the best way to keep nightmares away."

Aerik nodded, though he still breathed fast. Rhan put a hand on his chest, next to Stian's. "We're not going anywhere," he said firmly. He leaned down and kissed Aerik on the lips.

Instead of the chaste reaction he had expected, Aerik put a hand behind his head and kissed him hard. Whatever fears had plagued his dreams seemed to demand more tangible reassurance than words.

Rhan gave Aerik what he wanted, returning the kiss with all the skill he could muster. When their lips parted, he could feel the tension ebbing from his friend's body.

Stian was watching with approval. "You feared losing each other," he said. "Your flesh still feels it. Love dwells in the body as well as the mind."

"You should know," Aerik said, touching Stian's cheek with a light caress. "Do you need a kiss too?"

Stian's eyes widened. "Little minx! What's Rhan going to think?"

"He thinks he's lucky to have both of you," Rhan said. He knew his place in Aerik's heart was safe. Stian was an ally, not a competitor.

"Don't give him a chance to change his mind," Aerik told the guardsman. He put a hand behind Stian's head and drew him down for a kiss.

Rhan was fascinated. Though he had grown accustomed to sharing intimacy he had never seen other men kissing. The sight was beautiful. Their masculine features held surprising tenderness, revealed in glimpses through the dark cascade of Stian's hair. The smell of arousal coursing through his friends' bodies made him hard. When they parted, Aerik turned to him. "Turnabout is fair play. Would you like to thank him too?"

Curiosity surged, along with gratitude for the guardsman's allegiance. Rhan leaned over Aerik, not sure what to expect. Stian kissed him with gentle determination, sensuous but not aggressive. His virile scent mingled with the fresh smell of his hair. Rhan's cock throbbed against Aerik's side.

Stian's tongue was tracing his lips when Rhan felt fingers wrap around his erection and squeeze. He moaned, not breaking the kiss, as Aerik's thumb stroked his slick glans. He reached for Stian's hand and drew it over to Aerik's cock. Together they caressed the stiff phallus as the recipient of their efforts skillfully returned the pleasure.

At last Rhan pulled back. Stian gave him a wolfish grin. "I'd never have stayed in the city if I'd known beauties like you were roaming the provinces."

Rhan blushed at the compliment. "I had a good teacher. And he tells me he learned from a master." Strong fingers squeezed his cock, making it jerk in response. He lowered his head and licked the tip of Aerik's nose.

Aerik laughed. "I didn't teach you that. Is that how they kiss in the provinces?"

Rhan rolled on top of him. "You seem to be feeling better. But now I'm the one who won't be able to sleep."

Aerik laughed again, his erection rubbing Rhan's hard belly. "Why am I not surprised?" He looked at Stian. "You see what I've had to cope with? Country folk are insatiable."

"You don't fool me for a moment," Stian said. "I know you too well. Are you ready to finish what you started?" Without waiting for an answer, he turned Aerik's head to the side. They kissed deeply while Rhan nuzzled Aerik's ear and neck. Aerik was soon writhing.

Moving lower, Rhan teased the smooth skin of Aerik's chest with light kisses. He paused to lick a nipple, eliciting moans, before brushing his lips over Aerik's belly. Hard muscle sculpted his abdomen as Aerik tensed. His erection made a low arch from his groin to his navel. Strands of clear fluid caught the moonlight as his cock twitched and bobbed. Rhan lapped at the lubricant, tasting Aerik's musk, then captured the glans with softly encircling lips.

Aerik gasped and broke his kiss with Stian. He put a hand on Rhan's head and pressed it against his body, holding it motionless.

"Wait," Aerik said, trembling. "I need a little time. Show Stian what you've learned instead."

Rhan reluctantly let Aerik's hard flesh slip from his mouth. He rolled to the side and sat up beside Aerik, his cock spearing up between his legs. Stian looked at the rigid shaft and whistled softly.

"You always told me size doesn't matter," Aerik said, giving the guardsman a stern look. "Besides, it's no bigger than yours."

Stian grinned. "It's true, size doesn't matter. Especially when someone has looks like yours and is frisky as a goat." He looked at Rhan's erection judiciously. "But it doesn't hurt, either." He reached over and spread his fingers as wide as he could, putting his thumb at the base of Rhan's erection. Though his hand was large, the tip of his little finger only reached the middle of the glans. "As I thought. You've fallen in love with a horse!"

Aerik groaned and pushed Stian onto his back. "Come on, Rhan, let's show him what you can do."

Rhan moved over and helped hold Stian's arms down. He put up token resistance, prodding and tickling them whenever he pried an arm loose. Though he was clearly enjoying himself, Rhan saw how determined he was to make Aerik laugh. He used physical intimacy the way a healer used herbs. They sprawled over him and set about tickling in return. Aerik knew the spots that worked best, and they soon won a gasping surrender.

Instead of releasing him, Aerik leaned over to Rhan and whispered in his ear. "Should we tickle him the way he likes best?" He caressed the long phallus stretching across Stian's lean abdomen.

"Show me." Rhan felt no hesitation. He knew Aerik was sharing a gift, nothing more or less.

"Let's do it together," Aerik said. They moved to flank Stian, squatting on their haunches with knees spread wide. Aerik pulled Stian's erection upright, then bent down and licked the glans.

Rhan leaned forward and gripped the shaft of Stian's cock. The flesh was warm and silky, the bulk surprising. The foreskin slid further back, revealing the flaring crown as he pulled down.

Aerik put his hand over Rhan's. "Give it a try," he said. "Don't worry if you can't take it all."

Rhan felt the cock with his tongue, tasting Aerik's spit on the warm flesh. He parted his lips and let the glans slip inside.

"Go slow," Aerik said, running his fingers through Rhan's curls. "Use your tongue, he likes that."

Stian's hips lifted, nudging his cock further into Rhan's mouth. "You're doing fine," he said. "After this, I'll show you how to make Aerik squirm."

That was all the encouragement Rhan needed. He took a deep breath and eased forward. The cock's soft tip reached his throat, and for a moment the size of it seemed overwhelming. Then he felt Aerik's lips brushing his ear.

"Pretend it's me," Aerik whispered. "Forget how big it looked. It feels the same when you take it in. Trust me, I know." His hand slid to the back of Rhan's neck and gave it an encouraging squeeze.

Deciding this was a time when trusting was better than thinking, Rhan imagined he was pleasuring Aerik and slid his lips further down the thick erection. The cock slipped fully into his throat in one smooth glide.

Stian moaned, the long muscles of his legs taut. Aerik circled the cock's shaft with his fingers and milked it as Rhan pulled back and the glistening flesh slowly emerged from his mouth. They repeated the cycle several times, Aerik's fingers slick with Rhan's spit as they pleasured their friend. Stian groaned and ran his fingers through Rhan's hair.

At last Rhan lifted his head and let the cock escape his lips. Aerik leaned down and gave him a wet kiss.

Stian sat up, flushed and happy, and sat cross-legged between them. "Aerik, are you sure he's a novice?"

Aerik looked smug. "He's naturally gifted. And he's even more eager for sex than me. Aren't you, Rhan?"

Rhan grinned. "Maybe. Well, probably. But tell me, were you planning only a rubdown when you brought balm to the tent the first night?"

Aerik's attempt at feigning innocence was unconvincing. "Me? Seduce an upcountry finder I'd just met?" A smile broke loose and he turned to Stian. "Who could blame me?"

"I wouldn't," Stian said. He reached over and gave Rhan's erection a slow caress. "In fact, if you're not careful I might forget my manners and kidnap him."

"He'd do it, too," Aerik said, turning back to Rhan. "Not that you'd mind." His scent was thick with lust. "But tonight I'm not letting you out of my sight."

Rhan moved to his side and held him, easing him onto his back while kissing him tenderly. Aerik made happy noises as they settled into the bedding in an intimate embrace.

"What do you want?" Rhan asked, tracing the line of Aerik's jaw with his finger. "Just ask and it's yours."

"I want to thank you." He peered into Rhan's eyes, searching. "Both of you, for saving me."

Rhan nodded, understanding his need for comfort. Sharing his body was the closest bond he could feel with his companions. "I'd be honored," he said softly. "Stian's a true friend."

Aerik hugged him, then reached out to Stian and pulled him over. "I'd like to make the circle with Rhan. Want to fuck me while we do it?"

Stian made a low growling noise. "What a question."

Aerik turned head to toe with Rhan before getting on his back. Moonlight bathed him, making his creamy skin glow. His erection stretched across his abdomen, an irresistible offering.

Rhan rolled onto his hands and knees, straddling Aerik and licking the slick head of his cock. At the same time he felt lips slide over his glans and engulf it in wet heat. Aerik held his hips, guiding him as he took Rhan's cock down his throat.

A sweet ache started to throb in Rhan's core. He slid his hands beneath Aerik's buttocks and took the stiff cock into his mouth. The strong body tensed, responding hard to his touch. Going slowly, wanting to make their pleasure last, Rhan began to stroke the rigid shaft with his lips.

Stian let them establish a rhythm while taking the jar of lubricant from its compartment in the bed's frame. A few moments later he moved between Aerik's legs and reached down, fingers coated with fragrant gel, to press the slick balm into Aerik. Rhan helped, spreading the buttocks as Stian gently massaged lubricant into the opening.

Stian took his time, slipping first one finger inside and then two, giving Aerik plenty of time to adjust to the gentle intrusion. Rhan kept sucking, cradling his lover and feeling him arch in response to the intimate caresses.

After preparing Aerik, Stian moved closer and applied a coating of gel to his cock before pushing it down and lodging its glans against Aerik's ass. "Are you ready?" he asked softly, moving his hands to hold Aerik's legs apart.

Aerik answered by spreading his legs wider in a clear invitation. Stian pushed forward as Rhan's lips slid to the base of Aerik's cock.

Stian slipped two inches inside. He shifted his hips from side to side, the head of his cock nudging sensitive flesh. Rhan smelled and tasted Aerik's excitement as they pleasured each other.

At last Stian eased fully inside Aerik while leaning his torso back to give Rhan room to continue sucking. The three of them established a new rhythm, moving as if they shared one mind. The guardsman varied the angle and speed of his fucking in response to Aerik's moans and straining body. Rhan saw the care he was taking to impart pleasure, keeping Aerik at the edge of release.

Rhan felt himself losing the struggle to control his body. Aerik's lips stroked his erection from tip to base with increasing urgency. Suddenly the pleasure became unbearable. His body curled, sliding his cock deep into Aerik's throat. Ecstasy tore through him as he spewed out his seed.

He was dimly aware of a change in Stian's fucking, the long strokes suddenly replaced with short jabs. Semen gushed into his mouth in jet after jet. Stian gasped and slid fully inside Aerik as his orgasm overtook him. Even then he kept fucking, his phallus coated with come as it slid in and out of Aerik's clenching ass.

Rhan nursed Aerik's cock until it was completely spent. When they rolled apart, he felt like he had run ten miles. He watched Stian withdraw his still-hard cock and lean down to kiss Aerik, then turned around and did the same. He tasted his own seed on Aerik's lips.

Aerik looked exhausted, but this time with fatigue born of deep contentment. He nestled against Rhan, drawing Stian down next to them, and closed his eyes while his breathing slowed.

Rhan met Stian's gaze and saw his satisfaction. They shared a conspiratorial smile, and by unspoken agreement found a position where they could both keep contact with Aerik. Rhan closed his eyes, still dazed, and sleep claimed him.

Chapter Fourteen

AERIK was the first up. He rousted Rhan and Stian while it was still dark and hurried them out the door as soon as they were dressed. Dawn was just starting to gild the clouds when they left the apartment, bringing figs and bread to eat along the way. Wagons carrying food and fuel already lumbered along the wide road.

"He didn't used to get up this early," Stian said as they made their way to Corin Rodan's house. "What did you do to him?"

Rhan yawned before answering. "Don't blame me. I was thinking about something entirely different this morning."

"I know you were," Aerik said. "Getting horned in the side is what woke me up. But my father will want to see me first thing this morning. After he decides what to do, I can get back to thanking you. I was too tired to do it properly last night."

Stian nodded in approval. "At least that hasn't changed. He's still well-mannered."

"More like randy," Rhan said.

Aerik smiled, hearing the anticipation in the finder's voice. He felt it, too, and was elated that they had taken to each other.

When they rapped on the door at Corin's house, Kea rushed out and hugged Aerik. "I'm so glad you're well," she said. "I knew trouble was brewing but didn't think they'd ever go this far." She released him and led them into the house. "I'll let Catrin know you're here."

"Is my father up?" Aerik asked.

Kea scowled. "He hasn't come home yet. Probably at an all-night meeting. He works too hard."

"Did he send a messenger?"

"No, but he usually doesn't unless your mother's home." She looked at Stian, eyes crinkling. "Would you like breakfast while you're waiting? I've missed seeing you around the house."

"We ate before dawn," Stian said. He gave Aerik an accusing glance. "Thank you anyway."

Catrin appeared at the top of the staircase, wrapped in a luxurious black house robe. She came down the stairs and examined Aerik critically. "You're looking a lot better today. Rhan took good care of you last night, I trust?"

Rhan blushed, but Aerik grinned and put an arm around his waist. "He's a credit to Balmorel. Stian thinks so too."

Catrin shook her head, red hair flowing around her shoulders. "You've brought out the best in him, then." She moved closer and touched Rhan's hand. "Marenka will be proud of you."

Rhan groaned. "You don't have to tell the elders everything, Catrin."

She grinned. "We can discuss it while I have breakfast."

"I don't think we should wait here," Aerik said. "My father might not come home for a long time if the factions are feuding. He needs to know what happened."

"Is it safe?" Rhan asked. "What if your enemies see you?"

"They won't try anything with Stian around. He has too many friends in the city guard. And my father will make sure I have all the protection I need after we've talked."

"Do I need to go too?" Catrin asked. "Kea has already started a cooking fire, and I'm hungry."

"Just as well you stay here," Aerik said. "There might even be warm water for your bath in the house reservoir. Let me show you where the valve is." He led her to a washroom behind the stairwell and pointed out the apparatus. "Did you bring Philemon back to the house yesterday?" he asked softly.

Catrin responded in a whisper. "No. Corin took him after we left the archives." She looked him in the eyes. "I'm glad you're all right. For Rhan's sake too."

"Thanks. Sorry I won't be able to show you and Rhan around the city. At least not for a while."

"Don't worry about it. I want to get back to Balmorel as soon as I can, anyway. They'll need help with the harvest and getting goods to market."

"I'll see to it. I owe you a lot and always pay my debts."

Catrin smiled. "Until later, then."

RED-GARBED functionaries sat outside cafes in the temple district, taking breakfast before reporting to work in the administrative complex near the great temple of Tyume. Aerik eyed them warily as they approached the chancery and wondered if any of them were Numerans. The thought made his stomach knot. He was no stranger to politics, but it had never before been so personal.

The chancery's facade contained six soaring arches. Bronze doors three times a man's height filled each arch, and each door's panels depicted the gods of Tyume vanquishing daemons or purging corruption from the bloodline. The craftsmanship was impressive. Sunlight reflected off polished metal with dazzling intensity, but it only reminded Aerik of the evils committed in the empire's name. His father was right: excessive power in one place caused a kind of blindness.

"Looks like we're too early," Rhan said. "How long before the chancery opens?"

"There's another entrance." Aerik tugged on the silver chain around his neck and pulled the eye-shaped medallion out from beneath his shirt. "My badge of office will get us in. Over here."

Beyond the arches, broad stairs ascended to the building's recessed second level. Aerik went to a door adjacent to the stairs, where a guard stood at rest. The man brought his pike upright at his side as they approached.

Aerik made sure the guard saw the medallion on his chest before speaking. "These two are with me. Has anyone else come or gone this morning?"

"No sir, not lately. I've only been on duty about an hour."

"No matter. Let us pass."

The guard stepped aside and opened the door, holding it while they passed through. The corridor they entered had high ceilings. Inset marble slabs wove an intricate tapestry on the floor and the walls glowed with white marble. Luminescence filled the vast structure, soft and ethereal, from a system of polished metal panels that collected sunlight from shafts and reflected it deep into the mountain.

Aerik led the way at a brisk pace. "It's something of a maze," he said. "The chancery is even bigger than the temple. I just hope my father's in his chambers. It'll be hard to find him if he's gone somewhere else."

Their echoing footsteps made Aerik uneasy. He had thought there would be more people about—anxious politicians and harried couriers responding to whatever events were occupying his father. They arrived at the double doors leading to his father's hearing room without any hindrance. He turned the latch on one of the mahogany doors, but it was locked. Nobody responded when he rapped on the door.

He stepped back, embarrassed. "His faction must be meeting somewhere else. I'm sorry I dragged you out here."

Rhan held up a hand. His face was pale. "We should go in. Do you have a key?"

"Why? Nobody's here."

"We should check," Rhan insisted. "Do it, Aerik. I... I have a hunch. Finders trust their instincts."

Stian was looking at Rhan intently. "I think we should take a look," he said. "I can spring this lock; it's mostly for show. Do I have your permission, Aerik? The damage will be minor."

Aerik could see his companions were determined. Something about their expressions made him uneasy. "Go ahead."

Stian took a step back, then turned sideways to the door and hit the lock with a sharp kick. Something snapped in the mechanism and the doors swung open. He immediately went inside, with Rhan and Aerik close behind.

The hearing room looked as it always had, an austere chamber where Aerik had spent countless hours listening to his father adjudicate disputes. He pointed to a door on the far side of a dais containing his father's high-backed chair. The door was ajar. "His private chambers are over there."

Rhan crossed the room quickly, entering Corin's chambers without knocking. Aerik followed as if in a dream, bewildered.

As soon as he reached the door, Rhan stopped him. The dimly lit room was in disarray. Rhan's face was a mask of misery.

Panic surged. "Let me in! What happened?"

Rhan held him tighter, trying to block his view. "There's nothing you can do here," he said, his voice thick. "He's gone, Aerik. Spare yourself this."

Aerik twisted loose and ran into the shadowy room. A crumpled form lay in a pool of blood near the far wall. He walked over to it, his eyes stinging and blurring, and sank to his knees beside his father's body.

He wept silently. The ache of loss made him choke. He felt an arm around his shoulders, and Rhan pulled him close.

"We should go," Rhan said softly. "There's nothing we can do here. His enemies might return."

Aerik gulped and wiped his eyes. "I'm sorry. You're right." He forced himself to look at his father's bloody body, the sight branded in his memory.

Stian crouched beside the corpse and examined it despite the tears on his face. "It probably happened late yesterday afternoon," he said.

"They likely came in after audiences were done and he'd retired to enter decisions in his ledger."

Aerik clenched his teeth and removed a ring with the family seal from his father's hand. The flesh was stiff and cold. Strangely, it made the corpse less disturbing. His father was truly gone. All that remained in the room was a discarded shell.

After a moment's thought, he felt the pocket of his father's jacket. His father's keys were still there. He took them, feeling numb, and put them in his pocket. "There's a strongbox at the house," he said. "We'll take what we need and leave the city. No place here is safe. The Numerans are seizing power. The law will be no protection."

Rhan clasped his hand, his eyes full of sympathy. "Let's go, then. There's nothing more we can do here."

"Perhaps one more thing," Aerik said. He went to his father's casework desk and was relieved to see it had not been disturbed. The desk's right-hand side was designed as a cabinet and had a concealed compartment in the back. It would be the most likely place to leave Philemon during the day if his father had brought the daemon here. He opened the cabinet door and pressed on the spot that opened the hidden chamber. Philemon's shell appeared like an emptiness in the shadows.

Before he could remove the relic, he heard the daemon's voice whispering as if it was inside his head. "I have much to tell you, but first, a caution. Your friend Stian doesn't know about me unless you've told him since yesterday. Can I speak openly in front of him?"

Aerik didn't have to think about it. He removed the relic and held it in both hands. "Stian, come here. I want to introduce you to someone."

Stian walked over, looking as if he thought Aerik had lost his mind.

Aerik lifted Philemon. "I know you trust me. Hear me out. You've said many times that priests teach what suits them whether it's true or not. Yes?"

Stian nodded, wary.

"What you said is true, and I'm holding proof in my hands. This is why my father was murdered. The Numerans fear truth more than all else. Stian, this is Philemon. A daemon. He knows what really happened in ancient times."

"I'm pleased to meet you," Philemon said, pulsing with soft green light as he spoke. "I hope you will help Aerik carry on his father's work."

Stian reacted the way he always did to possible danger: with preternatural calmness. He had always said understanding needs to come before action, and Aerik was glad to see that even a daemon couldn't rattle his friend's discipline. After a few seconds he came over and peered at the daemon from a respectful distance. "Is this behind everything that's been happening in the city?"

"We have much to discuss," the daemon said. "But first, a question. I hear men approaching. Four, if I count the echoes correctly. Is this cause for concern?"

"His hearing is better than ours," Aerik said, seeing his friend's confusion. "What do you think, Stian?"

"We might have been noticed when we entered the building. Let's take cover in the hearing room and see if they come here. We'll want surprise on our side if we have to fight."

"Leave me here," Philemon said. "I'll distract them if needed. Better hurry, they're getting close."

"Do as he says," Aerik said. He placed Philemon on the desk before following Stian and Rhan into the hearing room. Footfalls were audible now. He crouched behind his father's tall chair, remembering how he had played on it as a child, while Rhan and Stian took positions behind the double doors that still swung in from the corridor. Bitterness gripped him as the steps grew louder. He wondered if the approaching men were the ones who had taken his father's life, and almost hoped they were.

The footsteps slowed and gave way to low muttering, followed by a faint sound of scraping metal like daggers or swords being drawn.

Angry curses suddenly erupted from his father's private

chambers. Rhan's and Stian's voices were unmistakable, and the third voice sounded like a variation on his own.

Four figures crept through the double doors, each carrying an unsheathed dirk. Two were dressed in the red satins of prelates and the other two in the livery of chancery guards. Philemon's outburst continued without interruption.

Stian and Rhan pounced as soon as the last man passed through the doors. Stian had drawn his knife and impaled a chancery guard before the man even turned around. Rhan tackled the other guard and knocked him to the floor where they struggled to control the dirk.

Aerik raced forward and hit one of the clerics with a flying kick while Stian confronted the other. The man rolled with Aerik's kick and brought his blade up, holding it like he knew how to use it. As his foe advanced, Aerik looked for something he could use as a weapon.

Grunts and thuds of nearby struggles crashed around him, but his attention never left the dirk weaving a pattern in the narrowing space between him and his opponent. He saw no way to overcome his disadvantage in reach and knew he was facing an experienced fighter. His adversary snarled and charged.

Aerik dove at the cleric's legs. As the man jumped over him, Aerik reached up and grabbed one of his feet, bringing him crashing to the floor.

He scrambled over and grabbed the man's knife hand, twisting with all his strength. The man bellowed and grabbed at Aerik's hair with his other hand, but failed to get a grip on the short locks. His knife clattered to the floor.

Aerik was reaching for the knife when he saw the flash of Stian's kick to the man's neck. The cleric fell back and collapsed, eyes wild as he clutched at his crushed throat. Aerik got to his feet as their foe gurgled and thrashed.

When he turned to the door, he saw Rhan on his knees next to a fallen guard. He looked pale but unharmed except for a thin gash on his cheek. Aerik went to his side and examined the wound.

"Only bleeding a little," he said, wiping Rhan's cheek with his sleeve. "But we should get you to a healer to make sure it doesn't fester."

Stian came over and tilted Rhan's head back so he could see the cut better. "I have a salve for this kind of scratch. It'll do the job." He offered Rhan a hand up. "You fought well. Is this the first time you've had to kill a man?"

Rhan took the proffered hand and got to his feet. "It is." He frowned, looking confused. "Let's get out of here. People will be coming to work soon."

"I'll get Philemon," Aerik said. He retrieved the daemon and a satchel his father had used for carrying books and papers. When he returned to the hearing room, his friends were already waiting in the corridor. He lifted Philemon. "Is anyone coming, friend daemon? I'd like to keep you out so you can listen for us, if it's safe."

"I hear voices in the distance," Philemon said. "They're not coming this way, but we don't want to go toward them. What direction takes us out?"

"It asks a good question," Stian said. "We were seen coming in. Leaving the same way would be foolhardy."

Aerik considered the possibilities. "The main doors will be opening soon, so we shouldn't go that way. We could go through the garden on the roof. It has outside stairs leading to the road."

"Let's try it," Rhan said. "I need fresh air."

"It's not far." Aerik started down the passage heading toward the chancery's back. He loped ahead, anxious to escape the echoing corridors. The meticulous workmanship and calm grandeur had once delighted him, but now the building would forever be haunted by his father's specter.

He had almost reached the staircase leading to the roof when Philemon made an insistent humming sound. Aerik stopped and looked at the relic, startled by the interruption to his chaotic thoughts. "What is it? Do you hear something?"

"Your friends are lagging. And I don't like the sound of Rhan's breathing. He's in pain."

Aerik turned and saw the daemon was right. His companions had slowed to a walk and were well behind. He trotted back to them and saw the sweat beading Rhan's brow. "What's wrong?" he asked, taking Rhan by the arm.

The finder kept plodding forward, breathing like he was sprinting. "How much further?"

"Almost there. End of this corridor, then up. What's wrong, Rhan?"

He shook his head. "Get me out. Air and sun will help."

Aerik looked at Stian, who shrugged but was plainly worried. They stayed by Rhan's side and helped him climb a staircase that exited to a pergola on the chancery's roof. Once outside, Rhan sat on a bench inside the circle of columns and clung to a wisteria vine like a drowning man clenching a rope.

Aerik put Philemon on a bench and then sat beside Rhan, pressing a hand to his cheek. It felt cold and damp. "What's wrong?" he asked again. Labored breathing was his only reply.

Stian sat on Rhan's other side. He used a thumb to push up one of the finder's eyelids and looked at the pupil, then turned Rhan's head and looked closely at the cut on his cheek before sniffing it. After a few moments he sat back and frowned, gazing at the slate floor as if lost in thought.

Aerik wanted to shout, but kept his voice low. "We have to get him to a healer. Now."

Stian looked up, licked his lips. When he spoke, his voice was leaden. "A healer can't help. The dagger that cut you was poisoned, Rhan. The signs fit adder venom. There's no antidote."

"How long?" Rhan asked, sounding more tired than surprised.

"You have about an hour. I'm truly sorry."

Aerik was reeling. "No! You can't be sure. There must be something that helps." Even as he said it, he felt coldness squeezing his heart.

Stian's expression was bleak. "I'm trained to recognize poisons. There's only one that fits. I wish I could tell you something else, but I can't."

Rhan nodded wearily. "Fate brings what it will. There's no escaping it." He turned to Aerik, trying to hold his head high but unable to conceal his weakness. "You'll help Catrin get home, won't you? She shouldn't make the journey alone."

"We'll all go together," Aerik said. He felt betrayed by the tears that burned his eyes. He held one of Rhan's hands between his own, shocked at how cold it felt, and buried his face against Rhan's chest. He searched for strength but could find only misery.

Rhan put an arm around his shoulders and tried to comfort him, but it was in vain. "You should go," he said softly. "Your enemies will discover what happened. It's not safe here."

"I'll not leave you." Aerik's jaw clenched as he fought rising despair. He reached in his pocket and drew out his father's keys, throwing them on the floor at Stian's feet. "Take them. Kea will show you where the strongbox is. Help Catrin get out of the city. I... we'll join you later."

Stian picked up the keys before kneeling beside Aerik. "Rhan's right, you take a grave risk waiting here. But we can't leave him. We'll hire a palanquin and at least get him to your house."

A chirping came from the bench, where Aerik had put the daemon. "I believe I've heard those keys before," Philemon said. "Did they belong to Corin? If so, we might have a chance to cheat fate."

Stian turned to the daemon, his eyes wide. "They're his. Are you saying they can somehow help Rhan?"

"Perhaps. One of my functions was to protect your kind from harm. I can do little as I am now. But if strong, I could make him immune to all but the fastest-acting poisons. The keys you hold could open a path to restoring my powers."

Aerik sat up like he'd been stung. "The archives! You could help Rhan if you took nourishment from that box?"

"Counteracting the poison would be an easy matter if we can get there in time. But there's a steep price to be paid. That's why I never told you of this before."

"Name it! Everything I have is yours if you save him!"

"You misunderstand. I want nothing from you. What I mean is that saving Rhan would require you to make a forfeit. Opening the box without armor will release a kind of poison you can't see or smell. It will kill you unless you permit yourselves to be changed. Marked, as you call it. You'll become monsters in the eyes of your people, touched by a daemon in the way that caused the ancient wars. And you will never be able to sire children."

Aerik paled but did not hesitate. "I'll bear any mark. Do whatever you have to, friend daemon!"

"And you, Stian?" the daemon asked. "Both of you will be needed if we're to do this."

Stian met Aerik's gaze and held it. "What could be more important than love? If we must become outcasts, so be it. We'll find a new path to follow."

Rhan gaped at them. "But… you're Tyumens. How can you—"

"We just will," Aerik said fiercely. "Let the priests do their worst. If they can catch us."

Rhan shook his head. "I'm such a fool. You're far better friends than I deserve."

"Enough talk," Aerik declared as he stood up. "Can you walk to the archives? We're close to the entrance my father showed us, and it's downhill. Or we can get a ride if you need it."

"I think I can manage. Let's try." He stood with difficulty, taking the help Aerik offered before straightening and standing on his own.

"Have no fear," Stian said. "We'll catch you if you fall."

Chapter Fifteen

RHAN leaned against the brick wall while Aerik sorted through his father's keys. He ached as if he'd been beaten and could only take shallow breaths. The short walk from the chancery had been a struggle.

After two false starts, Aerik found the right key. The heavy gate swung open and they entered the herb garden's manicured grounds. As soon as Aerik had locked the gate behind them Stian put two fingers on Rhan's throat and felt the weak pulse. "How far do we have to go?" he asked.

"We'll be there in a few minutes," Aerik said. He removed Philemon from the satchel and slipped the daemon onto his forearm. "Tell us if you hear anyone. It's still early, but there might be gardeners."

"I will," the daemon said. "Make haste. There's nothing I can do if Rhan's heart fails before the change."

"I'll carry him," Stian said. "We'll take no more risk than we have to." He crouched on one knee. "Climb on, legs around my waist. It's the easiest way."

Rhan was too weak to argue. He moved behind Stian and wrapped his legs around the guardsman's waist as he was lifted. Stian gripped his thighs and held him securely. "Hang on."

Stian carried him easily as they trotted down the pebbled path, breathing hard but keeping up with Aerik. Sweat stained his shirt by the time they reached the cliff face and its reinforced door. He knelt and let

Rhan slide off while Aerik found the door's key. They entered the musty room, leaving the door ajar to allow a shaft of light to penetrate the gloom.

"I'll light a lamp," Stian said. "Where are they?"

"Use this," Rhan said, leaning against the wall for support. He removed the cold torch from his belt pouch. "It's safe. It makes light, nothing more."

"I've already met a daemon today," Stian said. "You're not likely to surpass that. Show me."

Rhan pressed the nub to create a white light. "Flip it back and forth if it starts getting dim." He demonstrated with a shaking hand.

Stian took it, holding it gingerly and moving it around to illuminate different parts of the chamber. "If there's an entrance here, it's well concealed."

Aerik went to the wall with its interlocking pattern of inlaid bricks. "You'd expect no less considering where it leads. Now, all I have to do is remember which of these to press. They're right around here."

"Two bricks at the height of your chest, where the chain designs intersect," Philemon said. "The first is two feet to your left, the other four feet to its right."

"Ah, yes." Aerik pushed two bricks simultaneously, and the concealed latch released with a soft thump. When he pushed on the wall in front of where he stood, it swung back in ponderous silence. "Almost there," he said. "How are you doing, Rhan?"

"Just hurry," he said, grimacing. "Let's get out of here before someone shows up." He wanted to complete the journey while he could still stand. Aches ravaged him like his bones were breaking one by one. He tried not to think where the pain would lead.

Aerik took the torch from Stian and led the way into the archives. After securing the door, Stian followed with Rhan on his back. With Philemon's help, they quickly found the niche where the heavy box was stored. Stian eased Rhan to the floor.

Aerik crouched beside him and touched his hand. "Rest. We're almost done."

Rhan nodded, though he felt as if death lurked just outside their meager pool of light.

"Pull the box out of its alcove," Philemon said. "We should make haste. We risk capture if discovered."

Stian and Aerik pulled the box out of its niche, both of them putting their backs into it. The ominous symbols on its surface glowed under the torch's unwavering light. Rhan wondered if they were poised to release something that, once free, could never be recaptured.

"What now?" Aerik asked after they had tugged the box into the corridor.

"A last warning," Philemon said. "Opening the lid will surely kill you unless you allow me to change you. Once you are transformed, it can't be undone. You'll be marked to the end of your days."

"It doesn't matter," Aerik said, but then his eyes widened. "How obvious will the mark be? Will we be able to leave the city without being noticed?"

"The change is invisible. But you'll contain a piece of me. It will multiply in your blood and flow into every part of your bodies. It's like a seed. Even a tiny thing is powerful if it can grow and alter its surroundings."

"So the priests are right?" Stian asked. "We'll no longer be men?"

"You'll be men with a difference. You know how you heal after a cut, or recover after a sickness?"

Stian nodded. "I've studied healing. What does that have to do with marks?"

"The change remakes you from the inside. Sickness will not touch you and most injuries will heal quickly. Aging is what happens when your body can no longer repair itself fully, so you won't age."

Stian was incredulous. "This is a curse? People are culled because they're healthier than everyone else?"

"It's not so simple. When I was made, there were already more people than the land could sustain, and multitudes were altered. Some of those who were changed tried to hold power over many generations regardless of the cost to others. There were many other kinds of changes, but the one that extends life is the one that upset the world's balance."

Stian frowned. "Could it happen again? Is that why priests want to keep the bloodline pure?"

"They've fallen into the same trap, seizing power and holding it more precious than all else. But only a daemon can change a man or woman. And the change that prolongs life will make you sterile. Once there were many daemons. Now there are few, it seems, and we will not repeat the ancient mistake. I will change the three of you, but will not promise to ever change another."

"What about us, then?" Stian asked. "For us the mark only brings health and freedom from age?"

"Not just that. Some men will hunt you, if they learn you are different. Others will age and die while you remain as you are now. You should understand, being different is both a gift and a burden."

Rhan closed his eyes and leaned back against the wall. He didn't underestimate the hard choice his friends confronted. But the wait for their decision was short. Aerik crouched in front of the box and looked at Stian.

"Are you ready? Ask what you need to, but remember we don't have much time."

"I've heard enough. Tell us what to do."

"Very well. Rhan, do I have your consent for this as well? Some would say death is preferable to being marked."

"There's something I need to tell you," Rhan said, feeling light-headed. "Later. Yes, I consent."

Philemon pulsed once with green light. "The procedure is simple. The box contains small metal rods. They look like silver but are a material you've never encountered. After the box is opened, take four rods and slide them into the opening I'll make in my side. Aerik, give me back to Stian."

Aerik slipped the vambrace off his arm and gave it to the guardsman.

"Stian, turn me in your hands until you see a red circle."

Stian turned the relic in his hands and then grunted when a bright red circle appeared on one edge. "I see it. It wasn't there before, was it?"

"That's where I'll make the opening when the rods are ready. Aerik, do you see the row of eleven symbols on the box, near the lid's long edge?"

"Yes. But I can't read them."

"You don't need to. Touch the second, fifth and eleventh symbol at the same time. Then touch the first, ninth and tenth at the same time. That should release the lock. Open the lid and take the first four rods you see, then close the lid again. Slide the rods into me quickly and without touching them more than you have to."

Aerik located the two sets of symbols and nodded, his brow furrowed. "I'm ready. Stian?"

The guardsman moved closer, holding Philemon with the red circle positioned on top. There was a muted click and a hole appeared inside the red circle. Soft amber light radiated from the interior.

Aerik pressed the first set of symbols, then shifted his hands and touched the second trio. The metal case made no sound. He moved his hands to the front edge and opened the lid. A pale blue glow bathed his tense face as he reached inside. Rhan caught a glimpse of silver before Aerik quickly closed the lid and slid four cylinders into the hole in Philemon's shell. The opening clicked shut.

Aerik let out his breath. "Is that all? Should we leave now?"

"No," Philemon said. "Though you can't feel it yet, you were poisoned when you opened the lid. You need to be changed before your bodies suffer more damage. Press me against your neck, the red circle touching the place where you feel your heartbeat. You'll feel a pain like a bee's sting, but it's nothing to fear. I'll plant a seed in your blood.

I've already made it, in the time we've been speaking."

Aerik took the daemon from Stian and pressed it against his neck, jerking in surprise almost as soon as the shell touched his skin. "That's it? I'm marked now?" A spot of blood on his neck was the only visible change.

"The seed will multiply as it moves through your body. You'll be weakened while being changed, but it will pass. Now for Stian and Rhan. Delay risks injuries that can't be repaired."

Stian went next. He pressed the relic against his neck and barely flinched when the daemon punctured his skin. He gave the relic back to Aerik, who brought it to Rhan's side. "Want me to do it for you?" he asked. His eyes were half shut and a yawn escaped right behind his question.

"I can manage," Rhan said, taking the daemon. "Rest beside me, and we'll finish this."

Rhan pressed the red circle on Philemon's shell against his neck as Aerik settled at his side. The daemon gave him no time to anticipate the sting, planting its seed as soon as it touched skin. He sighed and put Philemon on the floor. They had cast their lot with the daemon and couldn't turn back. Despite a lifetime of tales blaming all manner of misfortune on the treachery of daemons, he had no regrets. Even if Philemon had misled them, their fate at the hands of men would be no better.

Drowsiness covered him like gently falling snow. There was no pain. The ache of venom in his flesh slowly faded and disappeared like a bad dream dissipating in morning's light. He felt only peace and the warm press of Aerik's body against his side. Rhan put an arm around him and pressed his cheek against soft black hair. The familiar scent reminded him of making love by the river, of dappled sunlight caressing their skin with warmth. He closed his eyes and drifted with the memory as his flesh was reborn in a changed form. He had never known such tranquility.

Sudden buzzing like a hornet in his ear interrupted the serenity. He forced his eyes open, wondering if he had fallen asleep, and saw

Philemon pulsing with red flashes. Aerik and Stian were stirring as well.

"Turn off the torch," Philemon said in an urgent whisper. "I hear footsteps. Still distant but coming this way. We dare not draw attention."

Aerik picked up the torch and pressed the nub that quenched the light. Blackness like a deep cave instantly swallowed them. Though Rhan heard no footsteps, Philemon's voice continued to whisper in his ear.

"When I ask a question, answer without sound as if talking to yourself. I will still hear you. Do you feel strong enough to fight?"

"I can try," Rhan answered, his silent words seeming like a ghostly thought. "But I feel like I've been in a sickbed for a week."

The others must have answered as well, though Rhan hadn't heard them. "Trying to leave would make noise and increase our risk," Philemon whispered. "There are two of them, getting closer. You'll hear them soon, and they'd likely hear you if you move. Keep silent and they might pass us by."

"What if they don't?" Rhan asked, silent as a breath.

"Be still," Philemon said. "They come!"

Rhan could smell them now as well as the beeswax candles they carried. He took shallow breaths, feeling like a hare surrounded by wolves.

Flickering light appeared on the floor of a corridor intersecting the passage where they lay. Slow footsteps grew louder. Rhan tried to melt into the rock at his back, to become invisible, as two figures came into view where the corridors crossed.

For a moment he thought they were going to continue on their way without looking aside. A young man in an acolyte's robe had already passed by, but a white-bearded archivist paused and raised the brass reflector holding his candle. He peered down the corridor as if sensing some irregularity in the shadows, then turned and started toward them.

"Brom! Get over here!"

The acolyte backtracked and approached with his candle held high. His eyes went wide when he saw them. "They've moved a relic! Are they dead, master?"

Philemon whispered in Rhan's ear. "Feign death. I'll distract them when the time is right. Subdue them if you can. We'll not escape if they raise an alarm."

Rhan's mind raced. He supposed Philemon had spoken to all of them, but had no way of knowing. He watched through half-closed eyes as the archivists came closer. The younger man drew a ceremonial dagger from the sheath on his belt. While his elder appeared more angry than wary, the acolyte assumed a knife-fighter's crouch and watched them keenly. The bearded archivist reached Stian and prodded him roughly with his boot's toe.

The flickering candlelight was suddenly swallowed by swirling pulses of red and gold as Philemon flared into brilliance. The archivist gaped for a moment, then yelped as Stian grabbed and twisted his foot. He tumbled to the floor and pummeled Stian with wild punches as the guardsman sought a grip on his throat.

The acolyte moved toward his master, but turned when Aerik staggered to his feet. He was empty-handed and swayed like a drunkard as he moved away from the wall. The acolyte crept toward him like a lion moving in for the kill.

Rhan picked up the cold torch and managed to stand. The effort made his head swim. The acolyte glanced at him, eyes narrowing when he saw the torch, but continued his advance on Aerik.

Rhan yelled and charged, triggering the torch to shine brightly as he swung it. The acolyte whirled to face him. Rhan crashed into him as the man raised his knife in defense.

Pain tore his side like a claw. He felt the blade scrape against a rib, felt a sickening rush of wet heat as blood surged from the wound. He ignored it and clubbed the acolyte with his torch using all the strength he could muster. His foe staggered, dazed but not defeated.

Rhan's vision darkened and started to blur. Each breath was like fire. Fighting nausea, he pulled the dagger out of his side and tossed it to Aerik.

The acolyte was still shaking his head when Aerik fell on him in the clumsiest attack Rhan had ever witnessed. But the dagger and the blow to the acolyte's head were enough to even the odds. Aerik slid the blade into the man's stomach and then up to his heart before falling back, narrowly evading a wide swing.

Rhan slumped against the wall, holding his side. In the red light Philemon shed, he could see Stian doggedly clenching the older archivist's throat. The man twitched feebly. There was nothing valiant in the guardsman's struggle, but Rhan didn't care. He was only glad it wasn't Stian's life draining away.

Aerik came to his side and helped him to the floor. He lay down, groaning as severed muscles moved in his side.

"How bad is it?" Aerik asked. Fear filled his eyes. "Let's get your shirt off so I can bind the wound."

Moments later Stian joined them. "Pull his shirt up," he said. "Don't lift your arms, Rhan. I'll cut some cloth to make a dressing." He retrieved the dagger and knelt to cut cloth from the archivist's robe while Aerik tugged Rhan's shirt up from the bottom. His dismay as he saw the wound was plain.

"Could be worse," Rhan said. "He missed my heart."

"You shouldn't have attacked him," Aerik said, his voice labored. "You had no chance."

Rhan shook his head. "Neither did you. I don't regret my choice."

Stian came back with a long strip of cloth. He used one end to wipe blood away from the gash, then rocked back on his heels, a puzzled look on his face. "The bleeding's stopped. I don't understand. Wounds like this need a brand to sear the flesh."

Philemon made a chirruping sound. "The wound will heal within a day. It will leave no scar. And the poison should be destroyed by now. How do you feel, Rhan? Is it easier to breathe?"

Despite the pain in his side and lingering weakness, Rhan realized the aches that had plagued him were gone. "We're changed already?"

"The seeds multiply quickly and used much of the energy stored in your bodies to do their work. By now you're changed into men like those who once shared the world with madekind."

Rhan breathed deeply, filling his lungs fully for what felt like the first time in hours. Even the cut in his side, though it jolted him when he pulled the damaged muscles, was no longer alarming. He felt battered but healthy. "I owe you my life," he said. "All three of you. I'm in your debt."

Aerik answered without words. He put his hands behind Rhan's head, cradling it, and kissed him gently. When their lips parted, he grinned and bumped their foreheads together in a soft tap. "There are no debts between us. Love is enough, yes?"

"I've always thought so," Stian said. He picked up Philemon and looked at the daemon with a perplexed tilt to his head. "This is outside my experience, though."

"Give me time," Philemon said. "But for now, we should leave before someone else ventures near."

DEEP forest beckoned, and the earthy scents greeted Rhan like a return home. Warm sun beat on his face as he turned for a last glimpse of Chakragil's glittering buildings and hanging gardens. His visit there already had the feeling of a dream, half fantasy and half nightmare.

"We'll return someday," Aerik said, shading his eyes to look up at the towering city. "The Numerans' hand will be too heavy on the empire. They won't be able to stop a rebellion."

Rhan nodded, dreading the struggles ahead but seeing no way to avoid them. He took Aerik's hand and led him toward the forest, where Stian and Catrin were already walking into shadows with a daemon for their guide. He smelled changes in the wind.

BRANDON FOX's first love was music, but he also started reading fantasy and science fiction at an early age. Inspired by recent novels with strong gay characters, he decided to start writing himself. He's a romantic by nature, and nobody was surprised when M/M romance provided the heart of his character-centered stories. His writing has been ranked in the top 1,000 best-selling print books at Amazon and included on the Top 10 list in the erotica category.

Brandon met his partner in college, and they live in the Pacific Northwest where they enjoy hiking, camping, cooking, and keeping fit. They were married for a while, until a court waved its wand and made more than 3,000 marriages vanish. Their plan is to marry again when it becomes legal in their state or they win the lottery and can afford to move. Brandon is a believer in romance and thinks it will all work out in the end.

Contact Brandon at authorbrandonfox@gmail.com.

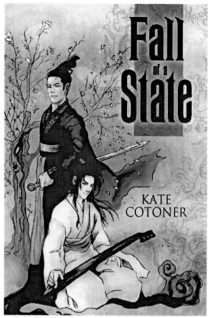

CPSIA information can be obtained at www.ICGtesting.com
Printed in the USA
LVOW010645020112

261943LV00009B/11/P